D0348891

The Whole of the Moon

Rogers, Brian, 1964-
The whole of the moon :
a novel /
[2017]
33305239758166
cu   02/16/18

The Whole of the Moon

A Novel

Brian Rogers

UNIVERSITY OF NEVADA PRESS | *Reno & Las Vegas*

University of Nevada Press | Reno, Nevada 89557 USA
www.unpress.nevada.edu
Copyright © 2017 by University of Nevada Press
All rights reserved
Cover design by David Ter-Avanesyan/Ter33Design

LIBRARY OF CONGRESS CATALOGING-IN-PUBLICATION DATA
Names: Rogers, Brian, 1964-
Title: The whole of the moon : a novel / Brian Rogers.
Description: First edition. | Reno : University of Nevada Press, 2017. |
Identifiers: LCCN 2016059984 (print) | LCCN 2017018816 (e-book) |
    ISBN 978-1-943859-40-5 (pbk. : alk. paper) | ISBN 978-0-87417-596-7 (e-book)
Subjects: LCSH: Interpersonal relations–Fiction. | Determination (Personality trait)—
    Fiction. | Failure (Psychology)—Fiction. | United States Highway 66—Fiction. |
    California, Southern—Fiction. | Psychological fiction.
Classification: LCC PS3618.O4564 W56 2017 (print) | LCC PS3618.O4564 (e-book) |
    DDC 813/.6–dc23
LC record available at https://lccn.loc.gov/2016059984

Excerpts from *Death of a Salesman* are from *The Portable Arthur Miller,* edited by
Christopher Bigsby, published by the Penguin Group, Penguin Books USA Inc.,
375 Hudson Street, New York, New York, 10014. U.S.A.; "The Surrey with the Fringe
on Top." Copyright © 1943 by Richard Rodgers and Oscar Hammerstein II. Copyright
renewed Williamson Music (ASCAP), an Imagem Company, owner of publication and
allied rights throughout the world. International copyright secured. All rights reserved.
Used by permission.; "Getting to Know You." Copyright © 1951 by Richard Rodgers and
Oscar Hammerstein. Copyright renewed Williamson Music (ASCAP), an Imagem Company, owner of publication and allied rights throughout the world. International copyright secured. All rights reserved. Used by permission.

The paper used in this book meets the requirements of American National Standard
for Information Sciences—Permanence of Paper for Printed Library Materials,
ANSI/NISO Z39.48-1992 (R2002).

FIRST PRINTING

Manufactured in the United States of America

For Colby and Mallory

the ploughman may

Have heard the splash, the forsaken cry,

But for him it was not an important failure; the sun shone

As it had to on the white legs disappearing into the green

Water

—W. H. AUDEN, "Musée des Beaux Arts"

CONTENTS

The Whole of the Moon

CHAPTER 0

The Fairfax Apartments (Present)

The door to unit 6 opened at the Fairfax Apartments and the Actor stepped out. The Actor was in his late twenties with a fit build—he had been to the gym the night before—and he wore swim trunks and a V-neck T-shirt, white. He had a towel and a water bottle and suntan lotion, a pair of headphones and a book. And his phone. It was not yet ten in the morning and already the temperature was rising past eighty degrees. The weather for weeks had been insufferable, like living in Phoenix or Nevada, not Los Angeles, a few blocks off Melrose Avenue, down the road from Paramount Studios where the Actor had sometimes worked as an extra.

He had no auditions today. No acting classes. The plan was to lounge by the pool and wait. *Do something every day for your career,* he had been advised, *even if it's just making a phone call or practicing a scene in front of the mirror.*

The book was *The Great Gatsby,* and he had checked it out from the public library. He planned on reading it for research purposes. He was up for a role in a television pilot, a period piece set during the Jazz Age. HBO had passed (it had been perfect for them, the creators thought, but the network did not bite), so they toned down the language and brought the script to FX, which took a flier. The Actor had read for the part of McKee, the muscular owner of the speakeasy where much of the action takes place. It was a decent role, and he would be a regular. If the series was picked up, it meant opening credits.

No one else was out by the pool, so the Actor had his pick of the chaise lounge litter. He faced the sun and stretched out. He was proud of his body, worked hard on it (his LA Fitness membership was one of his fixed expenses). His legs were muscular, his upper body developed without being ripped. He wasn't going to be one of those guys who only appeared as jocks, the dumb object of affection for some sleepy-eyed girl, come to deliver flowers and through a silly plot twist the shirt comes off. But the Actor could do a nude scene, would do it. If the role called for sex, he had the body. You had to be willing. The others in his acting class were mostly in agreement, with the exception of one whiny thing just out of USC who complained, "It's different for women."

The Actor reached down and adjusted the location of his water bottle. He placed the book underneath the chair, double-checked that the ringer was on, and set his phone on top of the book, protected from the sun. He squeezed out a measure of suntan lotion and began rubbing it over his legs and arms, his feet and face. You did not want to risk blotchiness, especially in this heat. Then he lowered the chaise lounge and closed his eyes. It could be a long wait. The call could come any minute. You just never knew.

CHAPTER 1

The Hikers (1964)

Should I kiss her?

That was his first thought when he woke that morning. He thought it again while he showered—and again as he drove to Ballard's Service Station where they agreed to meet. His car, an eight-year-old Pontiac, rattled a little as he drove down Foothill Boulevard, but the interior was clean (he had taken lemon water to the dashboard and seats the previous afternoon). The radio played the Supremes' "Where Did Our Love Go." His jaws worked two sticks of gum.

Will she be there?

He thought that too. What if it was all an elaborate prank? What if she was standing with her friends laughing at his gullibility? *You didn't really think that I was going to ditch school and go hiking with you! Oh my God, you are such an idiot!* Or what if her boyfriend was there, ready to blacken his eye and rip out his limbs? *What do you think you're doing with my girl? Spending the day together? Please.* And then he and the rest of the basketball team would descend like jackals in the wild.

But there she was, standing in a pair of shorts and a sweater and holding her books and a paper bag. His heart really did race as he pulled into the service station, and he knew that she had followed their plan: About ten minutes earlier her mother had dropped her off at school. She waited until the car disappeared and then turned and headed the four blocks away from the high school, to this service station with its Route 66 sign and "We Do All Repairs" painted in the window. There was always the chance,

of course, that someone would see them, but they agreed to ren-
dezvous at the side of the building, where she now stood, waiting. He pulled alongside her, and she opened the heavy metal
door to the Pontiac and got in. My God, it could have been a
dream. It absolutely had to be a dream. It was like something
out of a Beach Boys song or an Elvis movie, something fantastical and cinematic that this girl, Stacy Ann Moriarty, the girl
he spent day and night thinking about, was now next to him at
eight in the morning, the Supremes playing on the radio, the car
smelling of lemon, the inside of his mouth tasting like the Wrig-
ley gum factory.

"Hi," he said, lamely.

She tossed her things into the backseat, the books spilling
everywhere.

A Beach Boys song, yes.

Or maybe it was a dream, like this *Twilight Zone* episode he
had seen, a man being hanged who escapes but then is later
shown to be hanged and his escape only his last thoughts as he
dropped from the bridge to his death. Maybe it was like that.

Should I kiss her?

"You ready?" she asked.

They lived about an hour east of Los Angeles, just inside the Los
Angeles County line, where there was a strange mixture of scat-
tered lemon groves and parched land. To reach the trails—they
were headed into the mountains—they had to drive seven miles
east on Foothill, cut up Central and drive through the dust and
lemons, and then make the climb. In all it would take them about
an hour to make the trailhead.

The weather that late October morning was cooler than it
had been. A few weeks earlier the temperatures had climbed into
the nineties. Not unusual for California, but enough to make the
girl's father grouse that "it is too damn hot for October." Now it
wasn't. The weather had fallen into that predictable pattern of
being chilly in the morning, temperate throughout the day, and

then back to chilly in the evenings. It was, in other words, perfect hiking weather.

"Why did you bring your books?" he asked, as they were still making their way along Foothill Boulevard.

"I had to make it look like I was going to school," she said.

Of course.

What a dumb thing to ask. *Dumb. Dumb. Dumb.* He was always saying dumb things around her. And yet she never made him feel that way, not even in science class where they were lab partners. Theirs was a friendship borne over Bunsen burners and beakers, and when they were assigned to the same table, she took to him graciously, asking him questions about himself and whether he liked school ("it's okay") and what sports he played ("none") and did he have any brothers or sisters (he did not). Even so, he never imagined that they would one day ditch school together. A Beach Boys song. That's what it was. "Do you think Maureen has called in by now?" he asked, about the time they turned up Central.

This was the plan: her friend Maureen would call the school and pretend to be Stacy's mother, tell them that she was not feeling well and staying home for the day.

"Probably," Stacy said. "Maureen's pretty reliable, especially when it comes to anything devious. But even if she doesn't, it's not like we're going to rob a bank."

"No, we're not."

"You're lucky you don't have to worry about it."

"That's true," he said—and it was. His mother had started a new job that week, and he was certain the school did not have her work number, if they even decided to call and check on his absence. Sometimes they did, sometimes not.

After that they chatted aimlessly, the girl gossiping about some of their classmates, complaining about senior year, how she was ready to be done already. She wanted to "kill" her math teacher and she was sick of her "stupid boyfriend's friends." Sometimes, other times, when she mentioned her boyfriend, it would depress him. It would remind him that she *had* a boyfriend (as if he could forget), but the word *stupid*. . .well, he wondered if it was purposeful, or if she had just sort of said it. Is this what girls did? Was there a kind of code that he needed to unravel? My boyfriend is stupid. I am spending the day with you.

Should I kiss her?

The dry flatland, the weeds and cacti, gave way to trees as the road began to wind into the mountains. The transformation really was remarkable, how you could be on the set of *The Searchers* one minute and *The Olympian* the next. And pine trees! You couldn't find a pine tree in their neighborhoods if your life depended on it. Some palm trees sure, but pine trees—well, the air grew fresher, you could tell, even if their windows were rolled up. She took to staring out the window from time to time, and he would catch glimpses from the corner of his eye, her head turned toward the outside, lost in thought, her brown hair so goddamned beautiful he had to stop himself from clutching the steering wheel with too much force. And it was during these moments when he liked her best, not when she was talking—though he loved to hear her voice—but when she was staring out the window, obviously thinking, because he thought a lot too. He seemed to be always thinking, like he had been locked in a puzzle box and the only way out was to assemble the pieces, except you couldn't even find the corner pieces to get started. All the while the trees grew closer and closer as the Pontiac climbed. The radio began to lose its signal (no more Supremes, no more Beatles), and at one point Stacy turned to him and said, "I'm glad we're doing this."

"Me too."

"Do you know where we're going?"

He explained that there were some trails up the road. He was pretty sure he knew where (in fact, the night before, he had studied a map for the better part of an hour). He thought they could just park off the road and cut in from there. She was only half-listening and told him cheerfully, "You know what? I don't even care where we go. I'm just glad not to be at school."

He agreed. They went around a bend and the radio got reception. Was it Dean Martin? Then the signal was again gone.

Not five minutes later they were there.

He pulled the car off the highway into a clearing with enough room to park. He killed the engine and they got out. From his trunk he removed a small backpack. "I can carry your lunch," he told her.

"Sure," she said, and handed him the paper bag, weighted down by an apple. "Do we need anything else?"

"Should I bring a blanket?"

"Why?"

How could he tell her, that he thought maybe they would stop somewhere in the woods, spread out the blanket, eat their lunch, *should I kiss*—that he had played out the scenario in his head a thousand times, but what she must be thinking now. *You didn't really think*—Oh, God, what is wrong with me. *Dumb.* "Yeah, it's a pretty big blanket," he said. "I'm not sure it'd even fit in my pack."

"Whatever you want to do."

"No, we'll leave it here."

And with that he slammed shut the Pontiac's heavy trunk. The sound reverberated all around them. They walked to the trailhead. He was wearing jeans. She was dressed in shorts. They both had on sneakers. Without fanfare they entered the woods and began their hike, the air immediately growing cooler, the smell of pine enlivening, evident.

By the side of the highway the Pontiac glistened in the morning sunlight. Back at school second period was just beginning.

Felicity (1999)

Felicity stood in the kitchen of their two-bedroom apartment, located just a few blocks off Foothill Boulevard, and stared at her mother as she watched television. "Come on Big Money!" a contestant was shouting.

Wheel of Fucking Fortune.

You really had to give it to her. Her mother had honed the ability to watch the same television shows day after day without a trace of boredom. "My shows," she called them. Soaps in the daytime, and then game shows—*Hollywood Squares, The Price Is Right, Jeopardy!*—though she only partly paid attention to that last one, and then whatever slop the networks were serving up after eight o'clock. The habit was Sisyphean and she did it without self-censure. Most of the time, when she was not at work, Felicity would retreat to her bedroom and close the door, put on a pair of headphones and listen to music. She had learned years before not to play her music too loud—her mother would demand that Felicity turn it down. Thus there was no way Soul Asylum could compete with Pat Sajak.

When Felicity was not in her room, the smell of cigarette smoke nearly choked her to death. Two packs a day. But what did the Surgeon General know? Besides, it was too late—the cigarette companies had already gotten to her mother hook, line, and, one could assume, eventually sinker. (For now, her mother's only real ailment was a bad back, caused, she said, by a car accident some fifteen years earlier and not getting any better despite her state of continual rest.) If Felicity complained about the smell of smoke, her mother would say, "I have the thing on."

The *thing* was a little battery-operated device, no bigger than an ashtray, designed—"Patent Pending"—to draw in the cigarette smoke and keep it from polluting the room. It worked about as often as her mother, which is to say, not at all. But the *thing* was her mother's fortress against Felicity's occasional reminder that they both lived there. "I'm using the thing," "I have the thing on." And the device, which Felicity had picked up hopefully at Orchard Supply Hardware, would issue its small hum, powered by two double-A batteries, and do nothing at all.

Come on Big Money indeed.

"Mom, do you need anything?" Felicity asked.

"Oh, some more would be good." And her mother raised her glass, a few discolored ice cubes melting at the bottom, and rattled it.

Felicity retrieved the glass. Back in the kitchen she set it on the white tile countertop, refilled it with ice, and then cracked open a can of Diet Pepsi. If there was any salvation in this whole sordid mess, it was that at least her mother was not a drinker. Maybe because her first husband, not Felicity's father, had been a boozer of the highest order. Only on the rare occasion, Christmas Eve or a birthday, would her mother have a glass of wine, which she would of course complement with a Virginia Slim.

With the Pepsi still fizzing over the ice, Felicity set the glass back down on the side table on a coaster. The coaster was a terrific joke. The furniture was twenty years old, the same furniture Felicity had seen all her life, and not a single piece would have sold for five dollars at the Salvation Army store. But her mother insisted that they use coasters so that their glasses did not leave stains. Felicity set the glass on the Royal Cruises coaster—they had never been on a cruise and she had no idea how the set had come into their lives—and asked her mother, "Do you need anything else?"

Her mother was concentrating on a *Wheel of Fortune* puzzle and did not answer.

"Mom, do you need anything else?"

Her mother looked away from the television. "Why would she buy a vowel?"

"I don't know. . .when there's so many other things to buy in this world."

"Ha ha," her mother said, and looked back at the television.

"Do you need anything?"

"I'm good."

Felicity picked up her mother's finished dinner plate and took it into the kitchen. She poured a few drops of liquid soap over the plate and cleaned it with a brush, rinsed and set it on the drying rack. Sometimes, when she was washing dishes, Felicity liked to imagine that she was a nineteen-year-old peasant girl living in some small village in Mexico, working for the richest family in town. It was a weird fantasy that had come to her once—and returned every so often. She imagined that she was this peasant girl and that the woman of the house, some beautiful slender woman who had never smoked a cigarette in her life, recognized Felicity's own beauty and brilliance, pulled her aside one day, and sent her to school to become a doctor or a lawyer. And so she lived happily ever after. It was not impossible. Felicity had been a good student in high school. This was California. There was a community college on every corner. She could balance classes with her schedule at Orchard Supply—other people did it—and her mother, living off disability, could get her own damn dinner for a change. The few laps between the kitchen and the living room would be good for her circulation.

Or. . .imagine her mother was forced out into the world! Could she land a husband? She had done it twice before. Surely there was some kindred spirit out there, a soul mate waiting to bond over smokes and *Family Feud*.

Back in her bedroom, Felicity checked herself in her full-length mirror. She was wearing jeans and a white blouse, her brown hair pulled back and held by rubber bands. She wore no makeup. Felicity was blessed with gorgeous skin. It was the color of coffee that had been given a lot of cream, and she had never had a pimple in her life. Still, she knew she was not what boys called beautiful. She did not have arresting looks. (In high school she had barely been noticed.) She was "pretty enough."

Satisfied with her appearance, Felicity grabbed her purse off the dresser and opened the door. She waited until *Wheel* went to commercial and told her mother, "I'm going out."

"What time will you be back?"

"I don't know."

"I want you home by eleven."

"I'm nineteen years old," Felicity reminded her.

"Don't get smart with me. I'm still your mother."

"I won't be out late," Felicity promised. And she bent over and gave her mother a kiss on the cheek. "You'll be okay?"

"There's a new *Raymond* tonight. And a new *Becker*. I liked him better on *Cheers*."

"Okay," Felicity said. She had no opinion on Ted Danson.

Felicity was almost out the door when her mother reminded her, "Don't forget my smokes."

"I know."

At least two times a week Felicity had to buy her mother cigarettes. Once the clerk at the Circle K scolded her, "You shouldn't smoke, you're too young," and instead of telling him that the Virginia Slims were for her mother, Felicity said, "I like to smoke after sex." He kept quiet after that and rang up her purchase. She was enabling her mother, she knew. But at this point Felicity was committed to keeping the peace, until she figured out what she wanted to do or the heavens opened and served up some plan. Maybe one of those talent agents who roamed the mall would tap her on the shoulder and hand her his card (she didn't really want to be in the movies). Maybe she would become a champion equestrian. Maybe an astronaut. The world was her oyster. For now, however, it was a full-time job at Orchard Supply Hardware and smoke runs for her mother.

Felicity closed the door to the apartment and walked down the concrete stairs to the car. She knew what would come next. She would go to her boyfriend's apartment, which he shared with another man who worked at the shop. They were both older than Felicity, in their midtwenties. They would be drinking beer. Felicity would have one or two and listen to them complain about the shop owner, how he was "jewing" them out of raises, not appreciating their expertise. They would tell the same stories, like a CD playing on repeat, though somehow Felicity would find this preferable to sitting in a smoke-filled apartment and watching *Becker* with her mother. Her boyfriend was older and seemed wiser. He knew "stuff." Later they would go into his bedroom and have sex. And then she would leave, stopping at the Circle K for her mother's Virginia Slims ("I like to smoke after sex") and make her way back home by eleven ("I won't be out late"), where the local news would be covering some atrocity or some nonsense, the volume blasting loud enough that Felicity would hear it even before she opened the door. She would pause for a moment and then insert the key and open the door to discover her mother, as usual, asleep on the couch, mouth open, some drool probably, the *thing* issuing its small, useless hum.

Gatsby, the Musical (Present)

Dorothy Latham sat at her kitchen table waiting for her husband to return. She had a pot of coffee at the ready. Sometimes when he got back, he liked a cup of coffee, one cube of sugar, no cream. For years she would go with him on these morning jaunts, but her knees hurt her now and so she let him have his walks alone. He likes it better that way, she believed. Sometimes, though, she wished they still had the dog, just to have another living being at his side.

They had been in this Southern California home for nearly sixty years, having bought it the year after they were married. Her parents had helped with the down payment, money that George tried to repay but which her father refused. Her parents were not well-to-do people, but they could afford to help and they did. It pleased them. Still, for a good year, George and Dot scrimped and saved, buying no new furniture, taking no big trips. If they wanted to treat themselves, they would grab sandwiches from the market and go to the park. They kept their money in the proverbial cookie jar.

They wanted a piano. A baby grand.

Theirs had been a love affair sprung from a shared love of musicals, and Dorothy knew she would marry him from the very first time he sang "Oh, What a Beautiful Mornin'" to her. It was neither morning nor beautiful, but he held her hand and sang confidently as they walked the length of Shattuck Avenue. Not long after he left for graduate school in Southern California, so he could get his PhD in music theory. But George found the separation unbearable. Like Benjamin Braddock racing to retrieve Elaine Robinson—though that movie would not be released until much later—George drove north on the 101 and surprised her. They went to the top of Sather Hall with its panoramic views of San Francisco, the Golden Gate Bridge, the Oakland Hills. He proposed, and they were married the month after she graduated.

Dorothy rose and rinsed her breakfast plate.

She liked mornings best. There was so much clarity in the mornings. One's mind was not polluted by the passing hours, the fatigue, the medicines that nobody their age escaped. Later, she knew, her daughter would stop by, visit for a while. George would ask about her work, the grandkids. He might even play her a song on the piano. They would eat early, go to bed early, and she would rise as the sun was just making its way through the sheer curtains of their bedroom.

It had taken them a good year to save enough for the down payment, another two years to pay off the loan from Pat's Music. But when it arrived, Dorothy was without doubt. She had never seen her husband so happy. It was thrilling, like bringing home a baby, the feeling of something fresh and new, George the composer, Dot with her fine alto voice and boundless faith in her husband's abilities. And of course it had to be a Steinway & Sons. George would not have played on anything else. They were never drinkers, only a vodka and tonic (usually just one) every night at five o'clock, but for the occasion they bought a bottle of champagne. Cheap, because they couldn't afford anything else! They sat side by side on the smooth, lacquered finish of the piano bench, belting out show tunes—"Oklahoma," "I'm in Love with a Wonderful Guy," "Getting to Know You." How could they have not felt that life was a marvel?

> *Getting to know you,*
> *Getting to know all about you,*
> *Getting to like you,*
> *Getting to hope you like me.*

Dorothy sang joyously, while George's fingers moved effortlessly across the keys, his body pressed against his new wife. They sang deep into the night, past midnight, the sound of the baby grand filling the house.

The coffee pot turned off, and Dorothy stepped over to press the

THE WHOLE OF THE MOON

switch to keep the burner warm. She thought she heard the front door open, but it was just the rumbling of a truck from the street. George was late getting back, but she was not worried. He could take care of himself. Sometimes he went a little farther, all the way past the old train station. Maybe he was composing. He was a genius, you know. He was putting the finishing touches on his musical. Had been working on it for years. Based on F. Scott Fitzgerald's *The Great Gatsby*. The baby grand sat in the next room, its lacquered finish as shiny as the day it arrived.

Dorothy sat back down. George would be home soon.

The Hikers (1964)

Bobby was talking about baseball. Stacy was half-listening. Something about a Negro pitcher named Gibson. The World Series had ended a few weeks earlier, she knew, because her father had stayed home from work one day to watch the game on television. It had been all her boyfriend and his friends talked about. What was it about sports and boys? she sometimes wondered. But that was a little unfair to Bobby, who talked about other things, who as far as she could remember only talked sports one other time— and that was when *she* asked whether he played on a team.

They had been hiking for over an hour and she was getting hungry. The hike was harder, steeper, than she anticipated, but it was too early for lunch. She was a healthy but not especially athletic girl, the sort who could run a mile in PE but never felt the need to outrun the other girls. "They are batterymates," Bobby said.

"Who are?"

"Bob Gibson and Tim McCarver."

The baseball players. "Why do they need batteries?" she asked.

Bobby laughed. "No, that's what you call a pitcher and catcher. But I read that they are also good friends. I just thought it was interesting, because of everything that happened."

Everything that happened, she knew, meant the events over the summer, the civil rights workers that got killed down in Missis-sippi, the law that had been passed. They had black students at their school, but only a few. As far as she knew, nobody harassed them. But even if her family was not especially political—her parents would vote for Johnson, she was pretty sure—she under-stood that California was different. "I've never been there, to Mis-sissippi," she said.

"Me either. I've never been out of California."

"I have cousins in Washington. We go every summer. They live on a lake, canoeing, fishing, that sort of thing."

"You fish?"

"I can fish," she said defensively, before adding, "I just don't do it every summer."

"What's it like, Washington? You mean the state, right?"

"It's a little like this," she said, by which she meant the moun-tains. It was *green*. There were *trees*. It was not the dirt and dust of the Inland Empire, the miles of hard-caked land that stretched in every direction. "It's nice, you know. I like going there. I get a little bored, because my cousins are younger. That never used to matter, but now I mostly just sit by the lake and read or listen to the radio."

"Sounds pretty good," said Bobby.

"Do you think we could stop for a few minutes? To rest."

"Of course," he said, and he stopped like a train that had thrown on the brakes. Not like Sam, she thought, who would have teased her about getting tired and being "a poor sport." That was one of the things she liked about this other boy, Bobby, his eagerness about her. That, and he always dressed neatly, had his hair combed. Half the time Sam's shirttails were dangling at his side, his hair tousled from where he had been wrestling with his friends. They were in a state of perpetual warfare. Plus, when the subject of the civil rights workers came up, Sam would have made some bad joke. Everything was a joke to him and his friends.

She sat and rested on the trunk of a fallen tree, Bobby asking if she was all right, if she needed anything. He liked her, so obviously liked her. Would do anything for her. Stumbled on his words at times because he was always looking for the right thing to say. She thought it interesting, and even a little perverse, how much she enjoyed having this power over him, how she could make him inarticulate. When he suggested bringing along a blanket, she knew what he was up to, but she did not want to put him in that position, where he behaved clumsily. But what if he tried to kiss her. Would she let him? Probably. What could it hurt? And what was she doing out here anyway? If Sam found out she went hiking with another boy, and he probably would, they would have a terrible row. He might even break up with her out of embarrassment. Maybe it's what she wanted, to force the issue. For weeks she had been thinking about calling it off anyway. Her mind, exhilarated by the fresh air and the trees and the solitude (they had seen no one else on the trail), was buzzing with all these thoughts when Bobby asked her, "You're not getting blisters, are you?"

"I just needed to rest," she said, and she rose from the fallen tree. "Onward, Christian soldier," she announced, repeating a favorite phrase of her mother's. But Bobby did not understand the reference, she could tell.

The squirrel made her jump and shriek. It flew across the path like an acrobat at a circus. Bobby jerked a little too. It was just the surprise of it all, the sudden appearance of a small, flying animal. She was not phobic about squirrels. She was not a silly girl. But she had almost forgotten that they were in the woods, lost as she was in their conversation. They had both seen *Mary Poppins* and both liked the scene with the dancing penguins. She wanted to see Alfred Hitchcock's *The Birds,* but her mother would not let her, worried that it would give her nightmares. Bobby liked a new television show called *Bewitched,* about a witch who gets married and promises not to perform any spells, but of course she does. Then suddenly the squirrel appeared, its body stretched for aerodynamic effect, and she jumped and shrieked and realized... and then began laughing. "Maybe it's been following us," said Bobby, "and finally decided to make its move!"

"We should write a horror movie about a killer squirrel," she suggested when they began moving again.

"What would we call it?"

She thought for a moment. "*The Squirrel in the Woods.*"

"How about just *The Squirrel*, or *The Squirrels*, like *The Birds*"?

"*A Squirrel Among Us*," she said, which they both agreed was the best, most haunting title.

And so they got a good laugh out of the squirrel and kept walking and fell back into their easy conversation. At one point the trail began to thin out, grow rougher. This did not alarm her, or at least she did not give it much thought. If she enjoyed the power she had over this boy, she was content to let him guide them on their hike. He knew what he was doing and where they were going, or acted like it. Later she would remember they came to a place where the trail seemed to fork, and that they probably should have slowed down and absorbed that fact. She would most vaguely remember that a tree had been dabbed with a streak of yellow paint. They were both inexperienced hikers, so they could not have known that other hikers were marking the trail. They were so lost in thought and conversation that she never realized there was any danger in their decisions.

Bobby, for his part, never saw the painted tree at all. He was flush with adrenaline and possibility. He might as well have been sixty miles away, riding the Tomorrowland Jets at Disneyland, thrilled but safely strapped in with only one pervasive thought, *Should I put my arm around her, should I kiss her, should I—?*

CHAPTER 2

Cousin Billy (1985-91)

My cousin is dead. Of that I am sure. No one in our family has heard from him in years. Not that I would be the first person he would contact. ("Hey Coz, have slipped into Istanbul, in a bit of a pickle, send money.") If the FBI has news about him, some lead or sighting, they have not shared it with us. It has been three, four years since they last contacted me, to see if I knew anything, longer since they brought me in under the hot lights. The case is cold. My cousin is dead. Or he is living happily in some beachside villa, wearing bathrobes and sipping cocktails under an assumed name. My cousin was a social Houdini, a rare breed—and it might well be that he has gotten away with murder.

* * *

Growing up he kept a large map of the world in his bedroom. It filled an entire wall, and he had placed it so that the top edges of the map ran perfectly parallel to the edges of his walls and ceiling. Born William—he was Billy in those days—my cousin was always meticulous, his attention to detail pronounced. He also possessed that very American trait, restlessness, and that map on his wall fed his ambition and imagination.

We lived in separate towns, so I did not see him all that often. But once a month we would drive to my cousins' house or they would drive to ours (our parents were brother and sister) and have a meal and play games or be bored in the way of children. I always preferred going to my cousins. They had a yard that was like an enchanted garden, with nooks and crannies and a pond with real fish. It felt massive, all the more so because it backed up to a park, which you could glimpse by wading through the trees and bushes that lined the property. I am sure if I went back there now—and I have not been in years—that it would be much smaller than my memory paints, shrunken with age like John Knowles' trees at Exeter or any of the places where we imaginatively romped as children.

I do not know why my cousin should have been so restless. He did not come from hardscrabble conditions. He was no Horatio Alger. His father in fact had gone to law school and carved out a small but prosperous practice, as prosperous as one might find in the Central Valley of California. If anyone was an Alger, it was my uncle Donald. My mother and he had been born into pretty poor conditions. My grandfather—dead before I was even born—had been a lout who spent more time in taverns than in jobs. My uncle Donald rose above this, made his way to college and then law school, while my mother, younger by two years, got married almost directly out of high school. By a strange bit of timing, my cousin Billy and I were born on the same day.

The map, it might have come from the National Geographic Society, had different colors for each of the continents. During one visit (my cousin and I were about eleven or twelve at the time), Billy stood on his bed and pointed to various parts of the map. "This is Alaska," he said, "where all those Jack London stories take place." "This is Polynesia, Fiji. Right here is Tahiti, where Gauguin went and painted."

I knew about Gauguin. We had studied him in school.

"And this is Switzerland," my cousin said, gesturing. "They ski a lot in Switzerland. I'm going there first."

"When?" I asked. Maybe my cousins were going on a trip and I had not heard. My family, by contrast, never travelled at all, except the twenty miles north to my cousins' house.

"As soon as I can," he said. "As soon as I figure out how. I may fly there, or I may take a steamer. You can do that. It takes two weeks to get across the ocean, and then you have to take a boat *and* a train from England."

My cousin spoke with confidence and certitude. He moved that way as well. He led every game and adventure. He was an exceptional athlete. If he doubted his abilities, he never showed it, not then and not later. If he said he was going to Switzerland, he was going to Switzerland. You would have been a fool to bet against him.

During another visit, on a Sunday, he spent the entire time sitting in his backyard, legs crossed, looking for all the world like a grown man. His clothes were new and he did not want to mess them up. He had a pressed shirt and a cardigan sweater, a pair of crisp khaki pants and loafers, no socks. But most remarkable of all was this: he had purchased the clothes with his own money! Combining birthday money from our grandmother with some that he had been saving, he had spent most of that morning at Macy's. I could not fathom. Any money I received went to games or gadgetry. My clothes came from J. C. Penney, the only real department store in our town, or I wore whatever I received as gifts on my birthday or Christmas. My mother also sometimes ordered out of the Sears, Roebuck catalog (still around in those days). The thought of spending your own money on clothing was bewildering to me, and I thought a little bit weird.

Then he got his driver's license. My cousins were visiting us, and, as I said, such visits were never as interesting. We had no enchanted garden, no nooks and crannies or hidden park. Also, our visits with each other were getting rarer. Everybody was older (Billy and I were the youngest of the four cousins), and I think my uncle and mother had become less close. Maybe times were just changing, but visiting your cousins began to feel like an antiquated idea. At any rate my father was barbequing and needed something from the store. My uncle tossed the keys to my cousin and told him, "The store, only the store."

This surprised me. Even though my cousin and I were the same age, I still did not have my license. I did not even have my permit, was not yet done with driver's ed. My cousin, I imagined, had been at the DMV on the morning of his sixteenth birthday, licensed within an hour of the doors opening. But even if I had my license, I couldn't imagine my parents tossing me the keys.

The store was not far away. He rolled down the window, slipped a cassette into the radio, and took the longest route possible. If I told him "turn left," he turned right, "right" left, and so forth. When we were younger it seemed natural to be with him. We would play games or talk sports or watch television, but driving with him now, I felt awkward. "You like the Worms?" he asked.

"I've never heard of them," I admitted.

"Yeah, they're pretty new. This is their second album." And he turned up the music and kept his left elbow out the window, a gesture that somehow seemed both casual and eager. I don't doubt that if he had seen some girls, he would have honked. And I don't doubt that they would have honked back, maybe pulled over so they could all talk. My cousin, I knew, was a good-looking kid, with a sharp jaw and blue eyes. He had lost none of his athleticism—in fact, he was the star player on the football team—and he was taller than me by at least four or five inches. Probably I sound jealous and perhaps I was. He had a girlfriend I had never met, but I already knew plenty about her from overhearing my aunt and uncle talk to my parents. They were admiring of the girl while managing to be a little bit critical of Billy. My uncle, I would come to understand, pushed my cousin hard, in a way that my parents did not. They allowed me to drift through school, generally leaving me to my own interests, which were few in those days.

There in the car the Worms played on.

We came to a stoplight. When my cousin let the car start to roll, I said, "There's no turn here on a red light."

He tapped the brakes and looked up and read the sign. Then he looked to his left: no cars were coming. "Why?"

How did I know? Whoever made such decisions thought the light was needed.

My cousin waited all of a few seconds before announcing, "Such an unnecessary light." Then he made the right turn anyway—and took another ten minutes to make the short trip to the store.

When we got back to the house, my uncle was furious with him for taking so long. *You just do what you want, you never listen, how many more chances.* That sort of thing. While my cousin stood with slumped shoulders and my uncle berated him, my father looked sharply at me as well. All the while I thought, What the hell did I do!

* * *

For my cousin's high school graduation party my aunt and uncle reserved a large room in the back of a restaurant. It overflowed with family members and friends of his from school, including his girlfriend. By that time my cousin had made two important decisions: the first—he ditched the name Billy. He announced, ceremoniously, that he would be known as Bill (his given name being of course William). Billy was a boy's name, not to be taken seriously, and he forthwith would be known as Bill Goodwin. The second was that he had accepted an offer to play college football. Come the summer he would be leaving for the San Francisco Bay Area, summer practice, living in the football dormitory, a full ride. (By contrast I was planning on attending junior college and, if things went okay, transfer to one of the state colleges, probably the one in his hometown.)

At his graduation party my cousin was completely in his element, moving like a prince, charming everyone, especially our grandmother whom he insisted on treating regally. At one point I saw him pull up a seat next to her and reach over and refill her glass, pouring a bottle of champagne as if it were the most natural thing in the world. My grandmother nodded vigorously at whatever he happened to be telling her and looked like a smitten schoolgirl. He placed his arm on her shoulder, paternally, and kissed her on the cheek. Then he resumed his princely wanderings about the room, both the host and the hosted.

I spoke with him only once that day, having spent most of the party sitting next to my parents and being bored. His handful of friends paid no attention to me—why should they?—and at one point I saw them ease out of the room (I assumed someone had stashed a bottle of something in his clothes). There was nothing to do but eat chilled shrimp and wait to leave. I rose to go to the bathroom, and on the way there I passed my cousin in the hallway. "Coz!" he cried. "I haven't seen you at all!"

My cousin was nothing if not always exuberant with me.

"I've just been sitting with my parents."

"Do you need anything?" He leaned in. "You need a beer?"

"No, I'm good," I said.

"I think Antonelli and his friends went to get loaded, if you want to get high."

"I'm all right." (At that point in my life I had never smoked marijuana. I also had no idea who Antonelli was.)

In his usual way my cousin's attention spun. He looked out the window of the restaurant: you could see most of the downtown from where we were standing, a mix of old and new construction, a real metropolis compared to my small town twenty miles away. "Look at that piece-of-shit building," he said. "The design is horrible."

I really had no opinion.

"I'm thinking of majoring in architecture."

"Oh," was all I could offer.

"It's one of Marten's, you know."

"Who?"

"Marten. The guy who got into all that trouble." My cousin turned back toward me. "Did you hear? He skipped town."

I had heard. This was a rich businessman who had been arrested for embezzlement. He had developed a reputation as a kind of playboy, to use an old-fashioned term, so much so that even I had heard the rumors of his wild parties and extravagant activities, some too far-fetched to believe. Released on bail, he disappeared into the night, to South America or who knows where. "Oh, and get this," my cousin said, his mind spinning again. "I may become a model."

"What?"

"Or I may do some modeling," he said, tempering the announcement. "I'm meeting with an agent next week, in San Francisco. Her husband and my father went to law school together. I sent her some pictures and I'm going to be meeting with her. Pretty cool, huh?"

"Yeah."

"All right, back to the hoopla. We need to hang out more, you know. I haven't seen you in forever."

"Maybe before you leave," I suggested, though I knew we would not.

"Done!" he said, and he headed back toward the party.

Watching him walk off, I was again reminded why I always believed he was bound for a life beyond the Central Valley, beyond taking a steamer to Switzerland or any of those fanciful childhood notions. My cousin didn't just walk. He strode! And later, after everything that happened, I would remember the case of the rich businessman and wonder if he had taught William a lesson: that it was possible to wade into murky waters, to have the finger pointed firmly at you, and then to disappear into the night without a trace.

Felicity (2000)

Felicity always thought she would be one of those women who got prettier with age, like those girls who were plain Janes in high school and later became *Playboy* centerfolds and left boys shaking their head that they didn't pay enough attention when they had the chance.

That hope would have to wait, however, because she still felt twenty pounds heavy from the pregnancy. The baby, nearly six months old, was crying. She held it close, making a *click, click, click* sound in its ear. She read that babies could be comforted if you imitated sounds from the womb, and sometimes this particular clicking sound worked. Not tonight. Maybe he was teething. Maybe the breast milk upset his stomach. Maybe he was just pissed off.

Felicity was tired. When she had been on maternity leave,

caring for the baby had been a snap, but now she was back at work. Her mother watched the baby during the day, but as soon as Felicity got home, her mother would hand off the baby like a runner's baton and disappear into her bedroom. Sometimes Felicity would not see her mother again until the next morning. It was all she could do to grab a bite to eat, go to the bathroom, sit for a few minutes without *someone* needing *something* from her.

When she first told her mother that she was pregnant, the old bat seemed somewhere between stunned and amused. "You're going to be a grandmother," Felicity said, driving home the point.

"Ooh, your life is going to change," her mother squealed.

"*Your* life is going to change," said Felicity.

`Her mother would watch the baby, for starters. Felicity could not afford daycare and her mother was hard-pressed to argue, especially since Felicity paid the rent. Besides, what the hell else was her mother doing during the day? Then there was the matter of the smoking. Felicity made it clear that her mother was not to smoke around the baby, whether the "thing" was on or not. Thus her mother was relegated to smoking in her bedroom, supposedly with the window open so that the smoke blew outside, though Felicity knew that her mother often ignored this agreement. She also imagined that during the day her mother trotted the baby around the apartment with a cigarette dangling from her mouth, but what could Felicity do—she was busy at Orchard Supply Hardware helping people pick out five-speed fans and cans of paint.

And naturally Tony had been useless. When he found out he was going to be a father, he did a little dance around his apartment, announced that the news called for a toast, and cracked open a couple of beers, offering one to Felicity, who explained that she wouldn't be drinking anything while she was pregnant. After that he pretty much fell off the pregnancy planet. Yes, he was there when she delivered, but seeing his flesh and blood, and a boy on top of it, did not cause some great epiphany. Tony just kept drinking beer, smoking pot, working at the shop. He also didn't give her any money. The only time he helped was when she asked him to buy diapers and he showed up with the wrong ones. He had bought pull-ups. "He's four months old," Felicity said. "He's not potty training."

"How am I supposed to know?"

"Because I told you what to get."

"Excuse me for trying to help."

"Just watch the fucking baby," she said, handing him the child and heading out to buy the diapers.

But most of the time she was not angry with Tony. She had expected nothing from him and so was not surprised when he failed to materialize as father material. She thought maybe someday he might grow into the role. People change. Plain Janes become *Playboy* centerfolds. Stranger things have happened.

* * *

She knew the night it happened. They had been careless. Usually they were careful, or she was careful. She had left her mother home watching *Wheel of Fortune* and, as usual, went to Tony's apartment. She even remembered the song that was playing: Eagle-Eye Cherry's "Save Tonight." It was not so much that the song was memorable, or grating, or any of that, just that she had a strange capacity for such things—remembering what music was playing during some moment in her life. Of course, she would never again hear the song without thinking about Tony Donley impregnating her; and if the song came on the radio, she would almost always turn it off.

She labored over the baby's name. "Felicity" was the one thing her mother got right, she always thought. "Felicity." *An intense happiness. The ability to find appropriate expression for one's thoughts.* Not that her mother had any of *that* in mind when coming up with the name. She had simply seen a character on a television show that she could never recall but at the time had thought wonderful. It would have been enough to drive Felicity to madness except she liked the name, thought it was apt for her personality. It was a happy fucking accident, just like the kid.

Nicholas Norton Gomez, she finally decided.

Nicholas because she planned on calling him Nick. Norton because it sounded smart and she wanted that too. And he would be Gomez, like her, certainly not Donley, not after Tony, someone who thought they should celebrate her pregnancy by slamming back a couple of beers as if the Lakers had just won the championship.

And what of her own father?

Despite his bailing, another man in her life who did not want responsibilities, she had fond memories of him. Not insignificantly, he taught her how to ride a motorcycle. He owned a truck and kept a shabby trailer in their yard—they lived in a house in those days, a rented place right off the 57—and every so often he would load up a pair of dirt bikes and they would head to an open field. Sometimes they even went as far as Cabazon, the Indian reservation out near the desert. She was eleven the first time she got on a bike, a small Yamaha her father had acquired somewhere, no doubt under unscrupulous circumstances. "I got it from a friend" was his only explanation. Naturally Felicity didn't care. It was a toy. And she had never been a Barbie doll kind of girl.

She was also eleven the first time she crashed. They were riding in the hills around Chino and she leaned too heavily into a turn. The bike slid out from underneath her and down she went. She spun a few times before finally coming to a rest, hearing her father laughing over the sound of his idling motor. She was not badly hurt. Her head had not walloped the ground, and even if it had, she was wearing a helmet. Her father was reckless but not so reckless, or stupid, that he didn't insist an eleven-year-old wear a helmet. She was also not going very fast. But her jeans were ripped and her flesh was torn. It hurt more than she would admit. She was eleven: she didn't want to seem like a baby.

"You all right, Betty Cakes?" her father asked.

That was her father's name for her: "Betty Cakes" after Betty Boop, the pinup cartoon star from the 1930s. Her father thought

Felicity looked like Betty Boop, with her dark hair. No one else would have made the connection.

"Can we go home?" she said.

That night Felicity overheard her parents fighting. "You're a fucking idiot," her mother was saying. "You and your fucking motorcycles."

Her father said something that Felicity could not make out.

"Who puts a girl on a motorcycle?"

"That's racist," she heard her father say.

Felicity let it go at that. She did not press her ear to the door of her parents' bedroom to eavesdrop. Fighting was nothing unusual. She went into her bedroom and put in a CD, "Crazy" by Seal. It played constantly on the radio, but she had bought the single anyway.

Her father left about nine months later. "I know you, Betty Cakes, you'll be all right," he told her, before going. Felicity's mother had not begged him to stay. Things had deteriorated, the fighting more intense. Like any twelve-year old—she had had her birthday by then—Felicity had a better grasp of the situation than her parents thought. She would have told you it was for the best, if anyone had asked. Half the time her father was gone, the other half was a state of constant bickering. But she promised, maybe not that night but around that time, if she ever had a child, she would never leave him. Abandonment was for the birds. Your kids come first. Sacrifices are to be made. That is a promise, as she would later learn, that is sometimes easier made than kept. Also, when he left, her father took the Yamaha with him.

Gatsby, the Musical (1959)

Dorothy remembered:

George Latham stretched out on the couch in his stocking feet. He had a pad of paper and a pen. This is how he liked to compose. In those days he could still write with Dorothy in the house, and he was working on his *Gatsby* musical.

Dorothy brought him a sandwich—egg salad with a hint of

dill on white, a few potato chips, glass of plain water. She set the plate and glass on the coffee table, the secondhand furniture they used so they could save up to buy the baby grand. "What do you think of this?" he said, and he read her some lines:

> She has a voice full of money
> A voice that will break your heart
> A voice that can lead you anywhere
> A green light through the dark

"Daisy," said Dot.

"Yes, of course."

He was working on the "book" and the lyrics. He had not yet written the score. He added,

> And when I finally reach her. . .
> And when I finally reach her. . .

Standing in their front room, their window looking out to the nearly identical homes across the street, Dot sang the lyrics in her alto voice: "And when I finally reach her, and when I finally reach her." George got something in mind and he turned his attention back to his pad of paper, where he jotted down some notes. Dorothy let him be. He was in "a place," finally making progress. She was not a composer herself, but she sang beautifully, had been in a few performances at Berkeley, and of course it was their shared love of musicals that had brought them together. When George drove north to propose to her, and they stood atop Sather Hall, she said yes and broke into song, "I'm in Love with a Wonderful Guy" from *South Pacific*. George joined her. It was like something out of a musical itself, the two of them singing atop Sather Hall, the sun just setting (George was always mindful of mood), Oscar Hammerstein's lyrics drifting out into space.

George first got the idea for his *Gatsby* musical while in graduate school. He had seen the film adaptation, the one starring Alan Ladd, full of shootouts and Gatsby behaving like a Prohibition thug, and it occurred to him that it had the makings of a Broadway hit. When he spoke with Dot about it, he spoke animatedly, full of possibility. "I see Gatsby at the edge of the stage," he would say, "alone, single spotlight, singing out to the audience. It's his solo, the first time we learn about his obsession with Daisy. Nick appears stage left but does not approach. Gatsby turns from the audience and faces upstage, where the green light comes on, and stretches out his hand, his arm rising higher and higher, his fist slowly closing."

Other times George would see Gatsby reaching out over the audience, the green light imaginatively in the back of the house. He liked the dramatic effect of that, when Gatsby tells Daisy that he can see her house—he just had to work out the logistics. Dot was his sounding board in those days, and she would offer suggestions, always being careful not to say too much or be too critical. Secretly she wondered whether *Gatsby* was too dark for Broadway. Sure, the flappers dancing would be great fun and the conflict between Tom and Gatsby could drive the action, but there was no Emile and Nellie to sing together at the end. What would the audience think? But she had an unwavering faith in her new husband and believed if anyone could pull it off, it was George.

After he first told her of his idea, she had gone to the Carrolton public library and checked out *The Great Gatsby*. She had never read the novel (it was not the high school staple that it would become). She finished it in a day, found the book entertaining enough but wondered why Tom could never just say something plainly. Fitzgerald always had to add, "Tom said violently" or "aggressively" or "abruptly." Dot had been a good student at Berkeley.

For George, the problem was too little time. He had a full load of classes and was working as many hours as he could at a local music store. He would write in fits and starts and compose in snippets, but progress was slow. Then after graduation he took the teaching job at the college and was occupied with his classes, Music Theory and Beginning Composition. He was eager to make a good impression, so he concentrated on returning student work in a timely way. He secured an early reputation for that. Plus, he had the long work commute. They had bought the house in Greendale because it was more affordable, but it meant a half hour in the car, not as commonplace then as it would become.

One morning, before sunup, Dorothy found him in their front room, sofa and stocking feet. A single lamp illuminated his pages. Dorothy thought it the most romantic thing in the world, her composer husband, awake before the sun, finding the only possible hours in the day. She did not say anything, but slipped into the kitchen where she brewed a pot of coffee. She sat at their small round table until it was ready. Then she poured out a cup, dropped in a sugar cube, and set the cup on a saucer. She brought the coffee to him, all the while remaining silent. The time of day, the single illuminating light, seemed to demand silence. At least until George said, "Thank you."

"Good morning," she whispered, and returned to the bedroom.

They were only a couple of months away from buying the baby grand.

The day she brought him the egg salad sandwich . . . Dorothy especially remembered: After she improvised the music to his lyrics, he lowered his head and began making notes. Maybe he was composing, maybe he was writing more lyrics, she wasn't sure. She lingered for a few moments and then went to water the mint. She liked mint in her tea, so she had planted some right outside their back door. The yard was pretty barren back then, a single oak tree and some grass, the clothesline being the only real feature. Dorothy grabbed the green hose and sprayed the water over the small mint field. Her mother had done the same, kept a supply of mint at the ready, and these were some of Dorothy's most pleasant hours. She was young, midtwenties, married to a man who shared her interests, who had ambitions but was stable. With help from their families, they owned a home. The Steinway & Sons baby grand had been delivered and sat glistening in their front room.

The morning smell of wet mint reached her nostrils.

She had news to give George, but he was composing, and she wanted to let him be. He did not have to go to campus that day, so there was plenty of time. Maybe they would go for a walk and she would tell him then. Maybe they would splurge and buy sandwiches from the market and go to the park. Wherever, she imagined he would hear the news and say, full of wonder, like a line in the first act, before the complication, "A baby?"

And she would say, "Yes, George, a baby."

Cousin Billy (1994)

My cousin played football for only one season before he gave up his scholarship. His interests shifted. As he had mentioned on the day of his graduation party, he decided to major in architecture. He wanted to design buildings. He was meeting new and interesting people. And he was busy with his modeling career, so much so that he could afford to let go of a full-ride football scholarship.

I got all this from my grandmother. I did not see my cousin very often, and we certainly did not stay in touch. But my grandmother spoke glowingly of him, as if a bit of contact was benevolence beyond belief. "Bill sent me a card," she would tell me, using his preferred name. "Bill called me." "Bill came to visit." I guess I didn't mind horribly, even though it was a reminder of the humdrum circumstances of my own life. I had enrolled in community college, later transferred to the state college, shared an apartment with another student, worked in the evenings at a restaurant, and even managed finally to get myself a girlfriend, a shy English major named Carol. In short, my life was most *ordinary*.

My cousin, by contrast, was appearing on billboards, and one weekend my grandmother asked if I would drive her to San Francisco, so that she could see it and take a picture.

We set out early on a Saturday so that we were crossing the Bay Bridge by midmorning. I did not know my way around "the City" (I had been scolded by a classmate one day for calling it "Frisco"), and I made a handful of wrong turns, landing onto a number of one-way streets and nearly barreling over a pedestrian, before we made our way to where my cousin's billboard was supposed to be, in what I now know is the Russian Hill neighborhood. This was not the only location where he could be seen, but my cousin had informed my grandmother that this was the best place. "You can't miss it," he had written to her.

That was true. We had just pulled onto Chestnut when my grandmother said, "Oh there it is!"

I parked the car, and the two of us got out and looked upward. The billboard was atop a small building, and my cousin's image ran the length of the advertisement. He was stretched out, leaning on one arm, smiling confidently (thankfully he did not have one of those "come hither" looks that were all the rage in those days), and dressed in clothing that somehow managed to look formal and informal at the same time. I think the message was that you could and should look good even when relaxing. In the corner of the billboard ran the words "Burkes Cavanagh." This was a clothing store, foreign to me naturally, and probably my grandmother, but apparently known enough to others that the company name and my cousin's stretched-out body were all that was needed.

My grandmother took her picture and stared upward a little longer. Then she turned to me and said, "Let's get lunch."

She was always a lunch kind of gal, my grandmother, keen on a good but affordable restaurant.

Years later, after my grandmother died, I would come across that photograph in her belongings. It was in one of several boxes of pictures and postcards that I brought home for safekeeping. My grandmother had framed the Burkes Cavanagh picture in such a way that very little of the background could be seen; the billboard filled most of the print. You could make out that the billboard sat at the top of a building, but you could not have known it overlooked San Francisco. And the way my cousin lounged and smiled at his surroundings, he really could have been anywhere.

CHAPTER 3

The Comeback Kid (1993)

Mike Allison parked his car in the lot at Trinity University. He had never been to the campus before, never played on their fields. He knew they had a baseball team, and a pretty reputable one at that, but this Christian college seemed an unlikely site for his comeback. But then the whole lofty point of this was its unlikeliness, the long odds, the goddammit nature of it, the if I'm going down, I'm going down swinging attitude.

He was not out of his car before someone else pulled into the space next to him. Mike got out and retrieved his gear, his glove and bat (his batting glove was already shoved into his back pocket). The guy next to him did the same. "Do we need to bring our own water?" the guy asked Mike.

"What?"

"Water. Do we need to bring our own?"

"I have no idea," Mike said.

"Me either."

This other guy was about Mike's age, looked in fact a lot like Mike, not his skin color or his features but his build, the way he carried himself. Perhaps this was not so surprising. After all, they were both baseball players, or had played ball at one time, however you wanted to describe it. There was a *type*.

They walked together toward the field. Nice facilities. Mike could see that. Perhaps not the pomp of Angels Stadium but not some ragged community field either. Mike had made it a point to arrive early—show 'em you're eager—but already at least twenty other men were gathering in a line to get their number. Mike tossed his gear on the ground and did the same. They were a mix of ages, these other men, some looking as young as high school students, some, like Mike, in their early twenties. There was even one clown who looked about forty. Did he really think he had a shot at landing a major league contract? Had he lost a bet? But why the hell not? Unlikeliness was the order of the day.

By the time Mike made his way to the front of the line, at least two dozen more men had fallen in line behind him; and before they got started, another two dozen, at least, would turn out. There was no requirement. You just showed up was all. Mike knew that sometimes the head scout would winnow the field, and do so in a hurry, wean out the pretenders from those who had a real shot. This was Major League baseball, not some bullshit fast-pitch senior league being played for grins and beer.

"Twenty-six," the man told him. This was not the head scout but an assistant, maybe a volunteer. Mike took the slip of paper, and the man said, "Start stretching. We'll get started pretty soon."

Here and there some of the hopefuls were playing catch. Others were in various stages of loosening up, calves and hamstrings especially. That was the last thing you wanted, to tighten up and have to limp out of there, humiliated and injured. Mike had avoided surgeries, but he guessed a good many of these guys had been cut or scoped. The odds suggested as much. Baseball players have more scars than pirates. Tommy John had played just up the road before he got his famous surgery. It simply was an unnatural thing to do, to whip your arm, your wrist, sometimes your whole body, in a way that defied gravity, and to do so day after day, as hard as you could. But that of course was the pitchers, and Mike had decided he would not try out as a pitcher. He had pitched, had a fine fastball back in the day, but he judged that his best shot was as a position player. So when the check-in guy asked him, "Pitcher, catcher, or position," Mike had not hesitated. "Position," he said. Second base, he was thinking. He had not lost arm strength, he was certain. If anything, he was stronger than ever, but when he imagined himself taking the field inside a Major League park, fifty thousand fans cheering and the

PA announcer bellowing, "Please welcome your. . . ," Mike saw himself trotting out to second base, scooping up some dirt and wiping it on his uniform, his ritual, just like the good-luck Ray Corbin baseball card that sat inside his sock, placed there when he rose that morning.

* * *

Mike hated the song "Glory Days" by Bruce Springsteen. Hated it with a fucking passion. And not for the reason you might suppose, the sentiment of the aging athlete stuck in his high school past, getting a few beers in him and droning on about his good old baseball days. That was not Mike. He hated it because of the way it *sounded,* and because during *his* high school years it played constantly, the whole *Born in the U.S.A.* album, that poppy synthesized shit. And you were supposed to believe that Bruce was a genius. "He plays for hours, you know. His concerts are like marathons." Not that Mike had anything against Springsteen personally. "Born to Run" and "Thunder Road" were all right, but "Glory Days"—it might as well have been sung by Cindy Lauper.

It also annoyed Mike when people waxed poetic about baseball. He had attended Orange Community College for a year, and when one of his instructors found out Mike played on the baseball team, the man went on a sermon about how the baseball diamond was a shrine, perfect in its measurements like the Pythagorean theorem, how the game itself was holy and transcendent (he actually used the word "transcendent"), and he recommended to Mike several books by some guy named Roger Angell, whose name, Mike couldn't help noticing, was religious as well. It was not as if Mike was incapable of reflection or "transcendence," only that he preferred to *play* baseball rather than *read* about it. He never did check out any of the recommended books.

These were Mike's thoughts as the head scout addressed the players. Like the others, Mike already knew most of what the man was saying.

"Don't expect to get signed to a Major League contract. The odds are astronomical."

"At best you can hope we notice you, that you end up on our radar and maybe, maybe, we come watch you play somewhere."

"Keep playing, that's the key, wherever you can."

"But be realistic. We scouts know our territory. If you were really Major League material, we probably would have already heard about you."

"But, you never know."

And that's what every guy at the tryout believed, *you never know*, it could happen, had happened, when Tim Heinrich had attended an open tryout, caught a scout's eye, and two years later was playing in the major leagues. Every one of these players thought they were the next Heinrich. Mike included.

Then the head scout went over the day's agenda. They would start by running the 40 ("some of you will be sent home after that"). Next they would divide up: pitchers would go with catchers, and position players would run drills, take infield practice, or shag fly balls depending on their position. If you were still around after that, you would take batting practice and possibly be asked to stay for a scrimmage—if there were enough players still around to scrimmage. "Any questions?" he said.

"Yeah, when do I get my bonus?" somebody asked.

Even the head scout chuckled at that one. "All right, boys," he said, "let's do some running."

They ran the "boys" in pairs, side by side on the outfield grass. Because of his number, twenty-six, Mike was in the thirteenth group. He was not too worried about his time, especially after watching some of the guys who went before him. One oaf showed up in tennis shoes and slipped right out of the gates. Another guy lumbered his way across the grass, like a dream in slow motion. But he was a big guy, a power hitter, a Harmon Killebrew or Big Papi sort, and those kinds of guys weren't expected to steal bases. (Later in the day he would park three balls over the left-field fence, but it would not be enough to get him a contract.)

Mike moved along in the line. He had the Ray Corbin baseball card tucked in his sock. He did not think he would get sent home. He was fast enough. He could take the extra base when needed. True, his nickname had not been Speedy or Spider, but if he had played football, he would have been a halfback. He was faster than most.

"25, 26," the head scout called.

They were to run from a standing position, not getting down in any kind of crouch. One of the assistants would smack two bats together and that was the signal to take off. "Don't worry if the other guy beats you," they were told. "You're being timed separately. It's possible that you'll still have the faster time."

But of course you wanted to beat the other guy. You were competing. Your success meant his failure.

Mike stood and dug the toe of his cleats into the grass, better to push off.

A second or so passed and he heard the smack of bat on bat. He sprung out and stayed low. He pumped his arms and told himself, *Dig, Dig, Dig. Don't stop*. He practically flung himself past the assistant with the stopwatch. And when he turned around, not even breathing hard at all, they were already onto twenty-seven and twenty-eight.

He felt confident, having beaten the other player by at least two steps. As the rest of the hopefuls went through the 40, Mike tried to stay loose, stretching, moving his body left and right, smacking a ball into his glove. God, it felt good to be out here again, the familiarity of it all. "Nice job, Allison," someone said.

Mike turned: *Do I know him?*

"Carl Day. We played against each other in school. You struck me out."

"Did I?"

"Fastball. Inside corner. 1-2 count. I thought for sure you were coming curveball."

"I don't remember," Mike said, good-naturedly. And he could tell Carl Day was one of those guys who could recall every play, every pitch. He was like a golfer who could tell you what club he used on his second shot on the third hole at the crappiest municipal course but could not remember the dates of his children's birthdays.

"So what are you up to?" Day asked.

"You know, just giving this a go."

"You playin' anywhere?"

"Nah. Just cages, shagging flies at my old school. You?"

"I'm hoping to get on with an independent club in the spring, but if not, I may go back to school. I've got another year of eligibility."

"Yeah," Mike said.

This had been Mike's plan as well. Perhaps. If he didn't get signed at the tryout, and he knew the odds were long (*but you never know*), he thought he would go back to Orange Community College, play another year (*keep playing, that's the key*), see what happened.

"All right, man, good luck, good seeing you," Carl Day told him.

"You too."

Had struck him out, fastball, inside corner.

The 40s wrapped up not long after, and the head scout called them together.

If you hear your number, you're done.

The head scout read off eight numbers. Mike's was not one of them. He was moving on. He saw the guy with tennis shoes collect his stuff and head out of there. He looked unfazed. He's a joker, Mike thought, and grabbed his mitt and sprinted out to second base, where he bounced around a bit, scooped some dirt and wiped it on the back of his pants to get the feel. Every diamond is different, and the dirt varies, but it ain't no shrine. They hit the ball, you field the ball, you throw the guy out. It's not that complicated. "Glory Days." It's a shitty fucking song.

The Hikers (1964)

Lost. The thought had not yet occurred to them, not even when the path suddenly disappeared, like one of those planes over the

Bermuda Triangle. One minute it was there, the next a block of trees. They did not panic. They decided to eat lunch, and then it was a simple matter of retracing their steps.

Stacy, who had felt famished, ate only half of her tuna fish sandwich. This happened to her sometimes: she would be as hungry as all get-out and just a little bit of food would do the trick. "I'm going to save my other half for later," she told Bobby, who scarfed down his bologna and provolone sandwich, then ate his crackers and his chocolate pudding in a cup. He had water in a canister and he drank some as well. This was not part of his usual lunch, but because they were hiking, he had filled the canister that morning. He offered some to Stacy, but she was sipping juice and told him, "No thanks," and then they got on the subject of college.

She was going, wanted to go even if her parents were not insisting, just wasn't sure where, maybe San Diego, maybe Marymount, but that was pretty close to home still. "Do you know what you want to study?" he asked.

"Maybe nursing, but I'm not really sure."

"You'd make a good nurse," he told her, and he meant it. Of course at that moment in time Bobby Taylor thought that Stacy Ann Moriarty would make a good anything.

"What about you?" she said. "Are you thinking of going to college?"

How could he tell her: there was no way they could afford it. After his father died they had made adjustments. They were not impoverished, but there was no college fund. They lived in a house that their uncle owned and there was always enough to eat and he had clothes on his back, but he worked all summer, and after school, to be able to pay for his car and insurance and have money to spend. He didn't mind. He liked working at the grocer's. "I don't think so," was all he said.

"So what will you do?"

"When you turn eighteen you can become a butcher. That's union. There's really good money in that and a lot of job security, so I may do that."

He was speaking truthfully.

"That must be nice, to be able to spend your own money. I always have to ask my mother and father if I want anything. I wanted to work last summer but it was hard to find a job."

"How come?"

"Because we spend so much time in Washington. Nobody really wants to hire you when you're going to be gone for a month. I did help my dad out around his office, filing and that sort of thing, but it's not the same, I think, working for your father. What's he going to do if you mess up? Fire you!"

"Probably not," Bobby said.

Above them a chorus of woodpeckers continued their relentless pecking. They had done so all morning, like a song with too much radio play.

"What about Sam?" Bobby wondered. "Is he going to college?"

Immediately the old self-loathing kicked in. *Dumb.* Why would you bring up her boyfriend?

"Oh, I don't know. He thinks he wants to but he never studies."

"Do you think you'll stay together, after you go away?"

Stacy looked off into the trees. Then she looked back at Bobby. Such a nice boy. Was she being cruel? Her mother had warned her about stringing along boys. Is that what she was doing? She said, "Should we start heading back, so we get there before school ends?"

"Probably," he said, regretting he asked the question. She did not want to talk about it—that was fine. Maybe she didn't know herself. As they rose to go back, he pledged, *No more dumb questions, no more reminders of boyfriends.*

* * *

They never would know how it happened, how the woods became so Byzantine. It was simply a matter of retracing their steps, but then the path somehow led them to another dead end; so they turned around and retraced *those steps,* but no more than fifty yards later they were again greeted with another fortress of trees. Like funhouse mirrors, everything felt distorted and confusing and yet everything looked the same, tree upon tree, pines rising above them, unscalable walls, the kind prisoners face.

He remembered when he finally knew it. Ronald Reagan. The actor. That was his name. Bobby had heard him give a speech on the radio, telling everyone why they should vote for Goldwater. Bobby liked the way Reagan talked. "He sure is convincing," he said.

"My parents think Goldwater is whacko," Stacy told him. "They're worried what's going to happen if he gets elected."

"Mr. Evans doesn't think he's going to get elected. He talks about the election all the time." Mr. Evans was Bobby's history teacher. "He had us read this magazine article, by some guy named Hoff-something. It was kind of hard to follow, but basically the article said that some people were afraid that the communists were taking over the country, but that it really wasn't anything new. I guess there's always been people worried about that. People used to worry about Catholics."

That did not seem far-fetched to Stacy. She was thirteen when Kennedy had been elected and she remembered a lot of talk about him being Catholic.

"Mr. Evans said the other day, 'I probably should keep my politics to myself but you kids need to be really careful about people like Barry Goldwater. They do what's called fearmongering. If you don't stand up to them, nobody will. I know none of you are old enough to vote, but you will be someday, and these things matter.'"

"Mrs. Johnson never talks about the election," Stacy offered. "I think she's still sad about President Kennedy."

And it was about then that Bobby processed it, really processed it. Came to a stop and looked around. "I think we're lost," he said.

Stacy stopped as well. "You think so?"

"None of this looks familiar."

They both absorbed that fact, and then Stacy asked, "Which way do you think we should go?"

Bobby just didn't know. It seemed like they had tried every direction. He kept assuming that the right path would reappear. Outside of their brief exchange about her boyfriend, the day had been a dream, what he had hoped, an escape into the woods with Stacy Moriarty, the two of them. He had even abandoned his struggles about whether to kiss her. Just being with her was enough. It seemed like nothing could go wrong. But now—

"Maybe we should cut across here," he suggested. There appeared to be an opening in the woods, a place where somebody else had gone through. They set out. The terrain was hilly—they were in the mountains, after all—and before long a branch caught Stacy on the leg. "Ouch!" she cried.

She wasn't bleeding badly, the cut was no gash, but they paused so that she could press her lunch napkin against her flesh. "I'm all right," she told him, after she pulled away the napkin a third time and the bleeding had stopped.

And they continued on, but the opening really wasn't one, or at least it was not the answer. They might have been inside the Halloween maze that had been set up off Baseline Drive, the one made out of hay bales, but there eventually you found your way out or they came and got you and helped you out. Here there was no man in overalls and a straw hat to say, "Follow me. We got you good."

Yes, *lost.*

Even so, they were not overly concerned. They didn't think they would be lost forever. They weren't thinking about how the sun would go down in a few hours and the temperature would drop in a hurry, how it would be all the colder because of the altitude and the lack of light penetrating the trees. They didn't think about the fact that Stacy was in shorts (she would wish they had brought the blanket then) or that nobody knew where they were, not even her friend Maureen who only knew they were going hiking, or that all they had with them was a half-eaten tuna fish sandwich, a cup of Jell-O, an apple, some sticks of chewing gum, and, thank God, a canister of water.

Their only concern at the moment was that they would be getting back late. There was no doubt about it. School will have ended. At some point Stacy's mom would have parked the car and gone inside the main building. She would have been informed that Stacy was out sick. "You called, Mrs. Moriarty."

"I never called," her mother would say.

And then Stacy would be in real trouble.

Felicity (2001-3)

The kid was sick. It was not that big of a deal. Toddlers got sick. You gave them medicine, you held them, you put them in bed with you and rose in the night when necessary, rubbed their back, got them a cold compress, held the neck of their pajamas if they were throwing up. It wasn't that. It was Imelda. She would not let Felicity be. "Do you need anything? Do you want me to take the baby?"

I want you to leave me the fuck alone, thought Felicity.

"Is he still warm?"

"Did you give him the Johnson's aspirin?"

"I'll get more juice."

Can't win, that's all there is to it. Couldn't get my mother to even look at the baby after six o'clock when I got home from work, and now I can't get Tony's mother to stop mothering for a single damn minute. She had moved in with Imelda when things came to an impasse with her own mother. "I'm too old for this shit," her mother complained constantly. "I didn't ask to raise another child." And then Imelda, who was thrilled to be a grandmother, began showing up: first for an hour or two at a time, and then pretty much all day long, until the arrangement was made that Felicity would move in with her. It seemed like a good idea. First of all, Imelda did not smoke. Also, because she was eager to look after the kid, Felicity would be able to enroll in classes. Her mother was going to move in with her sister. It looked like everybody was on the right side of matters, but now Felicity stood locked behind the bedroom door, trying to comfort a sick child, while Imelda, with her braying voice, absolute nails on a chalk-board, stood outside like a forlorn lover.

Felicity opened the door and handed the kid to Imelda. "Here," she said. "I'm going to get more medicine."

"I have plenty," Imelda told her.

"Not the kind I need."

And Felicity grabbed a sweatshirt and headed out. She did not go far, the steps of the complex only. What she could use most of all was a drink, but she wasn't about to go into some bar alone. She thought about calling the guy from her composition class, and she even pulled out her phone, but she didn't know what exactly she would say. They had swapped numbers for homework purposes. He was a kid, eighteen, good-looking, sure, but living in a different world. Even if she did call him and even if he did say, "That sounds great, let's meet," what would she say to him? *Yeah, I had to get out of my boyfriend's mother's apartment because she was driving me crazy with all her Mexican mothering of my sick one-year-old.* It was not exactly a well-honed pickup line.

Felicity shoved the phone back into her pocket. Two years, she thought, give me two years.

She had not been nervous about going back to school. Even on that first night, after circling the parking lot for a good ten minutes to find an open space, after squeezing into a classroom jam-packed with every human being in the Western Hemisphere hoping to add the class, after seeing the instructor enter looking like he had stepped out of *Hipster Weekly,* she felt good and confident. She knew she could do the work. She decided to enroll in two classes to start, her required English class and math (after taking a placement exam, she had been put in a skills course, one level below college math, but this did not surprise her—she had never been a natural at numbers). She would take Algebra I in the spring and be on her way.

That first night the instructor cleared the room, allowing only a handful of students to hang around who were not on the roster. Then they got down to business. Felicity took notes and occasionally looked around her. The class was a real grab bag of humanity, a mix of recent high school graduates like the boy sitting next to her and some people her age and older; there was even a man who looked to be about seventy. Because it was a night class, they took a fifteen-minute break, and Felicity stepped outside with the others. Some students seemed to know one another; others went and got coffee from a kiosk. But Felicity just wandered a bit, and when she turned the corner to the building she came upon a woman, midtwenties, who was smoking, clandestinely because the college was a no-smoking zone. Felicity recognized her from class. "Don't tell," the woman said.

"I won't," Felicity assured her.

"You want?"

"Sure."

Felicity of course was a seasoned secondhand smoker, and she took a quick draw for camaraderie's sake and handed back the cigarette. The woman had dark hair, like Felicity, but her skin was lighter, almost pale, and she had big round eyes, saucer-like eyes that made her seem alert and alive, sexy. (I am attracted to women, Felicity realized, not for the first time.) The woman told her, "The smoke police are everywhere. You gotta be incognito."

"It's my first night," Felicity admitted.

"Nice. Pauline."

"Felicity."

"Felicity. Shit, that's a badass name!"

"I guess. I don't think my mother really knew what she was doing when she named me. There had been some actress on TV."

"You can rock the world with a name like Felicity, you know. Your Marys, your Barbaras, dime a dozen. But Felicity." Pauline held out the cigarette, but Felicity shook her head. "Pauline's not too bad, but that's only because I changed it. I wasn't so keen on being Paula."

Felicity smiled, and they talked for a while longer as Pauline finished her cigarette. Then Pauline said, "I guess we better get back. Education awaits."

So they walked back together. I could be friends with this

chick, Felicity thought, and in fact some nights Felicity would accompany Pauline while she smoked during break, but they never saw each other outside of school, at least not in those days, especially since the former Paula dropped the class about a month into the semester.

Felicity got a B+ on her first paper. This troubled her. She had been an A student in high school, in English class anyway. The instructor had written her a positive, even flattering note—and gave her a B+. The assignment had called for writing an essay based on personal experience, and Felicity had struggled with what to write about. She imagined the other students had wild and wonderful tales to tell, places where they had been, but what could she say? I work at Orchard Supply Hardware, I forgot to tell my dumb-ass boyfriend to put on a condom and now I have a kid, I like to listen to music. She finally decided to write about her father and how they rode motorcycles together. She told about crashing the bike (though she left out the part about her parents getting in a fight) and about ruining her pants. The papers were to have a thesis, something called the "delayed thesis," and Felicity knew enough not to write, "What I learned . . ."

Toward the end of the essay she wrote, "It's funny how people can go out of your life but leave a part of themselves, how you can remember the positives and put away the rest, or maybe some of us are just built that way."

The instructor liked that—and gave her a B+. As he suggested in his notes, she went to see him during his office hours. He was a young guy. She knew he had just finished getting his PhD or still had to write his dissertation or something along those lines. He was patient with her, pointed out some errors he had not marked, gave her some other suggestions. And then, she was sure, he even tried to flirt with her. But he was not obnoxious about it. She also got A's from that day forward. She was a quick learner and not bad with language. *Felicity. The ability to find appropriate expression for one's thoughts.* About the only thing her mother got right.

* * *

The boy Darren was late. For some reason this irritated Felicity. They had agreed to meet at the Coffee Grind, the one not far from campus. Felicity had not told Imelda where she was going—*Thanks for watching the kid, Imelda, I'm going to meet a boy from my English class, Don't tell your son.* But she wanted Darren to be on time, to appreciate what it meant for her to meet up with him, even if it was for a study session for finals. She did not go out much—ever, to be frank.

By then Tony and Felicity were barely together. She was too busy with work and school and the child to hang out at his apartment. It had been weeks and weeks since they last had sex. She was just not interested. Becoming a mother had the strange effect of sharpening her senses, while Tony kept on being Tony. He would come by his mother's apartment from time to time (he was like a little boy around her), but he still didn't do shit financially for the kid. "You need to take care of this child," his mother would scold, but Tony would flap his arms like a wounded duck. He seemed to be genuinely confused as to what he *could* do.

And Darren—Felicity could tell that he felt no responsibility of any kind. He lived at home. He didn't even work. He took a half-baked approach to the class. For all of this, Felicity was jealous. But he was also strangely likable; so after a semester of casual conversation and swapping phone numbers in case either had a question about homework, they agreed to get together, review the study sheet for the final, meet up at the Coffee Grind. And now he was late.

When he finally showed, he apologized but there was no meaning to it. Felicity tried to shake it off. Why was she so edgy? Why had she labored over what to wear? She wanted him to like her, maybe even *want* her; so she told herself to chin up when he went to get something to drink. All around them the tables were filled, mostly students, but there also appeared to be a prayer group, some six men and women, each with a Bible opened in front of them. Felicity herself had long ago abandoned any religious inclinations. "We believe," her mother told her once, but just what they believed was anybody's guess. In God generally, she supposed. They never went to church. Her mother worshipped at the altar of Richard Dawson and Pat Sajak.

Darren sat back down.

Later Felicity would tell herself that he deserved better, that it was her fault for wanting something from him that he could not have known or been expected to give. His mind bounced, his eyes darted, he seemed to have not been in the same class as her, confused as he was about the final and the teacher's expectations. And he was obviously more interested in Felicity than any essay by E. M. Forster. "So do you have a boyfriend?' he asked at one point.

"A boyfriend. No." It was not far from the truth.

"That's cool," he said. "Do you live at home then, with your parents and shit?"

"I live in an apartment."

"Nice, your own place."

"Not exactly."

"Roommates?"

"I live with my son's grandmother."

He had not heard correctly; she knew that was what he was thinking. "With your who?"

"My son. I have a kid. I live with his grandmother, my. . . ex-boyfriend's mother."

This news blew his mind. "Are you serious? You have a kid?"

"Yeah."

"Like it's actually yours. It's actually your kid."

Felicity felt the trouble brewing deep inside her, the anger percolating. She was surrounded by dumb-asses, even now, at college. "Yes, it's actually my kid," she said, fairly sharply, but the tone escaped him.

"That's wild."

Is he fucking stoned, she wondered?

"So you like have an actual baby? You're like really young."

The percolation was almost complete.

"I mean, how does that work?"

Felicity started to gather her things together. "How does that work? Well see, you have a penis, and you stick that penis inside my vagina, and you get—"

She was making no attempt at being soft-spoken and he got uncomfortable in a hurry.

"—a stupid look on your face, and then nine months later this thing comes out of me that looks like a skinned chicken. That's how it works. Consider taking biology. You'll learn all about it."

She left after that. She thought about sending him an apology, but she knew he was convinced she was a lunatic. "Dude, this crazy bitch from my English class," she could hear him saying to his friends. So she let it be. And when she came to class for the final, he had moved to a different desk, as far away as he could get. She did not make eye contact with him. She kept her head down, just as she would do for the next year and a half.

And eighteen months later. . .

Tony was confused.

"I'm transferring," Felicity said. "I'm moving to Los Angeles. You need to move in here with your mother, to help take care of Nick. She can't do it herself."

Tony paused before replying. "Why don't you take him with you?"

"Because I can't go to school full-time and take care of a kid, that's why."

"Isn't that what you've been doing?"

"Yes, with your mother's help. But she's not moving with me."

"So what am I supposed to do?"

If Felicity had hoped Tony would grow into the role of a father, it had not yet happened. He still spent his days at the shop and his nights drinking beer and smoking pot and watching whatever inanity was amusing him, cage fighting or the WWF. She was determined to force his hand, however. He was closing in on thirty. Come hell or high water, she was moving to the Westside. Through the Housing Office she had already located a house share with three other women.

"You know, Lis, this is a little messed up. A kid is supposed to be with his mother."

They were standing in the kitchen of the apartment. Imelda had taken Nick to the park, so that Felicity could talk to Tony without anyone else around. "Let me handle this," Felicity told her, and for once Imelda did not fuss and protest.

"Isn't he going to be confused when you're no longer around?"

She did not explode. Nothing percolated deep inside her. She spoke plainly and bluntly. "Here's what's going to happen. You are going to move in here. You are going to take care of your son. *Your son.* I am going to college. And I may go to graduate school after that. We'll see. I will come home on weekends, some weekends. And I don't want to hear shit from you about obligations. You owe me plenty. Do you know I could take you to court, right now, and the judge would start taking money out of your paycheck? So don't tell me about what I am supposed to be doing as a mother."

Tony understood that he was derelict on that front, that she could have forced him to pay child support but never had. "I guess you'll probably want to date some other guys while you're there," he said. There was resignation in his voice.

"I don't know," Felicity said. She really had not thought that much about dating. "But it's not like you and I are involved in some great love affair."

"Maybe if we had sex more."

"I'm sure you're taking care of that. And that's another thing—I don't want other women sleeping over here. Do whatever the fuck you want, smoke pot, whatever, but I don't want Nick walking in on you having sex with some chick you picked up at El Torito."

"I hardly go there anymore," Tony said.

"Yeah, well, you get the idea."

"Why are you doing all this?"

"Why am I going to college? Why am I going to have a life? Oh, I don't know. Maybe it's 'cause I'm twenty-three years old and that's what people do. Maybe I don't want to spend the rest of my days on planet earth helping people pick out spray paint. If that sounds selfish to you, I really don't care."

"All right," he said at last. "I'll let Bruce know I'm moving out."

Maybe it *was* selfish. She preferred to think that it was unconventional and ambitious. She wanted time to read. Go to the beach. And, yes, the more she thought about it, meet a few new guys, do whatever. Nicky would survive. Imelda would see to that, no matter how clownish Tony was. Felicity loved the child, but she had not wanted to be a mother, at least not at age twenty. She had borne her responsibilities well, she thought, but it was time. It was 2003. She was now twenty-three. She needed to look out for herself.

What had her father said before *he* left? *I know you, Betty Cakes. You'll be all right.*

The Comeback Kid (1993)

The Ray Corbin thing came about this way:

When Mike was five his uncle brought him a stack of *Sports Illustrated* magazines and a packet of baseball cards. Even though Mike could barely understand any of what was written in the magazines, he loved leafing through them and looking at the pictures, especially the baseball players—Pete Rose, Reggie Jackson, Tom Seaver. And when he opened the packet of baseball cards, Ray Corbin became his favorite player. There was really no reason for this, other than that a five-year-old can form his opinions on the flimsiest of grounds. Mike's family lived in Southern California; Ray Corbin played for the Minnesota Twins. Most children love the star player; Ray Corbin was a middling pitcher. He played only five years in the major leagues and, in fact, he didn't even play the year that Mike got his card: Ray Corbin had been released before the season began! But if you asked the five-year-old Mike Allison who was his favorite player, and people sometimes did, he would say, "Ray Corbin"—and unless they were the most die-hard of fans, they would have no idea who that was.

Then he forgot all about Ray Corbin. For many years. Mike

became a committed Dodgers fan (they were very good in those years), and the Corbin card got tossed in with the rest of Mike's collection, until one afternoon, when he was sixteen, Mike was looking through his old cards—a lark really, he had time to kill before a game that afternoon—and there appeared Corbin, the mitt at the ready, the right arm dangling, the picture looking like it had been taken during spring training, down in Florida.

And Mike remembered. He brought the card with him to the game and placed it between his sock and skin, right leg, the one he used to push off the mound. And that afternoon he pitched a one-hitter and went three for four at the plate with a pair of doubles. After that, he never played a game without the Corbin card tucked firmly against his flesh. Baseball players are superstitious by nature, a witches' brew of rituals: the sign of the cross before batting, the same meal before every game, and, in Mike's case, the baseball card of an obscure pitcher for the Minnesota Twins.

* * *

The drill was simple, no different from what goes on at every Little League field in every town in America: every player would get a half-dozen ground balls to field (*you catch the ball, you throw the ball*). If the scouts liked what they saw, they might give you a few more. If they didn't like what they saw, they'd probably send you home.

Most of the hopefuls who still remained were capable, scooping up the grounders and rifling the ball back toward home plate. The head scout, the man who really mattered, was rotating between the stations, watching the pitchers and catchers toss, then shuffling across the diamond to see the position players dig balls from the dirt. You had to wonder what he thought. The poor saps? Or did he find them admirable, this collection of men, most of them in their late teens, early twenties, believing in their dream, hoping to defy the odds? They had a better chance at becoming the next Wolfgang Puck, but here they were, on a Saturday morning on the finely groomed field of a Christian college, giving it one more shot.

Mike squeezed the ball into his mitt—his first grounder. A breeze. The second one was placed hard to his left, impossibly hard, but Mike moved on contact, saw what he needed to do and leapt out, his body in full extension to haul it in (he looked a little like the flying squirrel that had scared the bejesus out of Stacy Moriarty in the woods). The head scout seemed to take notice.

The next ball went the other direction, a hard shot to Mike's right. It one-hopped him, but he got his body down in time, grabbing it backhand, immediately jumping to his feet to wing it to home plate.

The man hitting the balls became determined to put one past Mike. But Mike was in rhythm. He had his confidence. The Ray Corbin card was pressed against his flesh. The next three balls were hit with increasing speed, and he grabbed all of them as if they were slow rollers to the mound. The man hollered, "A few more."

One time, in Little League, his coach had done the same. Hit the ball as hard as he could, but no matter what, every ball found its way into his glove. "Iron Mike," the coach had called him that day. The head scout was still watching. Mike tried not to think about him. *Just stay focused. There it is. One, two, into the glove. Move to your left. Stay down. Make the throw.* And when they were satisfied they had seen enough balls and called out the number of the next player, Mike did notice that the head scout was jotting down some notes.

He had passed that test, more than passed that test. He had *distinguished* himself. *The best you can hope for is to get noticed.* If only he hadn't squandered so many years, he thought, the years of partying and dicking the dog. But no worrying about that now. This was his chance. Today. A few months earlier Bill Clinton had been sworn in as president. Mike cared little for politics, hadn't even voted, but he remembered what someone had once called Clinton. Bouncing around on the outfield grass while someone else took their turn at grounders, Mike might have felt the nickname better belonged to him. He was Mike Allison, the Comeback Kid.

Gatsby, the Musical (1962)

Every year George and Dot Latham travelled to New York City for a few days, a getaway to take in whatever Broadway shows were the rage that season. They did so even after the children started arriving. Dot's mother would come and watch the kids, and George and Dot would take a room at the Belvedere, go to dinner, walk up and down Broadway. They saw *West Side Story* the year it debuted, and *My Fair Lady*. They bought decent seats—George had established himself as an associate professor and was making a good salary—and when they returned home, Dot kept the ticket stubs in a cigar tin.

It was during one of their first trips east. George's *Gatsby* musical was still being composed, and the two were sitting in a diner when George noticed. "It's Richard Rodgers," he said.

"What?"

"It's him. I'm sure."

George was sure, and he was correct. He had read countless magazine articles and seen any number of interviews and movie reels. He knew Dick Rodgers's face by heart.

"You should say something to him," Dot suggested.

"No, no," George said immediately.

"Why not?"

"You can't just go up to a man like that."

"George—"

"Dot, no."

But she could tell it was killing him. It was like a political junkie seeing Kennedy, just sitting there, eating a pumpernickel sandwich, or a Yankees fan stumbling upon Mickey Mantle as he picked up his dry cleaning. This was the most successful composer of his time, the man responsible for *Carousel, Oklahoma!, The King and I*. Good lord, Dot and George had sung "I'm in Love with a Wonderful Guy" together on the night they got engaged.

George tried not to stare—the man was not doing much anyways, just having lunch—and Dot said, "If you don't say hello, you will regret this for the rest of your life."

George looked at Dot. She was the measure of responsibility

and good judgment. The way she was dressed, well, she would have fit right in with the Mercury astronauts' wives on the cover of *Life* magazine. He rose.

Dot watched as George crossed the diner. She could not hear what he was saying, but she could tell that he was apologizing for disturbing Rodgers during his meal. The famous composer set down his fork and shook George's hand. They spoke for a moment, Rodgers nodding his head a little. George was offering his high regards, telling Rodgers how many wonderful hours he had spent listening to his music. But they did not talk shop. Rodgers didn't invite George to sit down, and George did not say, "You know I do a little composing myself." Certainly he did not tell Rodgers about his *Gatsby* musical. That was close-to-the-vest information. They spoke for maybe a minute at most, and then George turned and returned to the table.

He took a sip of his soda.

"Well?" Dot asked.

"He's a helluva guy," George said, beaming.

At the time Rodgers was in his fifties, George not yet thirty. His *Gatsby* musical was not finished, but he had made good progress. Most of it was written. He just needed to finish composing a few numbers. And when they got back to California, he worked like the dickens, rising early and staying late at his campus office. Richard Rodgers—in the flesh. He had shaken his hand. The man just sitting there, eating his lunch.

How could George Latham have failed to believe?

CHAPTER 4

Cousin Billy (1996)

I lost track of my cousin for a while. His calls and letters to my grandmother came less frequently, and so there was less news to learn. My grandmother would even ask me, Have you heard from your cousin, have you heard from Billy, using his childhood moniker, but of course I had not. When she would hear from him, she'd announce it as if the Pope himself had sent her a handwritten note. Not that my cousin was mischievous in any of this. He was just doing his thing, and that thing involved appearing on billboards, pursuing his design career (most of us in college had a major, my cousin had a career), attending the parties of a lot of big shots. He had even met the governor of California.

Once my grandmother showed me a sketch of his. He had sent it to her as an example of his work. The sketch was white ink on a black background, an original design of an urban building in a parklike setting—trees, fountains, people for verisimilitude. The sketch was fine, competent. But I did not look at it and think, Man, oh man, that is something amazing. (But then I don't know my Andrew Lloyd Weber from my Frank Lloyd Wright.)

Then there was the reception in his honor. It was right around the time we were both graduating from college. Remember, we were born on the same day, and I was finishing up my degree at the state college while my cousin was finishing his at a private school in the Bay Area, the one where he had been offered a football scholarship. Did he actually graduate? I don't know. I don't recall my grandmother, or anyone else, ever attending his graduation. Maybe he just did so quietly; maybe graduating from college was such a humdrum affair for my cousin, so *every-day people*, that he just collected his degree from the registrar's office and moved along.

His coming-out party, however, was an *affair*.

Again I drove my grandmother to San Francisco. Again we crossed the Bay Bridge and navigated the meandering and hilly streets of "the City." I parked in the lot at Union Square, and we marched a few blocks north to the Burkes Cavanagh store. We were early—my grandmother had insisted on leaving plenty of time for the drive from the Valley—and we passed the hour by stopping in at a few other stores, upscale shops and clothiers. They had names like Atkinson West, Fletchers, Buckley & Farrell. *Podunk.* That's how I felt. The neatly arranged silk ties, the jackets hanging with military precision on the racks, the impeccably dressed clerks (they knew immediately that I was not buying)—all of them reminded me of my outsider status. These stores were not J. C. Penney or Mervyn's. Even the jacket I was wearing (the invitation had indicated "evening casual," whatever that meant) was the one I'd worn for my high school graduation. It was a drab, gray piece of cloth, a poor match for my khaki pants and the flat-edge tie that people were wearing in those days, at least in my neck of the woods. Some of the clerks, especially one bone-thin girl, were not that much older than I was, yet they had acquired a sophistication that was foreign to me. They were *clerks*. I understood that much. But they possessed a sensibility, a snobbery, that separated them. But I was no Pip, come to the city to become a gentleman. The bildungsroman belonged to my cousin.

Burkes Cavanagh himself was an elegant man of maybe sixty. He had a mustache that looked freshly trimmed, and he greeted us warmly. No doubt he appraised my shabby attire, but he said nothing, told us "welcome," and invited us to look around. We were among the first to arrive, perhaps predictably. A server offered us wine, which we took, and we moved slowly about. Burkes Cavanagh's store was like the others on Sutter—impeccably arranged. There was not a single speck of dust, and even the light fell differently on each of the tables and the, well, "racks" is not the right word. This was no Filene's Basement.

Apparently what we were attending was a reception for my cousin. To use an old-fashioned term, I believe Burkes Cavanagh was making "introductions." Billy's work, his sketches of buildings and homes and bridges, lined the walls (whatever décor that was usually there had been removed for the evening). They were meant to be tasteful, and I suppose they were. I hadn't known what to expect. The invitation, sent to my grandmother, had been sparse on details—"An Evening at Burkes Cavanagh, Featuring the Architectural Vision of William Goodwin." My grandmother had told me he went by "William" now, a logical and inevitable progression. The invitation also featured a drawing of him. "Self-Portrait" read the small caption.

The store began to fill, mostly middle-aged men and women who looked like they *shopped* at Burkes Cavanagh, but also some younger women, early to midtwenties, beautiful all or at least dressed and made-up to suggest beautiful. They were my cousin's friends, I imagined. As for my cousin, he spent most of the time with an older woman on his arm. They moved like he was escorting her during cocktail hour on a cruise ship. Was my cousin a kept man, I wondered, like the poor screenwriter in *Sunset Boulevard?* But the woman was no Norma Desmond. There was nothing forced and sad in her mannerisms and dress. I would soon learn that she was Mrs. Cavanagh, Burkes Cavanagh's wife, and it occurred to me that perhaps the whole champagne shindig was her doing. Perhaps she had met William when he was modeling for her husband's store. Perhaps he had charmed her. At any rate, he had *some sort of relationship* with them, and here we were, marveling at his talents and evidently celebrating his very existence.

And what was William to gain from the event? I guessed the people there were the sort who built things, or knew people who built things, or employed people like my cousin to design their summer homes. He spoke to us only briefly, but he made my grandmother feel like the most important person in the room.

"There's someone you have to meet!" he told her, and began leading us to one of the middle-aged women. "Coz," he said to me, "I really appreciate that you came. It means a lot."

The woman my grandmother had to meet had family from Wisconsin, a town or two away from where my grandmother had been born. The woman was pleasant, friendly, even as she and my grandmother had little else to say to each other, but it pleased my grandmother to no end to know that William had been talking about her. "So nice to meet you," the woman said, before moving off.

I was ready to go. I had seen the designs, fulfilled my duties as grandson and chauffeur, been summarily ignored by the beautiful young women in their black cocktail dresses (this was evening casual?). But William had told us that he was "going to say a few words," and I knew there was no way my grandmother was leaving until his oratory was complete.

I had to wait another uncomfortable half hour for that to happen—and had another glass of wine while I waited. At last we heard the tinkle of silver spoon upon glass, William standing in the back of the store and asking us all to gather. "First, I want to thank you for coming," he began. "And I want to thank Burkes and Midge for hosting me and for their support for all these years. If there are . . ."

You get the gist. You have heard such speeches before. But my cousin's particular quality was this: he was no huckster, no salesman. He did not say, hint, hint, that he was available for their design and architectural needs. In fact, he made no mention of his drawings. My cousin simply *carried* himself. He concluded, everyone applauded, and we had to wait for ten minutes before my grandmother could reach him to say her good-byes.

"Nana tells me everything," he said to me conspiratorially, as he walked with us to the front of the store. "Every time I call her, she tells me everything you've been doing. It's all she talks about." He smiled at me.

I could not imagine. There was not enough in my dull life to fill a half-page short story. "Congratulations," I told him.

"Burkes is incredible," he said. "People think he inherited, but he built it all himself. He's practically a genius."

How could I not like my cousin? He had been thought a prick in high school, but he spoke without guile, with so much admiration in his voice. After he kissed our grandmother on the cheek, we stepped out onto Sutter. It was dark by then, and the city lights were on in full force. People were crossing the street and the late spring air felt cool, chilly even.

I would drive the nearly two hours home buzzed on white wine, but before we stepped away I glanced back inside:

The store glowed. There was nothing cheap and fluorescent about the lighting. My cousin was speaking with another man, older than us, perhaps late thirties. He had arrived at the reception only a short while earlier and had struck me as someone who would have been fussed over in those Sutter Street stores whose clerks had told me dismissively, "If you need anything, let me know," to which I muttered, "Thanks."

My cousin had a hand on the man's upper arm. It was an almost sexual gesture. The man was grinning wildly. I did not think much of it at the time, but I would recall the image some years later, when the news hit of the famous perfumist, when my cousin became "a person of interest."

Felicity (2004)

Felicity was drunk. Beyond tipsy, something closer to wasted. The boy—and make no mistake, he was a boy, a sophomore all ruddy-faced from dancing—was leaning into her.

"Felicity," she told him. This was the second time he had asked.

"Felicity," he repeated, but it sounded more like "Fa-litch-ity."

They were at her house share. She and the other women had decided to throw a party. They went to the liquor store and bought a bunch of gin and vermouth and limes, for something Kathy called Bombay Bombers. Ramona made a playlist. Then they started phoning people and telling them to come over, and somewhere along the way this boy appeared and latched onto

Felicity. She did not shoo him away. She was drunk. They danced for a while and then she tumbled toward the couch and fell into it. The boy followed her.

This was her second semester at UC. It had gone mostly as planned with one exception: her classes were easier than she had anticipated. Not that she was breezing through, but she had set her expectations very high. And she liked her roommates. Theirs was a two-bedroom unit, so two girls shared a room. Felicity had set her preference for an older student, and the college had been able to accommodate. Ramona was from Bakersfield, and like Felicity she had gone to community college before transferring. What Felicity liked best was their habit of talking deep into the night. Sometimes they would talk with the lights off, just shooting the shit about classes, the world, sex. One night Ramona crossed the room and climbed into bed with Felicity. They kissed—but then they started giggling. It felt silly, out of place. Ramona fell asleep in Felicity's bed but by morning was back in her own.

The boy asked a third time. "Imelda," Felicity said.

"I don't know why I can't remember," he confessed.

"Because you're fucked up!"

"I am."

"Betty Cakes," she told him the next time around.

He went to kiss her, but Felicity had no intention of making out in front of everyone, like she was some sort of junior high student. "Come on," she said, and led him toward the bedroom. There were about twenty-five, thirty people in their small unit, the music blasting, people dancing, a code violation's worth of people in the kitchen drinking Bombay Bombers. Felicity locked the door behind them.

Since transferring, she had had sex with just one person, a recent graduate she met at a Brentwood bar. Her roommates liked to go to the bars in Brentwood. Ramona and Felicity were about the same size, and Ramona let Felicity wear her clothes whenever she wanted. Felicity always asked—she was *that sort of roommate*—and she had been wearing one of Ramona's blouses when she hooked up with the guy. This night, too, she was in one of Ramona's tops.

They fell onto the bed. The boy smelled sweaty from dancing, but his skin was warm and electric. Felicity felt good, slutty. "I'm Going to Be (500 Miles)" by the Proclaimers was playing in the next room.

It was not a prolonged matter. They were both drunk, and after he left the party, she realized she had never asked *his* name.

At that point Felicity had not been home in three weeks. Going back to Imelda's had begun to be drudgery. Felicity was always happy, excited even, to see Nick, but the contrast in the two lives became painfully pronounced. In her one world she was attending classes, lectures, going to Brentwood bars with her roommates; in the other she was taking a four-year-old to the mall, the park, McDonald's, doing her best to give Imelda a break. And then there was the matter of Tony. He had moved into the second room, so whenever Felicity came back, she slept on the couch. One night he came home, drunk, and climbed on top of her. This was a couple of weeks after she had sex with the recent graduate.

"Stop," she said. Even if she had not been asleep for an hour or more, she would have wanted none of it.

"Why not?" Tony grumbled.

"Go to bed."

"Come on."

"Knock it off," she said, forcefully.

"Bitch," he told her, and rose and moved toward the bedroom. "I'll bet you're fucking plenty of college guys," he added.

"Don't let your imagination get away from you." She turned over on the couch and readjusted the blanket.

That was another thing. At school nobody called her a bitch, or if they did, they meant it in a fun way, like in the *Melrose Place* ads that she remembered from when she was a teenager.

And her mother. Felicity did her best to call regularly, see her mother when she was back, but every conversation was the same. Life was a hardship. Living with her sister was unbearable. And this was before Felicity's aunt encouraged, then insisted, that Felicity's mother get a job. Twenty-five hours a week on her feet in a gift store. You would have thought she was a migrant worker picking strawberries for three dollars an hour. During one visit, the same one when Tony called her a bitch, Felicity suggested they go to lunch, her mother, she, and Nick. "I can't afford it," her mother said.

"I'm paying," Felicity told her.

"How do you have money?"

They went to the International House of Pancakes, so that Nick could get chocolate chip pancakes. Her mother ordered scrambled eggs and bacon, Felicity a yogurt parfait, an order her mother somehow managed to pronounce as "high and mighty."

"You need to spend more time with Nick," Felicity suggested at one point.

"Why? He doesn't look like me."

"Mom, he's right there."

"He's eating. He's not even listening."

"Mom."

"Seriously. He looks like a brown bear."

"Well, his father is Mexican. So is his grandfather, so you know, he got their genes. It's how it works."

"Not for you."

"I'm not all that light."

"You're not all that dark either."

"What are you talking about?" Nick asked.

"Eat your pancakes," his grandmother said.

"We're talking about people's skin color, which doesn't matter— it doesn't have anything to do with who they are. Do you understand?"

"No," the child said.

"Never mind," Felicity told him.

"See," her mother offered triumphantly.

Seriously, it was enough to make you stay away forever.

Yet one time she brought Nick back with her to school. She cleared it in advance with her roommates. You would have thought that King Tutankhamen was coming to visit. They made all sorts of plans—they were going to take him to the La Brea Tar Pits, to the Santa Monica pier for hot dogs. Ramona went out and bought the game Candyland. When Felicity came through the door with him, they squealed.

"Oh my God, he's a doll," said Kathy.

And for the first full day they doted on him. They asked him question after question after question: did he know how to do addition, what was his favorite Dr. Seuss book, what did he think about the president. Felicity felt proud and wondered if she wasn't making a mistake by not having Nick live with her. Why shouldn't he be surrounded by this climate? She doubted that Imelda was reading to him at night (certainly Tony was not). She worried that he was falling behind cognitively. Did she detect dullness in him? That night, while Nick slept, Ramona said, "It must be really hard, not to have your child with you."

"I don't know," Felicity said, truthfully.

By the following day her roommates' attentions had abated. They were college students, after all. They had classes and study groups and boyfriends. Felicity took Nick to the botanical gardens. It was one of her favorite places to go to just walk around and think about all that vegetation, how every plant was its own kind. She tried to point out the different species to him, but he had no interest. He kept pausing to push his Hot Wheels through the dirt. I should have taken him to the zoo, Felicity realized, but she was too drained to do so; instead they stopped at McDonald's and then went back to the house share to watch television. Her roommates came in and out, while *SpongeBob SquarePants* played incessantly on the television. Felicity felt herself crumbling. She began to cry, wondered if she could drive him back that night, a day early, but realized she could not. Madison emerged from her bedroom, dressed and headed out the door. "What's wrong?" she asked, and came and put her arm around Felicity.

Felicity just shook her head.

The television blared its unholy noises.

"Can I do anything?" Madison said. "What's going on? Why are you upset?"

"I—," Felicity started. How could they understand if she did not understand herself? She felt like Prufrock, unable to put into words exactly what she meant. "I'll be all right," she managed to say. "I'm just having a crappy life."

The Hikers (1964)

Stacy's mother, Jill, sat in her car outside the high school for a good fifteen, twenty minutes, but she never did enter the main building. At one point, when Stacy did not emerge, her mother rolled down the window of the car and called out to a girl she recognized. "I haven't seen Stacy all day, Mrs. Moriarty," the girl said.

Probably Stacy had an after-school activity and had forgotten to tell her mother. Her kids were constantly doing this, though her son more than Stacy, who was generally organized. Maybe she and Sam had made plans. Maybe there had been some confusion about pickup and Stacy had gotten a ride home.

Jill Moriarty returned to the house and started dinner— Sloppy Joes. Her husband typically got home by six—he was good about that—and he would have a drink and watch the evening news, and then they would sit down as a family and eat. This was a Moriarty requirement. Unless there was some very good reason, they ate together as a family. Perhaps it seemed old-fashioned—Jill Moriarty knew plenty of families that ate in front of the television— but she and Bill determined early on that the dinner hour would be sacred, a chance for everyone to share their thoughts about the day. Her children would appreciate the routine when they were older. Everything was moving so fast these days.

The sky darkened and still Stacy had not returned. Her brother was in his room studying, or was supposed to be studying, and Jill tried to remember if Stacy had told her of some plans. Jill forgot things herself from time to time, a dentist appointment or something one of the kids needed for school, but for the life of her she could not remember Stacy saying anything about going anywhere. As usual, Bill got home a shade before six, and as he mixed a drink, Jill asked, "Have you heard from Stacy today?"

It would be unusual if he had, and Bill told her no.

Jill fretted, but she was mostly irritated that her daughter was being so thoughtless. They would need to have a "reminder talk" with the children about their obligations—to clean their room, walk the dog, be home by the dinner hour.

Then a short while later the phone rang: it was Sam calling for Stacy. "I thought maybe she was with you," Jill told him.

"I was calling to see if she was feeling any better," he said.

"What do you mean?"

And that was the first sign, first real sign, that something was amiss. "I have to go," she told Sam. Jill began making calls. She phoned a number of Stacy's closest friends. None had seen or heard from her all day. Because she was not at school, they all assumed the same thing: she had not been feeling good and stayed home. It was not until the sixth or seventh phone call that she spoke with Maureen, Stacy's friend who had phoned the school earlier that morning and pretended to be Mrs. Moriarty.

Maureen told her that she had not seen Stacy. "I'm sure she'll be home soon," Maureen said.

"Yes. If you hear from her, please let me know."

"I will."

Maureen was not the panicky sort. It was hardly that late. Maybe she and Bobby were just having fun and lost track of time. But over the course of the hour, strange thoughts began to occur to her. Why had they not gotten back as planned? What if there had been an accident? No matter how you cut it, Stacy was going to be in trouble. She had obviously lied to her mother, had played the truant, but Maureen just couldn't imagine a scenario where Stacy would come breezing through the door after dark, like she was some sort of rebel, like one of those platinum blondes who rode the backs of motorcycles. Maureen didn't want to implicate herself, or cause more trouble for Stacy, but about nine o'clock she phoned the Moriarty house. From the way Jill Moriarty answered the phone, Maureen could tell that Stacy was still not back.

"Mrs. Moriarty," Maureen said, "I have something I need to tell you."

Stacy was insisting that he eat half of her unfinished tuna fish sandwich. Bobby was refusing. He "ate enough at lunch," was "not hungry," was "okay."

She tore the remaining sandwich in half and forced it on him. "It's going to be a long night. You need to have something."

Finally he relented, but they agreed that they would save her apple and Jell-O, that they needed to space out their provisions. They needed to be stingy about the water as well. They knew they were done for the night; there was no more walking through the woods. It was dark. The ubiquitous woodpeckers were finally silent. Their best course of action was to hunker down and wait until daybreak. Then, they were sure, they would eventually make their way out of this mess, would face the consequences of their actions, and have a pretty interesting story to tell. But Stacy was cold. (Bobby was as well but tried not to show it.) He was in jeans, she in shorts. Thankfully she had worn a sweater, but the temperature had already dropped below fifty degrees and it was not yet nine o'clock. They thought about building a fire, understood the importance of that; it was just that they had no means to do so. They could rub two sticks together, but that was a myth, wasn't it? Bobby had never been in Scouts. Plenty of kids smoked at school, but neither of them did. They had no matches, no lighter. So all they could do was sit and shiver, there in the San Bonaventure Mountains, while Stacy's mother waited for Maureen to arrive.

Jill Moriarty had questions:

Where were they going?

"I don't know," Maureen said. She and her mother and Stacy's mother were standing in the entryway of the Moriarty house. "I don't think Stacy knew. They were just cutting school."

"Just cutting school," Maureen's mother sniffed. She was furious at her daughter, wanted Stacy to walk through the door so she could drive Maureen home, lock the girl in her room and let her out on graduation day.

What kind of boy is he?

"I don't know him well," Maureen admitted, "but he's not a bad kid—"

"How do you know that," Jill interjected sharply. "How do you know he's not a sicko?"

"They're in biology together. He lives with his mom. I think his dad died or something. He works at Kroeger's Market. You've probably seen him there."

Jill looked at Maureen's mother. "Do you know this family?"

"I don't."

"I don't understand why she would do this," Jill said, but it was to the air.

"Do you know anything else, anything you are not telling?"

Maureen shook her head. The only thing she had not admitted was calling the school and pretending to be Mrs. Moriarty. What good would it do to admit that? It wouldn't change anything. "Maybe they went to the movies."

"I hope you're right," said Jill, but she did not believe Stacy was at the movies or sitting in some bowling alley somewhere. Stacy's mind was a muddle at times but she was a dutiful girl, not the sort to wake up one morning and become a juvenile delinquent. So far Jill had been reluctant to call the police. It really wasn't *that* late. Maybe Bill would locate them. He was out driving around. There would be a perfectly good explanation. Jill had crazy thoughts herself when she was a teenager, had once stayed out past curfew. She thanked Maureen's mother for driving over, then shut the door. Peter had gone with his father to look for Stacy. The house felt empty.

* * *

Stacy was shivering, so Bobby put his arm around her and she pressed close to his body. She was smaller than he was, but she was not a slight girl, no body fit for a ballerina or a gymnast. Bobby himself was of average build, and he squeezed her upper arm, to try and curb her shivering. They were sitting in a cluster of trees—of course, the whole damn mountain range was a cluster of trees—and had pushed together some brush to make sitting more comfortable. This is where they would sleep, they had decided. It was as good, or bad, as anywhere else.

They stayed this way for a while, Bobby holding Stacy as close as possible. It seemed to work: the shivering subsided, not completely but enough so that Stacy began breathing normally. "This was pretty stupid," she said.

"I guess so. I should have paid more attention to where we were going."

"It's not your fault. Okay? Don't blame yourself."

"I just never saw the trail go a different way."

"Stop," she told him. "It happened. We're here."

She moved away from his embrace and stood up, walked around to get her blood moving. She jumped up and down, rubbed her hands together. "Do you think it will get much colder?"

"I don't know," Bobby said. "The sun has been down for a long time already. Maybe this is as bad as it will get."

"We should sleep holding onto each other," she said, "so that we retain heat. That's our best bet."

"I agree."

Moving again helped, even as she knew it was a losing battle. She was in the middle of the woods, wearing a pair of shorts, a sweater that had been selected to battle the morning chill, not the frigid night air. She looked at Bobby: he was trying to be brave, she could tell, but he was cold too. And troubled. Very troubled. She wished desperately that he had brought the blanket. "Can I ask you something?" she said.

"Sure."

She was going to ask him what he thought about her, why, when she had cut school to go hiking with him, he had not tried anything, to at least kiss her. How much more romantic could it get, at least until they got lost, alone out in the woods, the two of them doing something shared and illicit? Was he just shy? Sam was never shy, now anyway, once she had made the first move—after that he was as confident as Dean or Brando. Maybe all boys were that way, shy until they got their confidence, once you showed them you were interested. Then they behaved like swaggering idiots. But it was cold, and Stacy beat away these thoughts. She told Bobby, "You know what, never mind. We should try and get some sleep."

Gatsby, the Musical (1963)

If only he could write a song as good as "America," the number that would be in their heads as they headed into the New York night, the signature song. He had a few good numbers, he believed. The reunion scene between Gatsby and Daisy was touching, a good old-fashioned love song, and there was a terrific heart-breaking solo for George Wilson after Myrtle had been run over, but *that number,* the one defining the whole show, he just couldn't find it. Nick's first party at Gatsby's seemed a likely setting—built around the dancing flappers—but the problem was that Gatsby and Daisy are not together in the scene, and how do you have the song that defines *everything* when the two principals are not on stage? Maybe he could have Gatsby singing from the upper floors of the mansion, Daisy from her perch in East Egg. But the logistics were not the problem. Logistics could always be worked out. He just didn't have the tune, the one that made people say, "Have you seen *West Side Story?* You have to hear 'America'!" He knew it to be so, a fatal flaw. But he just kept waiting for the composing gods to bestow their good graces upon him. It would come. Maybe while he was driving. He read Dick Rodgers tell an interviewer that sometimes the tune popped up, like a bubble, as if it had been there the whole time, waiting to be captured. Sometimes George Latham thought he had it. A riff or combinations of notes would come to him. If he were by a piano, he would try and flesh it out. Otherwise he would write it down. He kept a scrap of blank sheet music with him always, in case the bubble appeared. One time he rushed into a coffee shop—to set down the tune before it disappeared back into the ether. He was the mad composer, divinely inspired, but when he got home and played the sequence on the piano, well, it just didn't work. It was not genius. But it *would come*. Patience and perseverance, that's all that was needed. Not everybody could be Sondheim at twenty-seven. George was only thirty, then thirty-one. The children were young. Dot was as supportive as can be, even if she did not always understand. He was never tart with her, but he sometimes wondered how he might fare if she was a greater critic. "That's good," she would tell him when he knew it was not, or not good enough. It had to be *genius*. Had to be *fool-proof*. But there was time. He would be walking, a thought would flash, followed by a tune that had been sitting there the whole time. He would have it, his "America." *One fine morning!*

The Hikers (1964)

What had been enchanted became a dark prison. Where there had been industrious woodpeckers, now there were hooting owls, low deep sounds like the throttling of an engine. Every now and then the brush would rustle, making them think, *snake, cougar, bear.* Even the croaking frogs were a reason to be startled. They might have stumbled into a Grimm's fairy tale, suspecting that any minute an old woman would appear, crooked nose with warts. They slept in snippets, if at all. Sometimes they would speak ("do you think they are looking for us"), sometimes they would rotate positions—the brush was hardly any cushion against the hard floor of the mountains. Stacy's legs were goose-fleshed and she would bury them between the coarse fabric of Bobby's jeans. It need not be said: there was nothing sexual in any of this. They were trying to survive. "Do you think it will get any colder?" Stacy had asked. It had. The temperature had dropped below forty, slipping toward freezing. Now and then Bobby thought of his mother. At some point she would have phoned his uncle, considered whether he had run away, worried about a car crash. (In fact his mother had already called all the local hospitals; and a little after midnight Stacy's mother finally phoned the police.) Then his mind would shift, uncontrollably, without will, and he would be back on the path, wandering, running into dead ends, back on the path, should I bring a blanket, Stacy cutting herself on the leg, the path, they were walking and wandering and every tree the same, her mind cold and cluttered, her bed, with its floral pattern and two big pillows, God, it's so cold, then darkness, only to wake shivering, pressing even harder into his body, and when was daylight, just darkness and darkness and darkness, we just have to make it to daybreak, then everything would be okay, the sun would warm us.

CHAPTER 5

The Fairfax Apartments (Present)

His name was W. and he had been born in Clyde, Ohio. You could write the rest. It is a familiar story. He did no acting in high school, played sports. But in college a girl he knew suggested he take a class, and he discovered that he liked being on stage. He did not become an Olivier in the making—he was never going to do Shakespeare in the Park—but he was cast in a couple of plays, Happy in *Death of a Salesman*, Corporal Barnes in *A Few Good Men*. He graduated with a business degree but had no real desire to go into sales or anything else. He thought he could become a star. He knew he was good looking. (From an early age women had paid attention to him.) And he thought he had a certain charm that set him apart. He admired Brendan Fraser, saw himself in that vein, a franchise guy. So he came west, changed his name, and registered with Central Casting. The drill.

* * *

About eleven o'clock, the woman from unit 2 joined the Actor by the pool. He spoke to her from time to time, nothing substantial, just hellos and apartment gossip around the mailboxes. She was friendly and flirted openly with him, was the sort of woman he could have in a minute, he believed, divorced no doubt, hard up, probably thought about him when she touched herself. But he was not interested. Have sex with a woman like that and she won't leave you alone. Would brag about it to her friends and do stuff like bake you cookies and bug you all hours of the night.

She settled in a chaise lounge across from him, which was

good, because he wasn't in the mood for conversation. He wanted to read for a while, tried to read, but the book bored him. There was very little about Prohibition or speakeasies—nothing that could really help with his role. *His role.* The thought thrilled him. He remembered when he arrived in Los Angeles and registered with Central Casting. His first job had been at Paramount Studios, for a medical drama. When he walked on set, it was like having a magician reveal his signature trick. There were the cameras, the matter-of-fact crew laying down tracks and tape, the hustling assistant director who was assigned to keep the background actors on task and in place. He felt he had arrived. They broke for lunch, and he went through the line with the others. "I was on set with Brad Pitt, last week," a woman said to him. "You can't believe how nice he was to all of us. He used to do background work, did you know?"

He hadn't known.

The woman talked a little more, and he examined her. There was something odd, but he could not place it, not right then. She was older, a little haggard, neither a Hollywood beauty nor someone who might be a character actor, the recognizable but elusive face. Later, after he had more extra work under his belt, he realized what he had missed: she had the look of desperation. Most of them did, these background actors. The woman had been at it for nearly twenty years, twenty years and still grinding away for a hundred dollars a day. And it was not always Paramount or Warner Bros., that's for sure. Over the next couple of years the Actor spent long days in high school gymnasiums and cafeterias, the Elks Lodge parking lot in Pasadena, any number of public parks. But he would not be doing background work forever. He was never going to end up in Tarzana doing porn shoots. He was going to be Brendan Fraser.

And now, yes, here he was, five years later, up for a role in the pilot for a series that had a legitimate chance to get picked up. His agent said so, and the Actor had read about it in *Deadline Hollywood*. Unless the showrunners screwed the pooch, they would get the order. Thirteen episodes.

A short while after the woman from unit 2 settled into her chaise—and he was not so disinterested that he did not watch as she removed her wrap and sprayed down her bikinied body with lotion—the Armenian man who lived near him took a spot at the north end of the pool. The man removed his shirt. Good God, he was a fur ball! He drove an airport shuttle, the Actor knew, because sometimes the man parked it in the apartment lot. It took up space and annoyed everyone. And a short while after that, one of the brothers who lived in an upstairs unit appeared, dressed in a blue hooded sweatshirt and jeans. The brothers looked Persian or Middle Eastern or something. (Geography had never been the Actor's strong suit. He wasn't even sure the Armenian man *was* Armenian.) They kept late hours and had all sort of sketchy characters coming and going. They probably dealt drugs, but what did he care? To each his own, so long as they left him alone. The Actor was not into drugs, some pot in college only, was just not interested in polluting his body with impurities. He took testosterone pills sometimes, on the advice of one of the guys at the gym, an actor like himself who said it helped with energy and form, but was otherwise about healthy food and free weights.

The brother, the one in the hooded sweatshirt, bounced down the stairs without looking anyone's way. A sweatshirt. In this heat. The Actor had been out here for an hour and the temperature must have climbed another five degrees. The Armenian man was reading a magazine, wearing a pair of plain-colored swim trunks, a pair of sandals still on his feet. The woman from unit 2 was sitting with her hands folded behind her head, her eyes closed. Mrs. Brownmiller, the elderly woman who lived in the unit next to the Actor, came through the entryway holding a bag of groceries. The Actor rose and hustled over to help her. She was a spry white-haired woman who appeared to have no family, and the Actor helped her whenever he could. He carried her groceries up to her unit, and they made some small talk about the heat. He refused an iced tea and then made his way back to the chaise lounge.

As he settled into the chaise—and it was not yet eleven-thirty in the morning—a startling thought came to him. When he helped Mrs. Brownmiller with her groceries, he had left his phone. *What if?* He reached below him, where his phone sat on top of the book. But there was neither a text nor a phone message.

The Actor set his phone back under the chaise and decided to go for a swim.

Felicity (2004)

Ramona went with her friend to Planned Parenthood. She never told the sophomore, in fact never saw him again, did not even know his name. Once she thought she recognized him across campus, but she was not sure—she had been drunk, he left shortly after they emerged from the bedroom, the rest of the party dancing wildly to Tag Team's "Whoomp! (There It Is). " But what would she have said anyway? She had made the mistake once before and would not do so again. She loved her child, but Felicity had no intention of becoming a mother two times over. She would graduate from college.

Ramona was patient and sweet. She had aborted a child herself several years earlier, when she was in high school. She drove Felicity to and from the clinic, settled her into bed—the same one where she had gotten pregnant—and asked if she wanted anything to drink.

"Maybe just some water," Felicity said.

"All right."

They had not told their other two roommates. Madison was less nimble on these matters. While she would not have tried to convince Felicity to keep the child, there would have been judgment in the air. And Kathy would have been *too* solicitous.

Ramona got the water and brought it to Felicity, closing the door behind her. "You know what song?" Felicity said.

"What do you mean?"

"The song that was playing."

"When you were—"

"Yeah."

Ramona sat on the edge of the bed. "No."

"The Proclaimers, that '500 Miles' song."

"Okay."

"What do you think about that song?" In a very tired voice, Felicity sang a little bit of it. "I would walk 500 miles, and I would walk 500 more."

"I don't know. You need some sleep." Ramona reached over and pulled the Target-bought comforter toward Felicity's neck.

Felicity closed her eyes. "I think it's a good song," she said, "but it's ruined now. Now it's the Felicity did a dumb-ass thing song."

"You were not a dumb-ass. You were drunk. And horny."

"It was dumb. And I'm a shitty mom. I should stick to women. They can't get you pregnant."

"You like men," Ramona said.

"I like you."

"You'll feel better after you sleep. Get some rest."

Felicity muttered something after that, but it was incomprehensible. She fell asleep and Ramona let her be. She slept for several hours, woke and watched some television, and went back to bed. When she rose in the morning, she showered and attended class. She moved numbly for a day but then found her stride. She placed a call to Imelda's and spoke to Nick. He was doing fine. Felicity was a few months away from graduation, an achievement when you consider her origins: a chain-smoking mother who rode disability like a log down a free-flowing river, a father who could not be bothered to raise her at all (he would come back into her life), and possessing a womb that evidently was as fertile as the Nile Valley.

Not long after, Felicity made her first visit to the Getty Museum. It was a rite of passage for students of a certain temperament. She went alone, rode the tram, walked the grounds and the gardens, and moved through the different wings. It was midweek, so the museum was not very crowded, just a few stray bodies at the opposite end of the room and an indifferent security guard in a brown coat. She came upon Cezanne's *Young Italian Woman at a*

Table, and the sight of it arrested her, the way art sometimes can, like seeing Michelangelo's *David* for the first time, or rereading *Gatsby* at thirty, or hearing a song you loved as a child but had long forgotten. The woman's beautiful but forlorn features, her head resting heavily in her hand—the painting grabbed Felicity by the throat, poured concrete at her feet.

Felicity had studied Cezanne in her art history class—*The Card Players,* of course, and *Mont Sainte-Victoire*—but the painting before her had not been part of the curriculum. How did I not know this existed? she thought. What if I had not lived long enough to have this moment? She had come alone but suddenly found she wanted someone by her side. It need not be a lover ("lover," a word that Felicity hated, with its saccharine sound), just someone who could commiserate, who would *get it.*

She must have stood before the painting for a full ten minutes. Had she been a different sort, she might have made notes, jotted down thoughts in a journal. "Young Italian Woman at a Table—sad, inexplicable, me." But Felicity was never that way, not even later when everyone, it seemed, felt the need to record every moment on their phone. Felicity preferred the contours of her memory, experiential, fleeting if necessary.

At last she moved along in a kind of trance toward the exit of the room. The man in the brown coat ignored her—he was like a security guard at Buckingham Palace—and Felicity turned to take one last look at the Cezanne. She would come other times, but none ever had the force of that first visit. The woman would always be sad, her head resting forever in her hand, the yellow scarf endlessly beautiful, but Felicity would never again slip into the woman's flesh, experience her for the first time.

Felicity left the room and went downstairs to the cafeteria, where she bought a Caesar salad and a Diet Coke and ate alone.

The Comeback Kid (1993)

Mike woke in the girl's bed, began to reassemble the pieces: the shots at the bar, the way she threw back her head whenever he said something funny, her black bangs swaying, the drive to her apartment (he should not have been driving, he realized now), and—

It came to him just in time. *Jacqueline.*

"I'm hungry as shit. I could eat an African safari," she said, stirring next to him.

They went to a café down by the harbor. Mike had never been there. They both knew what was what: they would eat breakfast, swap numbers, and suggest that they stay in touch, and that would be that. Maybe they *would* text each other. It was possible that they might even see each other again, but basically it was breakfast and then onto their respective Saturdays.

Jacqueline ordered a latte, and Mike ordered a Coke. He was not a coffee drinker, never had been. The other guys on the crew drank it by the bucketload. Their wives sent them to the job site with huge thermoses of the stuff, which they powered through while they drywalled their way around the homes of Orange County. "So do you think you'll do it?" she asked him.

"Do what?"

"The tryout thing."

"Oh, right." Mike had forgotten that he had told her—the Angels tryout, his thoughts about giving baseball one last go. "So you go to Fullerton," he said.

"Shhhh!" she whispered dramatically, and looked around for comic effect. "It might get back to my parents."

"What?"

"Typical Asian parents," she explained. "Piano lessons when I was still in utero, math tutors and SAT classes before I was menstruating. Then I got kicked out of school."

"College?"

"High school. Alcohol. The first time I stood before a jury of my peers and got put on probation."

Mike looked at her, confused.

"It was a private high school. Where did you go?"

"Benton," he told her.

"I remember. You told me that."

"The second time I went straight to the Head's office, no

more jury of my peers. When my parents picked me up, they looked like I had just been sentenced to San Quentin. Fullerton was the only place that would take me."

"What's so bad about Fullerton?"

"Thirty thousand people can't be wrong," she said, raising the latte to her lips.

The waiter brought the food and Mike ate hungrily, beating back the hangover. Despite her earlier declaration, the girl Jacqueline picked over her food, taking small bites as if she were eating cheese squares on toothpicks. She was watching him eat, he could tell, and it was making him a little self-conscious. "What's up?" he asked her at last.

"Did you know that other animals don't experience regret?"

"What?"

"Yeah. Humans are the only animals to feel regret. It's been studied pretty widely."

"I didn't know." Mike assumed she was talking about the night before, about their hooking up at the bar. He started to worry that she was going to get weird on him.

"We studied it in my psychology class. There's something called the lost opportunity principle, and existential regret, all kinds of crap. But animals, no such experience. Not even other primates. They just do their thing, eat, fuck, whatever. Your gorilla never wakes up in the morning, saying, What the hell was I thinking?"

"I have no idea what you're talking about," he said, "but I could use some more Coke." He began looking around for the waiter.

"You should do the tryout. That's the point. Otherwise you'll regret it. I never regret anything. I'm like an animal that way. But most people . . . regret's as basic as breathing. You sound like you're a pretty good baseball player. Not that I know shit about it, but if you have a chance and you don't, you know, you'll sit around the rest of your life wondering what might have been, like George Bailey."

"Who's George Bailey?"

"It doesn't matter. Your business, but there's nothing more annoying than listening to people talk about what they used to be or what could have been. I had to get past that, last night."

"Was I doing that?"

"A couple of times. I think you were just trying to impress me with your athlete past."

"Bullshit."

"Don't get mad. It worked, didn't it?"

"Some more Coke," Mike said, when he got the waiter's attention. "I never do that. Was I doing that? Talking about the past."

"You were drunk," she told him. "Everybody gets on that train sometimes. 'I coulda been a contender!'"

He didn't get the reference, and they moved on to other subjects, happily so for Mike, while they finished their breakfast. He never did see the girl Jacqueline again. She was nice, if a little funky, but a relationship had not been the point.

* * *

That afternoon, after he got back to his apartment, Mike dug a bat out of his closet and went down to the batting cages on Seventeenth Street. He fed a handful of quarters into the machine, and the balls started jumping off his aluminum bat, the old familiar *ping, ping, ping.* He had not swung a bat in ages, but the knack returned to him in a hurry. Sixty miles an hour. Seventy. The machine ratcheted to the maximum of eighty, Mike in rhythm, the barrel meeting the ball every time, the balls flying into the mesh. Effortless. It was like patching a hole in the wall or picking up a girl at a bar.

Gatsby, the Musical (1963)

George Latham walked ceremonially into the post office, an envelope under his arm. He had parked several blocks away, not because there were no spaces out front but because he wanted to take his time, be aware of the moment. Years in the making— you didn't just dump the thing in some indiscriminate mailbox.

There were several people in line in front of him. A woman at the counter was buying stamps, a man was mailing a package. Inside George's packet was his musical.

One Fine Morning.
Music and Lyrics by George H. Latham.
Story by George H. Latham, based on *The Great Gatsby* by F. Scott Fitzgerald.

George had never found his "America," the signature song, the surefire hit, and it disquieted him. But other songs were good, and the ones that were so-so, well, he hoped they at least moved the story along. It was not as if every number in every Richard Rodgers musical was brilliant. Songs had roles to play. And eventually he had to finish. At some point you have to drop your line in the water and see what bites.

The woman buying stamps moved away, and George inched forward in line. He was sending the work off to an old acquaintance in Los Angeles, a classmate who was now the artistic director at the Arcade Theatre. George had phoned him up a few years earlier, explained what he was working on, and the man said, "When you have it finished, send it along. We'll take a look."

If everything went according to plan, the show would open at the Arcade, be well received and move to Off-Broadway, then Broadway itself. George hoped, dreamt, that the next time he went to New York City, it would be to work on his own show. How many times had he sat inside the Belasco, the Lyceum, and imagined that very thing. So it had taken longer than he thought it would (Dorothy had just given birth to their third child). He wasn't the sort to sacrifice others at the altar of his artistic creation. They needed to eat. He enjoyed teaching. He wasn't going to run off and squirrel himself away in a cabin in the woods, live off the handouts of others so he could compose. He did it on his own time, in his own way.

When his turn came he handed the manila envelope over to the clerk, who weighed it and announced the postage. "Manuscript?" the man said.

The transparency took George by surprise. "Yes," he answered.

"Looks like a manuscript."

"A musical," George explained.

"Ah."

But the man did not ask the subject and George would not have told him anyway. He had learned never to tell people the subject of your work. It was like telling them what you planned on naming your baby. They would smile uncomfortably and say, "That's a nice name."

George watched as the clerk dropped the envelope into the pile of outgoing mail, then stepped away. There was nothing more to be done. His fate was in the hands of others. He walked the several blocks back to the car, but when he reached it, a compulsion came over him and he kept on walking. It was a beautiful September day and he had no other obligations. Possibility was in the air. He was a thirty-two-year-old associate professor of music, a father of three young children, and the composer of a musical that, he felt, was both heart-breaking and inspiring. It had flaws, he was aware, but wasn't that the whole point of Fitzgerald's novel, or one of the points, that we try and make it perfect but we never can.

For nearly an hour George Latham walked the streets of his adopted hometown, thinking, hoping. He was a long way from his native New Jersey, where in a few weeks the weather would turn cold, the leaves would start to fall, while Southern California would suffer a bout with the Santa Ana winds, blowing hot through the hills, the streets, the trees.

Felicity (2005)

Felicity stood in front of the mirror and admired the way she looked in her graduation gown. The gown was black and seemed a perfect match for her dark hair, her walnut complexion. It hugged her chest, her hips (she was in good shape in those days), and though she was not obsessive about shoes—too girlish for her tastes—she even liked the way her flats poked out from underneath the hem of her gown. She was not one of those graduates who would wear Converse high tops or flip-flops or military boots. She had worked hard to get to this day and she would dress the way people were supposed to dress.

An hour later, she sat on an aluminum folding chair in the middle of the football field. Graduation was a colossal affair, a cast of thousands, like extras on the set of *Titanic,* and she half-slept while the commencement speaker hit the usual notes: the self-deprecation ("the Administration has clearly made a mistake by inviting me"), the inside jokes ("the boys from Sigma Nu know what I mean"), followed by the earnest dispensing of wisdom ("I envy you, I really do, you are entering a world where anything is possible, where you can be a tech billionaire and a rain-for-est-saving scientist—all in one lifetime"). Somewhere out there sat Felicity's family—her mother, Imelda, Tony, and Nick. As the ceremony limped on, she wondered how Nick was doing. He did not like to sit for long periods. This had been well chronicled throughout the year—his kindergarten teacher sending various notes home, the kid's card pulled yet again. Felicity supposed that Imelda had risen several times during the ceremony to let the boy run wild in the area near the goalposts. She hoped anyway.

At last the provost began dispensing degrees, and when Felicity's name was called, she marched confidently across the stage (no pumps, no stumbling) and shook the old man's hand. She had never met him in her life, had never even seen him, and found it amusing that he was sharing this most important moment with her, when she heard—

what sounded like Tony, a catcall from somewhere in the crowd. "You did it, Girl!"

She might have been horrified. She might have wanted to shut herself within the leather-bound holder of her degree. But she was in such buoyant spirits that not even Tony's hijinks could knock her back. She stepped down from the stage and retook her place on the aluminum chair—and waited another forty-five minutes for the ceremony to be done.

They went to lunch at the Olive Garden. It seemed logical. What were they going to do, hit some trendy place on the Westside, watch as Nick ran wild and Tony whistled "look at these prices" and her mother said something like "Miss High and Mighty." The Olive Garden had bread and familiarity.

And almost instantly it depressed her. She had of course removed her graduation gown and was wearing a dress that Ramona helped her pick out, but no one else in the place had been at graduation. That was clear. They were just families out for lunch. And none of the others could seem to remember that the day was about *her*. Tony rambled on about the shop, and her mother complained about having to be on her feet all day at the store, and Imelda kept scolding Nick. "Keep still . . . Stop playing with the sugar . . . Behave yourself."

At one point Felicity caught the eye of a man at a nearby table. He smiled grimly at her, seeming to appreciate her misery. It was as if he *knew*.

A short while later, while they were eating their food, Nick hid underneath the table. "Sit up here," Imelda said.

Felicity was at the breaking point. Four years for this, to be eating Stuffed Chicken Marsala at the Olive Garden, her mother cutting her own meal short so she could go outside and smoke, Imelda with her unrelenting parenting. "He's fine," Felicity said, and thought her voice showed restraint.

"He needs to keep still."

"He's five. And a boy. They have a hard time sitting still."

But Imelda was undeterred. She reached under the table and grabbed him by the collar. "Sit up here and behave."

"Really, he's fine."

"How would you know?"

The accusation hung in the air. It had seemed to come from left field. Even Tony noticed. And on her graduation day, her goddamned graduation day. The bitch taking shots. Felicity let loose. "I know because I'm not an overbearing Mexican grandmother who can't let the boy wipe his own ass." Then she reached for her cruelest imitation of Imelda's voice. "Nick, sit up straight.

Nick, stop playing with your Legos."

"What does being Mexican have to do with it?" Tony interjected.

Imelda shot Felicity a hard look, the likes of which she had never seen before. "For five years I have raised your kid, five years so you can do whatever you like. Too good for my son. Too good for all of us. But now I guess we know."

"Know what?"

"How you feel, about all of us."

"Oh, how do I feel?"

"I just said."

"No, tell me again. How do I feel, if you know, because I'm really interested in hearing how *I* feel, since you have such keen insight into my character. You're a regular B. F. Skinner, Imelda. You could teach Freud a thing or two. Am I suffering from repression, guilt, displacement? What is it? Maybe I'm Nora, just so selfish that I can't be bothered to raise my own kid."

Imelda's small eyes hardened, her cheeks grew flushed, her lips pursed. "He's your kid. Do what you want," she said at last.

And just then Felicity's mother returned from her cigarette. She sat and everyone was silent, the tension clear. "What's wrong?" she said.

In the parking lot Felicity apologized to Imelda. "I'm emotional," she said. "It's a weird time."

"Enjoy your night," Imelda said. Her voice was conciliatory but cold.

Felicity helped buckle Nick into the back of the car and watched as the four drove off, headed back to the Inland Empire. Felicity, who had driven her own car to lunch, was tempted to go back inside the Olive Garden and have a drink, but the thought was odious, lonely. Instead, she returned to the house share. No one would be there, she knew. Ramona's family had come down from Bakersfield for graduation. They were going to a restaurant in Pacific Palisades. Felicity was not even sure if Ramona was coming back that night. Madison had another year before

she graduated and had already gone home, and Kathy had practically moved in with her boyfriend.

She threw a bag of popcorn into the microwave and went
into the bedroom and changed into sweatpants and a T-shirt. It
seemed incredible: two years and she had no one to call, no usual
crew to rouse and hit their favorite bar with. What is wrong with
me? she wondered. Who am I? Her unloading on Imelda was not
the worst of it. Felicity had already determined that she would
move back, get an apartment, and move Nick in with her, start
undoing the damage inflicted by the four years with Imelda. But
she had not told Imelda this. She was not sure how the woman
would take it. She had invested time and love, was well-meaning,
but Felicity would be damned if her kid would grow up to be like
Tony, a pot-smoking idiot who had not read a book since *Green
Eggs and Ham*.

Popcorn in hand, Felicity settled on the couch and flipped
through the stations. *Top Gun* was on, and Felicity watched as
Tom Cruise grinned at her through the television. She understood that she was feeling letdown, that no matter what happened
during the course of the day, some deflation would be natural.
But it was not even three o'clock in the afternoon. Graduation
Day. *Graduation Day.* She could pack. She could find a lecture in
town. She could go to the Getty, ride the tram and admire Monet
and Renoir. Maybe some beautiful man would lean into her, his
breath hot in her ear, and suggest they grab a bottle of wine and
watch the sun as it fell below them, dropped off the edge of the
Western world. They would talk about foreign films, Spanish lit-
erature, Cezanne's *Young Italian Woman at a Table*, the melancholy
posture, the beautiful blue scarf. It was possible, yes? Instead she
munched popcorn and watched Tom Cruise and Kelly McGillis,
the scene sanitized because it was on network television, Berlin
singing "You Take My Breath Away."

CHAPTER 6

The Hikers (1964)

A police officer stopped by at daybreak, to see if Stacy had come home over night. Jill and Bill had not slept. They stayed downstairs waiting for the creak of the door. Stacy's brother, younger by two years, waited with them, nodded off now and then. Possessing a younger brother's irrational disposition toward his sister, he assumed her disappearance was a ploy for attention, that she had something in the works. But by the morning even he knew there was cause for concern.

Satisfied that the girl was still missing, the officer informed the Moriartys that he would issue the all-points bulletin, notify the radio stations that a search was on, request that they broadcast the make and model of Bobby's car, the license plate number. About eight o'clock that morning a man driving down the mountain heard the report, saw the Pontiac parked on the side of the road, and pulled over. He jotted down the license number, and when he reached the tiny town of Gardner, he called the police. A park ranger was notified and made the trip to where the man had seen the Pontiac, confirmed that it was the missing car and made the additional calls—so that by nine o'clock that morning they knew that someone had driven and parked the car at the old trailhead off the highway.

When they got the call, Stacy's parents raced out of the house. Then Jill, remembering Bobby's mother, turned and went back inside and called her. Surely the police would notify her as well, but Jill wanted to be sure to pass the news as quickly as possible. She would want the same. After that, they headed up the mountain, leaving Stacy's brother at home to man the phones, and arrived an hour later.

A ranger was leaning against his truck when they arrived. He was older looking and had a grayish mustache that dropped around the corners of his mouth. Jill jumped out and began peppering him with questions. The Pontiac sat there, shifting with every glance, first an object of hope and promise, then something foreboding, then a ragged piece of metal that offered no clues. The ranger had experience dealing with frightened parents, thought himself to be an honest man. He said, "They may have had an old map."

"I don't understand," said Bill.

"These are old trails. The new ones are another mile up the road. They may not have known that. People still use these, but you really have to know where you're going."

"Do you think that's what happened?" asked Jill.

"We just don't know," the ranger told her. "It's easy to get lost in there, on these old trails. Hell, it's easy to get lost anywhere in these mountains. We don't even know that they drove the car here."

"Why would they—" Jill began to ask her husband, but she cut herself off. No one knew anything, other than that the boy's Pontiac was sitting on the side of the road, some indication of something. She beat back the worst thoughts. They needed to stay levelheaded.

"What now?" Bill said.

"I've got two guys in there right now."

And as if on cue, two rangers on horseback emerged from the woods, their unperturbed horses bobbing their heads and whinnying. The rangers looked at the ranger with the gray mustache—because of his older age, Jill assumed he was in charge—and just shook their heads. Obviously they had found nothing.

It was now past ten o'clock in the morning. The sun had made its way above the ridgeline on the east side of the mountain range. Even so, it gave off little heat.

The ranger thought for a moment and breathed heavily. He

looked first at the dim sun and then the sky. "Okay," he said. "I'm going to get some aerial support."

Cousin Billy (1998)

After my cousin's coming-out party at Burkes Cavanagh, the one in San Francisco, I saw him only once in the ensuing years, at my uncle's house for a Christmastime celebration. My uncle had divorced by then, so we were at his *new* house, not the old one with its enchanted garden. He and my other cousins were sore at William because he had not made it to their annual ski vacation at Lake Tahoe. My cousins were skiers, avidly so, and their ski vacation was the one time of year, even more than Christmas, when they were expected to be together. "The command performance," my cousin Barbara had always called it.

William arrived late at my uncle's house that Christmas season, looking thinner than I remembered, his features sharper. He had lost the bulk from his football-playing days, and he had an alertness that was almost animal-like. "An accident," he said, by way of explaining his tardiness. "Some dipshit family flipped their car. The traffic was backed up for miles. All it takes is one mistake and the rest of us get screwed."

And with that he removed his jacket and set it gently on the edge of the couch.

I was surprised by the callousness of his remark. It was Christmas, after all, and a family had flipped their car on the freeway.

"Well, you're here now," my uncle said, with some judgment in his voice.

My cousin visibly tensed, and he went and sat next to our grandmother. He spent the next hour telling her about a recent trip to China, his third time to the East. His furniture designs were in high demand there, he said; he was mostly working off referrals. I already knew that he had a connection with some kind of specialty furniture company, but I had no idea he had been going to China. Our grandmother had never mentioned it. Maybe she did not know herself, though later I would wonder how much she knew of his travels. But as my cousin spoke, boasted even in his usual "you can't believe this" way, I could hear the restlessness in his voice. The things he wanted were not happening fast enough. The furniture company owner liked to play "small ball," was obsessed with the mainland when all the money was in Taiwan, treated William as if he were some sort of hourly employee. Predictably our grandmother was charmed. She had slowed in recent years and was getting ready to move into a retirement center, but William had an unflagging ability to entertain her.

"I bet you're going to like your new digs," he said. "I hear it's a sex party over there every night."

I could never imagine saying such a thing to our grandmother, but she laughed.

"You're going to have at least two boyfriends before you unpack your suitcase."

"Oh Billy," she said, and he did not obnoxiously remind her that he went by William now.

The evening was otherwise uneventful. I have not said much about my other cousins (one wrote a well-received book on feminism, the other followed his father into law), but both were there with their spouses, and my mother and father had driven up from Hamilton, and my uncle's new wife was busy trying to make everyone comfortable. She asked about my job, and I explained that I had accepted a teaching position with a boarding school in Southern California, that I would be starting in a few weeks. Another teacher was going out on maternity leave and they needed someone in a hurry—this helped them overlook my lack of experience. But if all went well, there might be a position for the following year. My parents of course knew all this, and my mother said dimly, "He's going to teach history."

Later, after we ate and exchanged gifts, my grandmother announced that she was getting tired and was ready to leave, so I rose to drive her home. This was my job; I was the responsible one who, to that point, had stayed close to home. But I loved my grandmother. She was good to me always, had helped pay for my schooling, and I was happy to drive her.

As I went to get her jacket, William said, "I'll ride with you." The pronouncement irritated me. Now I would have to drive him back to my uncle's house, rather than head directly to my apartment. But it was more than that. I knew he would assume the role of escort, be obsequious in his mannerisms, affected in his conversation. He would be the Billy he always had been. Showtime.

But it did not happen that way. As we drove through his hometown, and where I went to college and now lived, William became reflective, saying things such as "there's the old clothiers," "there's Merrill's liquor store." And then we passed what had been De Luca's, a delicatessen that had been shuttered for at least two years. The place was once famous for its raviolis. "What happened to De Luca's?" he cried.

"They closed down," I said. "It's been awhile."

"Why would they do that?"

"All the businesses are moving to Creekside," my grandmother offered ruefully.

"Is the old man still alive?"

"I don't know," she said.

"I went to school with his granddaughter."

"Oh, yes, what was her name?"

"Anna. I can't believe they closed down. It's just an empty building now. What's going to go in there?"

My grandmother sighed. "I don't know. There's nothing but empty buildings around anymore. It's a shame what's happening. They build these new places and all the old buildings go unused."

"They shouldn't have closed," William said, clearly saddened. "They shouldn't have let them close down."

Even today William's sentimentality about De Luca's strikes me as odd. Maybe it was just the time of year, Christmas, which invited nostalgia about an old restaurant shutting its doors, something that happens every day. Here he was, a person who from an early age had itched to see the larger world, yet wanted, apparently, his hometown to be preserved in a wax layer.

Well, he did not say anymore after that. We dropped off our

grandmother and got her settled into her apartment for the night. On the drive back to my uncle's, I told William a little more about my new job (I would be teaching freshmen and sophomores) and where I would be living (I was being provided a small apartment on campus) and how long I had known I wanted to teach (I had not planned on doing so, but it was, you know, a history degree). And when we reached my uncle's house, William wished me well and jumped out of my used Toyota Corolla.

Watching him move toward the front door, I could see that his eagerness had returned, any sadness about a silly old delicatessen was short-lived. Without looking back, he opened the door and disappeared inside. Three years would pass before I saw him again, for the last time in fact; and when I did, it was inside a Los Feliz mansion.

The Comeback Kid (1993)

If one of those baseball writers that so warmed the philosophizing heart of Mike Allison's instructor at Orange Community College were to describe the open tryouts, it might go like this:

> On a brilliant morning in June, the kind of morning where heavy machinery plows the deep brown earth and children take lazily to fishing in ponds, dozens of men have come to this baseball field at Trinity College to find their pathway to the major leagues. Trinity is a four-year college "dedicated to deepening faith and equipping students for a Spirit-filled life," and while it's doubtful that many of these baseball cap-clad men are so dedicated, perhaps it's fitting that the tryouts are being held at a Christian college, as a prayer is all most of them have. They are like aging ballerinas, these ballplayers, giving it one more shot in hopes of performing *Swan Lake* with the New York City Ballet, even though most would not make the lead in the Peoria Ballet Company. Not that they are all clumsy Keystone Cops. Some have the chops to at least raise the eyebrows of Ed Miller, the head scout for the California Angels. Miller is a forty-year veteran of professional baseball, and he can sniff out

talent like a sommelier opening a bottle of Cabernet Franc. Just now he's walking toward one Mike Allison, a twenty-three-year-old resident of North Orange County who dazzled during grounders. Allison is built a little like Sandy Alomar, and his story is not so different from others—star player in high school, had a scholarship offer to play college ball but an injury sent him to community college instead, and now finds himself face-to-face with the man who in a minute could have Mike's signature on a piece of paper officially making him part of the California Angels baseball organization. Could it be that—

Someone more blunt might have put it like this:

Pathetic. Grown men donning baseball uniforms long past the "sell by" date, to try and scratch the balls of a man, the head scout, with a balding head and paunch belly who will go back to his apartment that night—his wife left him years ago—and fall asleep on the couch to a bucket of Kentucky Fried Chicken and the television blaring. They come mostly from Los Angeles and Orange County, these latent trick-or-treaters in their spikes and caps, and compared to real major leaguers, they look like community theater actors doing *Lear.* Consider the guy over there: Mike Allison is his name. Twenty-three years old. Does drywall for a living. Fair player in high school, just like the rest of them. Made All-League. Got him laid a few times. But then the draft came and went and nobody called his name. Nobody was *ever* going to call his name. A Division Three college showed some interest, a school out in Wyoming, Wyoming of all fucking places, a partial scholarship, but yeah, man, the dream lives on, until one spring afternoon he feels something twist, and down he goes, nothing too major, but the Wyoming college is no longer interested. So he goes to Orange Community College, plays some ball there, but he's a fuckup, a partier, would rather spend his nights hanging out in bars doing shots and the occasional line of coke and hooking up with girls, so he drops out of school, can't live at home anymore, his parents are getting impatient, and a buddy of a buddy knows a contractor and it's

Mike and three first-generation Mexicans (sometimes they call him "bambino," and not because he is Babe Ruth, other times they call him "Negra Modelo," after the beer) and it's drywall all day and six Bud Talls after work and a burrito at Three Amigos or a couple of slices of Chicago's Best, but you know the old itch is there, and he hears about an open tryout—all the major league teams do them, community service shit, for America, the land of opportunity—so he laces up the old spikes. They all think they're Rocky. Just give me a chance and I'll show Creed what's what. And he moves well, shows some of the old swagger. The head scout with the balding head and paunch belly takes notice. Mike kicks around some dirt like it's nothing, I could do this stuff in my sleep, and the head scout comes over, and if you were an optimistic sort—

* * *

The exchange was brief. How many hopes and prayers have been predicated on the most threadbare of evidence, the slight smile of a girl, the single word of encouragement? The head scout came over to where Mike was milling about in the outfield, waiting for the other players to run through their drills. "You showed good range there," the head scout said.

"Thanks."

There was something nonchalant in Mike's mannerisms.

"Pro range," the head scout added.

That got Mike's attention.

"Let's see what you do at the plate. If you can hit, we'll talk some more."

And the head scout sauntered toward where the pitchers and catchers were working out. *The best you can hope for is that we notice you. Tim Heinrich got a contract. Was in the Majors within two years.*

Second base. It wasn't even Mike's natural position. He had handled everything they hit his way. He tried to stay within himself. Now it was up to his hitting. *Hitting,* for the love of Pete. Mike could hit in his sleep. Hitting was his game. There wasn't a pitcher who could get the better of him. But most of all, Mike

believed. Believed now. It was real. The head scout had said so—
"pro range." The man did not drop chestnuts like that unless he
meant it. Mike Allison could see it all out in front of him: the contract, the minor league assignment, the steady climb through the
ranks, and then Angels Stadium, the place he had passed so often
in his life, sometimes on his way to work in the morning, sometimes on his way home from the bars at night. No longer would
he spend his days cutting out holes in walls, setting mesh in place
with masking tape, sanding and texturing, suffering through the
crew calling him "Bambino, Negra Modelo."

Mike *believed.*

The Hikers (1964)

The ranger with the gray mustache was coordinating the efforts,
driving up and down the highway, working the radio, keeping an
eye out. He had sent teams of two at two-mile intervals, trying to
estimate how much ground the children could have covered in
the course of one day, create a kind of lasso around them. The
problem was that you could not attack from the west—there were
just no good access points from that direction. And there was his
other lingering fear: that the children were not in there at all,
that someone had taken the car and dumped it on the side of
the highway. Those two kids could be anywhere. Hell, they could
have sold the thing to some drifter for a song, boarded a bus for
Mexico, and be sitting on a beach in Ensenada. He had been
around long enough to know that kids were unpredictable. They
got crazy ideas in their heads. They acted on impulse. Especially
if they were in love.

Jill and Bill Moriarty were asked to wait at their car or, better,
to consider heading into Gardner and waiting there. They were
not to go into the woods. "The last thing I need is for you to get
lost too," the ranger had told them.

This applied to other people who began showing up, friends
of the Moriartys, classmates, strangers who felt the compulsion to
help. At one point the ranger gathered them together. He said,
"Listen, folks. I can't keep you from going in there. I don't have

any jurisdiction to do that, but it will only complicate matters. Let my team do their job. They know these woods. They know what they're looking for."

Some people formed a prayer circle, a man ran back down the hill to buy donuts, and Bobby's mother arrived. Jill knew who she was immediately. The woman looked frazzled, sleepless. A part of Jill wanted to slap the woman, yell at her, "What has your child done with my daughter!" Instead she hugged her. The woman trembled a little. "I don't understand what they were doing," she said. "Bobby's never been here before in his life."

"Well, we can't know that," Jill said, rationally.

"What do you mean?"

"Who knows what kids do."

The woman broke their embrace.

"He's a good boy. He's not the sort to lure a girl into the woods."

"I'm not saying that."

"He works hard."

"I'm sure he does. We need to help each other out."

The woman nodded, agreeing. They both knew their nerves were raw.

A few minutes later the ranger with the gray mustache returned from his rounds. He left his engine running, the truck making a heavy growl, and he walked toward the Moriartys to let them know he had no news to share. "This is Bobby's mother," Jill explained.

"Ma'am," he said, and tipped his cap.

Bobby's mother looked closely at the ranger. "It was cold last night," she said.

"It was," he agreed.

"Below freezing."

"Yes."

"My boy was never a Scout. He wouldn't know what to do."

"Kids are resourceful. And they are both in good health, so, that helps."

"Yeah, but freezing is freezing."

It had been cold, no doubt about it, not January and February cold, but cold enough to be dangerous. And the weather station had informed him that more of the same was coming, lower by at least five degrees. The ranger felt confident that they could survive a single night, roughed up, yes, but nothing a night in the hospital would not remedy. Two nights, well, that was a different matter. There was the issue of food. He doubted they had any. And their body temperatures going down and then up and then down again, and if the parents' account was right, the girl was wearing shorts. He even had concerns about a bear attack, doubted they would know what to do if they came upon one.

Just then a prop plane flew overhead, the one the ranger had ordered. It passed at low altitude, its engine working in a kind of symphony with the ranger's rumbling truck. Reflexively everybody's head turned upward, and they watched as the plane passed and headed out over the woods. The ranger's radio crackled. While still watching the plane, he said confidently, "Believe me, if they're out there, we'll find 'em."

And Bobby's mother said, "What do you mean, 'if'?"

Gatsby, the Musical (Present)

Dorothy fixed herself a sandwich, low-sodium sliced turkey and Swiss cheese with nonfat mayonnaise on wheat bread, two precut tomato slices and a bit of lettuce. She used a butter knife to cut her sandwich, and while the knife did not slice neatly, it did the trick. She poured herself a glass of water and sat back down at the table.

George was running behind. He must have decided to go past the red building, where he usually turned around, and walk clear to the end of the path. It was a good sign, that he was feeling healthy enough to push himself a little. He had always kept himself in good health, but of course they were old now and certain ailments were out of your control. As Dorothy sat at the kitchen table, she wondered whether she had choir practice that afternoon—then she remembered that it was Wednesday and choir met on Fridays. Then she remembered that she no longer sang in the choir. I'm getting to be a dodo head, she thought.

For years she had sung with the Methodist choir, her alto voice much in demand. She needed to arrive early, a good hour before services, and George would drive her, before heading to the shopping plaza that sat adjacent to the church, where he would drink a cup of coffee, read the Sunday paper, sometimes do a little bit of work. He always returned in time for services.

Dorothy loved her years with the choir, the camaraderie and sheer joy of making music. Her favorite hymns were "A Mighty Fortress Is Our God" and "Joyful, Joyful, We Adore You" and "Give to the Winds Thy Fears." Certainly she knew that George was listening with a trained and appraising ear; and while he never said so, she could tell that he was oftentimes underwhelmed by the choir's performance. On several occasions the head priest had tried to recruit George to become choir director, but every time George refused, politely. He was not above leading a local choir through Sunday services, but he was busy with his duties as a professor, had a long work commute that would have made rehearsal difficult, and of course for years he was working on his *Gatsby* musical. Dorothy was glad that George never took the job, though certainly *she* never said so. She thought George would have been too critical and too taxing on the choristers. Church choirs are political affairs that make the US Congress seem uncomplicated, and George would have lacked the necessary diplomacy. Still, there he was every Sunday, sitting in the pews while Dorothy and the others marched their way through the *Methodist Hymnal*.

But bit by bit George stopped attending services. He had never really been a believer. He appreciated the history, the ritual, but over time he began opting out. At first he would drive Dorothy to the church, drop her off, and pick her up afterward. Later he just sent her off in the car—she was a capable driver—and when she returned he would ask politely, "How did it go?"

Dorothy was always able to place when George stopped attending: around the time he got the rejections. He waited months to hear from his acquaintance at the Arcade Theatre, his class-mate from graduate school who had become the artistic direc-tor. The work, the man said, was interesting, George always had talent, but he just did not see how they could make it fit. He wished George well and recommended that he perhaps record a couple of numbers, to send along with the book and sheet music.

George bore it very well. This was one theater, after all. He began querying every New York theater, agency, and producer he could locate. If none of them bit, there was always Chicago and Philadelphia. It would pop. You only needed one person to be-lieve in your work.

Dorothy finished her sandwich and rinsed her plate. She looked down at her hands. She had battled arthritis for many years, tried every remedy in the book, but nothing worked—until, almost overnight, the pain subsided. But her hands were crooked things now, like those of a Halloween witch. But better that than the pain.

She thought she might clip some mint for her tea. She walked—not shuffled, she refused to shuffle—from the kitchen through the front room, where the baby grand sat luminescent as always, and moved toward the back of the house. The washer and dryer were in the garage, something she used to love about this house, but now it meant a trip outdoors, hauling a basket of clothes. George needed clean underwear and socks. It would give her something to do this afternoon, and George could help with the basket.

Outside the mint had become unruly.

Mint will grow like a madwoman, and Dorothy Latham's once tidy mint field had overrun the borders. You could have sup-plied every mint julep for every Kentucky Derby with the amount of mint that was growing. Still, the leaves were a lovely green, and Dorothy leaned down and plucked a small branch of the stuff. She took a heady sniff. She never tired of the smell of mint. How long has it been since I trimmed this, she wondered. She thought she might take some to Helen, her next-door neighbor, who was always bringing Dorothy limes and tangerines from their trees. They were good neighbors, Helen and Doug, even if the four of them had never become best friends. They looked out for each other, exchanged Christmas gifts, at least until Helen had died, and then they certainly did not expect Doug to carry on the tradition.

Mint in hand, Dorothy went back inside. Yes, I should have gone with George today, she considered. He should have taken the dog with him.

But her knees would not let her walk great distances anymore.

He liked to walk alone.

A letter arrives from Philadelphia. A producer out there. George opens and reads, as if expecting. "I'm going to go out for a while," he tells her. He tosses the letter in the piano bench.

After he leaves, she retrieves the letter from the bench, reads, invasively, walks not shuffles past the baby grand piano, remembers when it arrived, champagne, they were never champagne drinkers, "I'm in love with a beautiful man," they sing, Susannah should be here soon, a baby, George, yes, a baby.

The luminous Gatsby on stage, his hand outstretched toward Daisy's place on the opposite side of the Sound, Gatsby singing

And when I finally reach her . . .
And when I finally reach her . . .

CHAPTER 7

The Fairfax Apartments (Present)

Picture Los Angeles from above. Like an airplane arriving into LAX. Or imagine that you are floating, arms stretched out like a superhero or a flying Christ. Maybe you know the neighborhoods. Maybe you don't. You linger over a patch of real estate. This is no suburban neighborhood. The homes are mansions. And *real* mansions, not some 6,500-square-foot job constructed in a day. These are palaces from the twenties and thirties, the kind of places that movie people built. Their pools are elegantly designed. You can't see the marble from your distance, can't see the Greek statues, certainly can't see the nearly naked starlets, the actor you love who got a DUI the night before in Malibu and is sleeping it off poolside. You would be tempted to think that they are all movie people, but they are not. These mansions belong to lawyers, and software people, and that guy who owns half of the jewelry district, the one who had the trouble two years ago you saw on television. You wish you could float downward, settle in next to one of those lovely girls with their nearly naked bodies, sip something cool, rest up for a party that night, read your name in *People* magazine, but the air is too thick for you to breathe, so you float on until you come to another part of town, and see below you an apartment complex. It has a pool—this is a Los Angeles story, so there must be a pool—but the pool is regular, rectangular, built in the fifties. All the doors in this complex are painted red, and there are a few palm trees, but the place is not kitschy enough to be called retro. The water is blue, wonderfully blue, the chlorine could clean your nostrils, and you are close enough now to see a man rise from his chaise lounge. He steps to the edge of the pool, hesitates, and dives in. The water parts around his body. When he emerges, he beats a breaststroke to the opposite end of the pool. He is an athletic but not especially graceful swimmer. His back is muscular, his hair dark brown. He appears tanned, but *artificially* so. He turns and beats his way back through the pool, and you strain to see his face. Do you recognize him? Have you seen him somewhere before? You are just about to place him, or are you, when a sudden wind, a Santa Ana maybe, blows you away, like a scrap of paper being blown by a leaf blower, some Mexican gardener having a laugh at your expense, as you blow out to sea or maybe back to a place in the middle of the country.

* * *

The Actor grabbed the metal ladder and pulled himself from the pool, water beads falling all around, hitting the concrete and evaporating on the spot. For a few fleeting moments he felt chilled, surprised by the sudden cold, but he knew it would pass, and it did. Almost by the time he situated himself back onto the chaise lounge, he was dry. Only his black swimming trunks and his dark brown hair retained any wetness, and both would be dry soon enough. The Actor reached under the chaise lounge to check his phone, but no one had called.

The Armenian guy was still reading at the end of the pool, but the woman from unit 2 had disappeared. Her towel was there, her bag as well, so she was obviously not gone for good. Where did she work? he wondered. He could not remember if she had told him. He had learned not to take anyone for granted. Everyone in Los Angeles was someone's sister, assistant, favorite barista. You never knew. It was one of his cardinal rules: Don't be a jerk.

As it happened, the woman from unit 2 had gone inside and fixed a pitcher of margaritas. She emerged from her apartment wearing her wrap, and waved the pitcher at the Actor. *You want?*

She was smiling.

Well, why the hell not? It was not yet noon and already a hundred degrees.

The Actor rose and made his way to her (bringing his phone with him). Even before he reached her chaise, she was pouring some margarita into a blue plastic tumbler, the ice rattling as it fell from the pitcher. Isolate on that for a minute. Hundred degrees out. The cold ice and the green liquid. The Actor grabbed the adjacent chaise lounge, and it made a scratching sound as he pulled it over the hot concrete. He took the tumbler of margarita and pressed it against hers.

Cheers.

My personal recipe.

He could have downed it in a single gulp, very nearly did.

Plenty more where that came from.

She called out to the Armenian man. He seemed confused at the offer but then declined, smiling slightly. *Let me know if you change your mind.*

The woman set down her tumbler and removed her wrap. She had a freckled chest, and he saw that she was in better shape than he first thought. Was she an actress?

Nooooo.

She worked for a medical supply company, did sales, was taking the day off.

Fridays are for shit when it comes to sales, afternoons anyway.

Even before the Actor finished his margarita, she had taken his tumbler, filled it to the brim. He was not used to drinking tequila—the body is a temple—but in this heat you could drink a gallon and it would hardly affect you. The woman leaned back in her chaise lounge but the Actor sat upright, facing her. Small beads of sweat dripped off both of their bodies, and they talked for a while. He did not say anything about the FX show, about his waiting for the phone call that might or might not come that day, but he told her about a CBS show he had done, about another audition he had coming up for a commercial—a national. She listened cheerfully. She had lived in Los Angeles a long time. Her ex-boyfriend had been an actor. *A real creepo.*

At one point she took a call. It was work-related. She spoke in a lingo, about unit prices, and PSOs, and vendors. The Actor was buzzing from the drinks. He looked down at her crotch, her legs, her painted toenails. She finished the phone call and he said something about her taking the day off.

Right you fucking are.

We need more of this.

When she went inside to mix more margaritas, he went with her.

Her apartment was almost identical to his, right down to the lino-leum counters. Lime green. But where the Actor had nothing on his walls (he had read once that Brendan Fraser kept nothing on his walls), the woman had decorated hers with a large French print, some photographs of Seattle, a decorative spoon. Her fur-niture matched, and a few of the pieces looked like they might have been heirlooms. She had an espresso maker on the counter. The woman pulled the tequila bottle from the freezer, and the Actor realized he did not know her name.

Susan.

She pulled down two shot glasses and filled each with tequila, pushed one of them toward the Actor. He balked.

Come on, it's Friday. You don't have any auditions.

She was taunting him.

The Actor clinked the shot glass next to hers and they threw back the tequila. The liquid was icy cold going down, but then it began racing through his body, warming him. She grabbed the bottle and began pouring tequila into the blender. She added other liquids that he did not recognize, limes as well, limes on the lime-colored linoleum, and she mixed it all up and hit the blend button.

The Actor stepped away from the kitchen, walked into her living area. He was shirtless, wearing only his black trunks and flip-flops. Susan came around from the kitchen holding their two plastic tumblers. The Actor was feeling cooler now, she had on her air-conditioning, and he took the tumbler from her and figured they would head back down to the pool. But Susan turned on music. He did not recognize it.

They're a band from Minnesota. I saw them a few weeks ago at the Echo.

And she began to move around, dancing, tipsy. She had not bothered to put on her wrap, so tits bouncing. She wants it bad, the Actor thought. Have sex with a woman like that and—

But the tequila had washed away his inhibitions. He began moving his muscular body, an Adonis.

She let out a whoop.

And he began moving a little deeper, rolling his shoulders. He gave her his look, the one he used in auditions, and moved closer to her. She rolled and swayed her body. She was not wearing her wrap.

They're good, right?

The Actor was more a pop guy but, sure, he liked.

She spun away and he stepped toward her. An afternoon fuck. Why not? Give her a story to tell her friends. His mouth tasted of tequila. He swayed toward her and put his arm around the base of her back, pulled her toward him. Her head shot away and she pushed him gently from her body.

Slow down there, Captain America.

Wants it so bad. He moved toward her.

Drink your tequila.

She stepped toward the music player and lowered the sound. Then she went back into the kitchen. He came and stood in the frame of the door and watched as she filled her tumbler and—

She gestured toward the outdoors.

Shall we?

So it really wasn't going to happen. These LA women drove him nuts. Like he wanted to dance in the middle of the hottest fucking afternoon of the year. Fine, her loss, this forty-year-old with her sagging tits and her leathery skin, her medical supply job.

When they went back outside, it was like getting hit by a special effect, heat from an exploding car or a window being blown.

He thanked her for the drinks—

Gotta beat the heat.

And returned to his side of the pool, settled into the chaise.

A horn honked from the road.

The Armenian man was gone.

The Actor realized he had left his phone in her apartment.

Felicity (2007)

She found someone to whisper in her ear, but it did not come at the Getty Center while she was staring at *Young Italian Woman at a Table*. It came in the form of a woman at Starbucks, where Felicity had gone to work on her application to a PhD program.

"Felicity."

She looked up to see a woman with jet-black hair and round eyes, a single pierced loop around the left brow.

Felicity tried to place her.

"Pauline. We had a class together. Or at least we did until I dropped. I smoked." And the woman made a motion with her fingers as if she were waving a cigarette.

Then Felicity remembered. She said, "I can't believe you recognized me."

Later Pauline would say that she recognized her because she always thought Felicity was "fucking hot," but that day she told her, "I'm good at remembering faces. I keep trying to figure out how I can make money off it, but so far politician is the only thing that comes to mind."

Without being asked, Pauline sat, and while it was unintentional, her leg brushed against Felicity's, who felt a sudden thrill. "What are you working on?"

"Graduate school application," Felicity said.

"No shit. Are you already done?"

Already—it had been six years!

Felicity explained that she had graduated two years earlier, that she had moved back from Los Angeles so she could take care of her kid, was working at Orchard Supply Hardware where she had worked before, that they were living in a two-bedroom apartment just around the corner. She could tell that Pauline was getting bored. "How about you?" Felicity asked. "You still in school?"

"Pauline, the perpetual student. My dropping that class was not an aberration."

If time had accounted for some of Felicity's difficulty in placing Pauline, her ever-shifting looks did as well. Felicity said, "Your hair is different."

"Oh yeah. I don't even know what it was when I first met you. Was I blonde then?"

"I don't remember."

"Liar."

Felicity laughed. "I just remember that it was on the darker side. I can't believe you recognized me. That was so long ago."

They talked for a few minutes longer, about nothing in particular, but in a way that felt natural to Felicity, and Pauline said, "So we should do something, you know."

Felicity was not a woman to whom trust came easily, but she agreed. "We should," she said, and pulled out her phone to get Pauline's number.

"No, I mean now. We should do something now."

"Right now?"

"Why not? Is that application due tomorrow or something?"

In fact it was not; Felicity had several more weeks to complete the application. She had always been dutiful when it came to school and deadlines, giving herself plenty of time. It was a beautiful day out, she was inside a Starbucks, alone, typing out answers to questions such as, *If you had one day to spend anywhere, where would it be?*

She said, "Sure, let's go do something."

The old zoo at Griffith Park was Pauline's idea.

Felicity had never been there, though she had heard about it—the stone caves and concrete cages that you could climb through, these places where animals had lived. The zoo had closed down in 1965 when the new one was built, and it had become a kind of makeshift shrine to a past era, part of the city's early years. At the very least it was a place where people ate picnic lunches and teenagers went to get stoned.

But even before they got there, Felicity was jazzed. It was an hour drive into the city, and she had made that drive hundreds of times, returning to the Westside after a weekend at Imelda's to see her son. Each one of those trips had been a kind of escape— she never made it with a heavy heart—and driving now with the girl Pauline (and Pauline really did seem more like a girl than a woman, she had recklessness and freedom about her), Felicity felt the rush of going to the place that had always felt like *freedom,* and doing so with Pauline, who acted like she could make anything possible. She was new. She was mysterious. She had stories to tell and layers to be unfolded. Her jet-black hair. Her round eyes. The way she sat propped with her legs folded underneath her and faced Felicity during the length of the drive to Griffith Park.

They parked and began walking toward where the caves and cages sat in their rotting conditions. But a few steps in, Pauline began running. "Come on!" she screamed at Felicity without looking back at her.

Felicity began running as well. Because it was the middle of the week, only a few other people were around, but even if they had been surrounded by hundreds of strangers, Felicity would not have felt self-conscious. She laughed and chased Pauline into a graffiti-covered cave—everything everywhere was covered with graffiti—and they trotted down some steps. "Can you believe they used to keep animals in these crap conditions?" Pauline said. "Look at all this shit. It's like living in a shoe box."

For the better part of the next hour they climbed in and out of the cages. Someone had thrown a bed into one, but it was so worn and disgusting you would have caught a disease just sitting on it. Several of the cages still had bars, and naturally people were posing as if they were in jail. Alone, Felicity and Pauline made their way inside one cave, and Pauline asked her, "Do you believe animals have spirits?"

Felicity said, "What?"

"What? What? There are people who think this place is haunted, you know, like you can feel the spirits of the animals."

"I don't know."

"You don't know if animals have spirits, or you don't know if you can feel their spirits *right now*." And Pauline made little ghostly movements with her fingers.

For as little as she understood Pauline, Felicity did not think she was the sort of person who would believe such things—that animals had spirits, that places were haunted. Felicity said, "I don't think animals have souls. They have bodies. When they're done, they're done. I don't think Simba really appears in the fucking sky to tell you what to do."

"Who?"

Felicity smiled. "If you had a kid, you'd know. It's from *The Lion King*."

"Ah, Mother Felicity. But I don't think so either. It's nature. Just like us. It's all about survival and attraction and doing whatever you have to do."

Graffiti filled every bit of space, including some massive lettering—a tagger's ID maybe, some sort of urban code. You could look at *Young Italian Woman at a Table* and know what you were seeing, but with the exception of a Mickey Mouse head or a bit of poetry, most of the graffiti around them seemed like gibberish, random initials, broad swaths of paint. Felicity was examining a wall, attempting to decipher, when she felt Pauline's hands on her shoulders. She turned to face her. Without additional warning Pauline kissed her. Felicity did not resist. They kissed for a good long time, and then Pauline said, "Come on, let's check out the other cages."

* * *

Within the month Pauline had moved in with Felicity (and Nick). This was as much out of need as passionate intensity: Pauline had been staying with friends, they were getting ready to move, she could not afford her own place, and . . .

The idea was Felicity's. They had spent the better part of the month together—Pauline had become Aunt Pauline to Nick—and Felicity of course knew about her housing situation. "You should stay here for a while," Felicity told her one night. They were in Felicity's bedroom; Nick was asleep in his. The bedroom door was locked.

"You don't want that," Pauline told her. "I have a job. I can get my own place."

"You sell pot."

"I work at a marijuana dispensary. Speaking of."

And Pauline rose from the bed and went to Felicity's dresser, where she pulled out some weed. "Open the window," Felicity told her. "I don't want it stinking up the room."

Pauline did. She took a few tokes and offered some to Felicity, who passed. Sometimes Felicity would smoke with her, but more often she would not. She had been surprised to learn that Pauline worked at a dispensary. Felicity knew such places existed—the law had been passed—but they seemed like they belonged to a subterfuge world, that if you were to walk into one, red lights would flash and government agents would ask for your ID. That night she made the suggestion a second time, an insistence almost, and Pauline accepted. She was practically living there already.

It had been a heady month. Pauline possessed a free-spiritedness that bordered on recklessness. They would be driving and Pauline would suddenly yell "pull over" and jump out of the car and go sprinting off somewhere, toward an object she had seen, a cowshed or a towering metal structure. The strangest things piqued her interest: the rock quarry off the 210, where they spent a good hour climbing around until an employee came and kicked them out, a restaurant where they saw several police cars parked and Pauline insisted that they go inside and sit in the booth next to them, even though Pauline was loaded. Probably because she was loaded.

Then there was the night they were driving back from a movie and Pauline directed them into the hills and through a neighborhood, where she had Felicity park off the side of the road. "What are we doing?"

Pauline was out of the car before she answered. "Come on," she said, and led Felicity across the length of a greenbelt, moving her arms like she was some kind of stealthy bird.

They reached the back of a large house. The house was dark, pitch-black, and there was a pool with a waterfall, although the waterfall was turned off. "I used to live around the corner," Pauline said, as she reached over and unlatched the metal gate.

"Where are you going?"

"Swimming."

"What?"

"The owners are never here. I used to do this all the time."

Felicity did not want to follow—it was, in fact, breaking and entering. She stood firmly at the gate.

Pauline was almost to the pool when she realized Felicity had not come. She turned back and said, "I swear I've never done this with anybody else."

"It's not that, it's—"

"Look, they're not home, okay. Not a single light. It's not *that* late."

With Felicity still hesitating, Pauline began backing her way toward the pool, making a reeling motion as if she were pulling in a fish on a line. Felicity finally gave in and joined Pauline at the pool. They undressed and slipped into the water (they did not jump in and splash around—Pauline allowed that much for caution's sake). It was autumn in California, and so warm enough that they did not freeze, and Pauline swam the length of the pool and came back toward where Felicity was treading water. "You're in the deep end," Pauline said needlessly, and she led Felicity through the dark waters, away from the silent waterfall. "See, no one's going to slap on the lights and rat us out."

Felicity began to believe it as well; and even if they did, what would be the big deal? They were two women swimming; they weren't lifting jewelry. They'd probably go tearing out of there like streakers at a sporting event. They stayed in the pool for ten, fifteen minutes, and then they were on the concrete and headed back to the car. Both were shivering, but it passed.

Driving home, Felicity would have been content with silence, but Pauline rarely was. She turned on the radio. The song was "Birth, School, Work, Death" by the Godfathers. Despite the noise Felicity felt at peace, full of promise—a PhD application in the mail, Pauline's hand on her leg, and the California night encasing her like an amniotic sac.

Cousin Billy (2001)

One day, out of the blue, I got a call from my cousin inviting me to a party. I had not spoken to him since the Christmastime gathering at my uncle's house, when we drove together to drop off my grandmother. The phone rang in my small campus apartment and the old familiar "Coz!" came over the line.

"William?" I said.

"I'm in LA," he told me. "How close are you?"

I explained that I was an hour east, more or less, depending on traffic.

"I *thought* you were near," he said. Apparently an hour was "near" by his reckoning.

He said that he was staying in Los Angeles, that Aldric (I had no idea who that was) was renting "a place" in the Los Feliz Hills and there was a party that Friday and I should come, that "some really prominent people will be there," that at any rate it would be great to see me, especially since I was so close. His voice was characteristically urgent. He made it sound as if he had just deboarded a plane at LAX and the first call he made was to me. In fact, as I would later discover, William had been in Southern California for over two months before he decided to ring me up.

I had no obligations that Friday. I was a prep school teacher living in a small campus apartment—I had never moved out of the one originally provided to me; it suited me fine and I am a creature of habit—and a party in the Los Feliz Hills sounded like a good antidote to poring over student papers or eating spicy tuna rolls alone at Shogun's. "I'll be there," I said.

"No need for a tuxedo," he told me. "It's nothing formal."

The Friday of the party was an unusually bright day, none of the dull hazy light that characterizes the Los Angeles atmosphere. It's the smog, of course, that casts this pale illumination, and you can find yourself transfixed by it. New Englanders can boast that their weather captures their essence, the hardy dispositions and whatever else, but Los Angeles weather is perfectly suited to the town itself precisely because it feels *so fabricated,* as if someone really did attach klieg lights to the heavens.

Anyway, these were my thoughts as I made the hour drive into the city. Los Feliz sits on the eastern edge of matters, and the Hills just below Griffith Park, and I found the estate without too much trouble. I was surprised there was no security at the gate, and I drove up the driveway—well, let me stop there. A driveway is what I grew up with, a rectangular bit of concrete that cracked over the years (at least until my father repaved it—himself). Here you were led to the property by a long cobblestone road that wound twice before you arrived at a Mediterranean-style villa, lit up from room to room, gleaming and marvelous.

A valet took my car, and I walked the marble steps into the house.

I began to mill about, moving through a few rooms and nodding at people and smiling slightly. I thought I recognized an actor from a film (it had not been a very good one), but otherwise these were all strangers to me and after a while I began to feel self-conscious. My cousin was nowhere to be found. I felt like a gate-crasher, saved only by a bar set up by the pool, where I ordered a drink and struck up a conversation with a man who took to calling me "professor." I explained that I was not—I teach at a boarding school, we are called simply teachers—but he liked the term and used it another two or three times. Then he moved along and I was again left alone.

I might have left. Not because of the opulence or because everybody else seemed to know somebody, but because I am no good at such affairs, at diving in and introducing myself. Weddings are torture. So are mixers. I try to avoid both at all costs. Then suddenly I spied my cousin talking on the other side of the pool. He saw me as well and immediately broke off his conversation and headed my way. "Coz!" he cried, and we embraced.

He looked well. Fit and lean. All his handsomeness was intact, and his hair, which was always somewhere between California golden and Central Valley brown, was carefully trimmed. "How long have you been here? I've been looking for you."

I doubted that, but I told him "an hour or so," and then he asked if I had seen the house and before I could answer he was determined that I would.

"Are you living here?" I asked, as we filtered through the rooms, the furniture looking as if it had never been used, every vase and every candlestick carefully selected.

"Aldric is just renting the place," William said. "Twenty thousand a month. It's called the Geoffrey Meade Estate. It was built by some guy who owned a shipping company about a million years ago."

"Who's Aldric?" I asked.

"Aldric. Aldric Chardin," my cousin said. "You know, Jean Gerard Chardin. Aldric is his given name."

So my cousin was working for Jean Gerard Chardin, the famous perfumist! Anyone my age will remember the commercials. Jean Gerard turning toward the camera, the exotic European look, the bottle of fragrance superimposed over the screen. In some commercials two women joined him on each side; in another a woman simply led him to bed. Fade out. Jean Gerard. He became a kind of television cult figure in a way now reserved for YouTube stars. His commercials were spoofed on *Saturday Night Live,* and Johnny Carson had a recurring bit on the *Tonight Show.* All of this was surely good for business, even more so than I could have imagined. As I came to learn, he was a very rich man.

A short while later William and I stepped out onto a balcony—every room it seemed had a balcony—and looked at the party below: the lit-up pool, people playing bocce ball, a gazebo in the near distance. The party, by anybody's account, was hopping.

I asked, "So what do you do for him?"

William thought for a moment, then said, nonchalantly, "Really, whatever he needs."

Whatever he needs. Was he a personal assistant? A body man? Was he now mixing fragrances the way he had designed furniture? The notion that he was Aldric's lover came to mind. I didn't ask any more about his job, it felt like it would have been intrusive to do so, and we headed back inside and downstairs. A waiter passed with a silver platter full of champagne flutes and William grabbed a pair. "Cheers," he said, and we drank, or rather William sipped. This was something I noticed over the course of the evening: he held a glass regularly, but he never actually drank. On the other hand, I was on my third drink, or was it my fourth, when William said, "Come on, let's find Aldric. I want to introduce you."

We moved through the rooms, back through some of the same ones we had visited earlier. People were everywhere, and my cousin knew many of them and introduced me always as his "favorite cousin." They were prominent business people and minor celebrities, these people that I met, and it was assumed that I knew who *they* were, including a county supervisor who would later run for Assembly and be arrested on bribery charges. And it was strange, because I began to get the feeling that my cousin wanted my approval. These introductions and the way he pointed out that the chandelier had been imported at great expense by Aldric himself, even though he was only renting the place, and that the catering company was the best in the city. . . William seemed to want to impress me. But why? Did he want me to report back to our family, to our grandmother, my uncle, tell them that I saw William in Los Angeles, you won't believe. . . Certainly I had nothing to offer William other than the fact that our parents were brother and sister.

And maybe it was just the booze, for I had another glass of champagne, maybe two, but the party opened up for me. I began to see the radiant possibilities of such a lifestyle, why William would be drawn to the opulence. There were fabulous people in their fabulous clothing talking about—

"How could you be so fucking incompetent!"

We had found Aldric.

He was in the kitchen—a long, involved space, as you might imagine—and he was standing before a woman of twenty-five or so, part of the catering company, and I believe she was attempting to explain something, but Aldric would have none of it.

"Oh no," William said.

"Get the fuck out of here!" Aldric said to the woman.

I did not follow William into the kitchen. In fact, I backed away into the next room. The charming Aldric from the fragrance commercials had given way to a guttural nastiness, and there were no other party guests in the kitchen (it was not that kind of party).

I could see fairly clearly: William approached with the intent to intervene. Is this what he did? Pour water on whatever fires the famous perfumist happened to light? But when William said something, and I could not clearly hear what, only a "maybe we," Aldric turned suddenly and went after my cousin. He hit William with two hands, square in the chest. Then he did it again. He did not knock my cousin down. He could not have done that. Aldric was not a large man. But he moved into William so that he was within inches of his face. My cousin noticeably flinched, ready to strike, and left the kitchen.

"Honestly, I could kill that fucker sometimes," he said to me, and kept walking.

I did not follow.

My cousin disappeared into the morass of the party, and I was again left alone.

I had enough of my wits about me not to drink any more, and the charming buzz I had enjoyed earlier was drained. I wandered aimlessly for a short while (again encountering the man who insisted on calling me "professor") and wondered, Should I leave, should I not leave, shouldn't I at least try and track down my cousin, wouldn't it be strange to leave on that note?

I began to move toward the front of the estate, and was near the main entrance when William appeared again. He was not quite the William of old, but I could see that he had cooled. He even had a glass of champagne back in his hand. "Aldric can be a bit of a prick," he said, "especially when he's been drinking."

"Has he been drinking?"

"Always."

"What was he so upset about?"

"Oh, who knows," said William. "Somebody forgot to put a toothpick in something probably. He's a perfectionist and expects everybody else to be that way, too."

"Right."

"Anyway, I don't plan on working for him forever."

"No?"

"I got something cooking. I just need a little more time. Then I can be free of Aldric and he can go shit on someone else."

These days of course I regret not asking my cousin what he had cooking—it might help explain things—and before I could say more, he observed, "I think you were going."

"Yes," I said.

"I'll walk you out."

My cousin did—he was always the perfect host—and left me only when the valet had brought around my car.

There is really not much more to say about the night except this: At the time I did not give any weight to my cousin's words— "Honestly, I could kill that fucker sometimes." Why would I? It was colloquial, a throwaway phrase. It was a reaction in the heat of the moment. It was a million different things, but a genuine threat was not one of them. Right?

The Hikers (1964)

When the ranger with the gray mustache called off the search for the night, Bobby's mother dropped to her knees and began sobbing uncontrollably. Bill Moriarty was the first one to her, and he said, "It's going to be all right, it's going to be all right, they'll find them."

But Bill, like everyone else, had his doubts: the kids had been gone for nearly a day and a half, dozens of rangers and police officers had been looking for them, and there was still the question of whether the children were even in the woods. *If* they're in there, the ranger had said.

They loaded Bobby's mother into a patrol car, and the officer drove her down the hill, to the hospital where they sedated her and kept her for the night.

Jill Moriarty was determined to be stoic. At first she refused to leave the search site, the place where the boy's Pontiac sat off to the side of the road. She had been there the entirety of the day, waiting, hoping that the children would appear like Glinda the Good Witch, a bubble come floating in, deus ex machina. The ranger convinced her that she needed to go home. "I'll have men here all night," he assured her. "If anything, anything at all, happens, we will call you immediately."

So she and Bill drove back down the mountain. Bill had checked in earlier with Stacy's brother, so they were not surprised to find him keeping his assigned vigil: to wait by the phone in case Stacy called. "Did you eat?" Jill asked him.

He had. The boy was fifteen and could manage a peanut butter and jelly sandwich. But he was clearly worried. Of course he was. He and his sister were close. For all their bickering, for all their jostling for their parents' attentions, they retained affection. They never failed to buy each other Christmas gifts, could sometimes be found sitting on the couch together watching a television show and laughing.

"She didn't run away," the boy said.

"I don't think so either," agreed her father.

"I found out a little bit about that boy. He's a senior. He works at Kroeger's Market."

Bill knew all this, and he told his son, "They don't think he's a dangerous kid. They think they probably went hiking and got lost."

Naturally Bill did not share any of the other concerns—that the children had been harmed and the car abandoned on the side of the road.

Jill listened for a few minutes and then walked numbly into the bedroom. She went to the sink and splashed water on her face—cold, she did not wait for it to run hot—and glanced into the mirror. She already knew what she would see: haggardness, dark circles, worry. She tried to remember what it was like to be seventeen, what would drive her daughter to skip school and run off with a boy she barely knew. They were under enormous pressures, these kids, with the race problems and the president being shot and the music that played day and night on the radio. She and Bill had provided Stacy and Peter with stability and love, yet she remembered a day when Stacy came home and found her dancing. It was a song, a remake, that belonged to the children, "Not Fade Away," but it came on the radio and Jill felt the compulsion. She turned up the Magnavox transistor and began whirling, whirling so that her hair was flopping around and she was dancing wildly and freely and—

suddenly there was Stacy, standing just inside the front door, watching her mother.

Jill did not say, Come on, dance with me.

She did not apologize.

She did not explain.

She quietly walked to the Magnavox and lowered the volume. Then she went into the kitchen and pretended to be busy.

Such a small thing, Jill thought now, for your daughter to discover you dancing, and dancing to *her* music. But as she stepped into the shower, with Stacy out there somewhere in the world, in the woods, hopefully only cold in the woods, unharmed, not frostbitten, not suffering from hypothermia, not come to any harm—maybe this boy Bobby was protecting her—she turned her back to the showerhead and the water hit her shoulders, a hot stream that felt good.

Then with a sudden jerk she shut off the water. She was ashamed of herself, ashamed to feel any measure of comfort. She stepped out of the shower and dressed hastily and went back downstairs to resume the wait.

CHAPTER 8

The Hikers (1964)

The boy Bobby heard the plane first, looked up and waited for it to appear. It was a prop plane, but there was no way for them to be seen, not with the thickness of the trees where they were. And anyway, Bobby did not think that the plane was looking for them, or anyone else; he figured it was just some pilot taking out his plane for a spin.

But then the plane circled back around and began to make loops, smaller to larger, as if it *were* canvassing the area. By then Stacy had noticed as well. "We should try to get to a clearing," Bobby said.

"Yes."

And with as much speed as they could muster, they moved through the woods, trying to find a place where they might throw up their arms and wave. Perhaps the pilot would see them, if he was looking for them, and they began to believe that this was a search plane. *They found the car,* thought Bobby. *That's how they know.* And he moved a little faster, not so fast that he left Stacy behind, certainly not, but measurable steps ahead of her in the woods. A clearing. They needed to find a clearing.

That morning, before the man had heard the report on the radio and saw the Pontiac and phoned the police, Bobby and Stacy woke before dawn, if they had really slept at all. They shivered their way through the night. They could not have known, but this was a good sign: had either one of them gone into a deep sleep, it would have been a sign of hypothermia, of their bodies going into that dangerous protective crouch. So they shivered and held each other, and Bobby said a silent prayer from time to time, and Stacy tried to distract herself by thinking of poems and song lyrics. Sometimes the most pedestrian thoughts would occur to her. She had to write a paper, and she had checked out a book, *The Great Gatsby,* from the public library. It was overdue. She thought about Herbert Hoover, who had died a few weeks earlier. She thought about the movie *From Russia with Love.* Other times the strangest images appeared—a woman she had seen in *Life* magazine, well-dressed and holding a martini for her husband as he entered the door, some shimmering fish she had seen the summer before when they were in Washington.

Then the sky began to brighten, and it felt colder still. They kept their embrace. "We just have to wait for the sun," Bobby said.

Stacy answered with a shivery "yes."

They did not wait, however, because the sun was slow in coming—so low in the sky this time of year—and they began to move through the pillared light (the woodpeckers began moving too, peck peck peck). Their bodies ached, but walking helped shake out the cold, so much so that they almost felt human again and began to speak and plan. "We should eat," Stacy suggested. "That would help."

Bobby wasn't so sure. He was hungry, no doubt about it, but he thought it best to hold out for as long as they could. Stacy insisted, so he pulled the apple out of the knapsack and handed it to her. When she bit down it was like biting into a frozen TV dinner—hard and cold. Then she handed it back to Bobby, who did the same, and back and forth they ate until the thing was gone, core and all. All they had left now was Stacy's Jell-O and her sticks of chewing gum.

"Something is wrong with my mother," Stacy announced a short while later, after they continued their movements through the woods.

Talking helped. Kept their minds occupied.

"What do you mean?"

"Well, one day I came home from school and she was dancing

around. She had the radio turned up really loud and it was like she was in a trance, her head was pointed down and she was whirling about."

Had they been in better circumstances, she might have imitated for him.

"What was she doing?"

"Dancing. I mean, just dancing, by herself in the middle of the day."

Bobby did not think it all that strange, but when he tried to imagine his mother doing the same thing, he just couldn't.

"And another day I came home and she was crying. Sitting at the kitchen table and crying. Normally I wouldn't think that was a big deal, we all get sad at times. It was just that, I don't know how to describe it, there was something really peculiar about the way she was crying. It was like hearing a dog bark when it's hurt. You know it's not just barking for the sake of it."

Bobby did not say anything in response.

"You think I'm a loony tunes," Stacy said.

"No," he told her. "I just don't know why she was crying."

Stacy considered that for a moment and said, "Me either."

Later, after they had hiked another half mile, Stacy said that she couldn't go on, that it was all hopeless, there was no way out, and she began crying herself. This was not the hysterical sobbing of her mother that she had described, but something closer to a measured sadness. She had held out for so long, tried not to be fatalistic, but she could no longer hang in there.

Bobby brought her into his embrace. Twenty-four hours earlier that would have been unthinkable, Now, however, without any hesitation, he held her close to his chest and she let him. Had she been another inch or two shorter, he might well have kissed her on the head (*should I—*). Instead he felt her cold brown hair press against his cold cheek, and as if some Greek goddess wanted to signal her approval, the sun appeared above the tree line.

Stacy recovered quickly and broke the embrace. She grabbed both of his hands and said, "We're not getting out of this hellhole by standing around, Mister."

Bobby said, "Onward Christian soldier."

And she smiled.

The plane circled above them for about ten minutes while they scampered to find a clearing. But by the time they reached one that might have done the trick, the plane had moved along, circling away until its engine could no longer be heard.

It would come back. It had to. It was a rescue plane. There was no doubt about that now. They agreed that it was best not to move for a while, not to outsmart themselves, wait for the rescue plane to make its way back toward them, and then they would throw up their hands and arms and *it* would see them, somebody with a pair of binoculars sitting in the passenger seat of the aircraft would see them and cry, "There! There!"

They would not be like those people on deserted islands or rafts out at sea, futilely screaming as the person on lookout duty says, "Let's go. There's nothing down there."

Gatsby, the Musical (1964)

George Latham stood alone inside the Encore Theater. He had arrived early. Eight folding chairs sat evenly spaced on the stage, and three standing microphones were positioned at equal distance—two on the end, one in the middle. There were no props or set pieces, though the lighting in the theater would allow for a shifting of moods. One of the theater's crew members had volunteered to come in and work the lights, and George took him up on it. He offered to pay the man, but was refused. "When this gets to Broadway, I expect to get paid back, big time," the man said to him.

This had all happened a few days earlier—when he and the man went through the cues, when to spotlight, when to brighten, when to wash the stage in green, and so forth. It was really not that complicated. This was a staged reading, word-of-mouth invitation mostly, even as George had notified the local papers and had a placement in the "Things to Do" column.

Standing alone now, inside this theater of one hundred and ninety-five capacity, George reminded himself that it was not a vanity project. It was *not* a vanity project. He had recruited faculty members and some students (and two people who appeared regularly in productions at the theater), and they had rehearsed a few times and would now read and sing for as many people as showed. Yes, he was paying the Encore Theater for the use of their space, but all theatrical productions did that—it was part of the game. He wouldn't make his money back (he wasn't charging anyone to attend), but the idea was to finally hear the words spoken, some (not all) of the songs performed, and make a recording (that was costing him too) and send it off to theaters in Seattle, St. Louis, New Orleans (he had exhausted New York, Chicago, and Philadelphia) and see if the spaghetti stuck against the wall.

No matter what happens, I am a lucky man, George reminded himself. I am a tenured professor with a family that loves me, children who are healthy. He thought about the two teenagers who had gone missing. It had been all over the radio that day, their car discovered on the side of the road. Apparently they had gone hiking and gotten lost in the woods, and driving to the theater George heard that the rescue mission had been called for the night.

But of course he wanted it to go well, wanted *One Fine Morning* to be *Hello, Dolly!* or *Funny Girl* or *Pal Joey*. And he still believed it could be. He had his bumps and bruises, sure, but wasn't hope the whole point, the ceaseless faith that some day soft winds would blow through the trees and alight upon your presence, that because you either worked hard or got lucky the earth's axis would at last tilt in your direction. And when it did you would sit in the back row of the theater, arms crossed and a satisfied smile on your face. No one would know you were the composer, you would have *no need* to tell anyone, and if that took root here at the

Encore Theater, then good. There were many roads to heaven.

"Oh, it looks terrific."

The voice snapped George from his reverie, and he turned to see his wife, Dot.

She was the first to arrive.

A little more than an hour later some sixty to seventy people had settled into their seats at the theater. The technician, Robert, lowered the house lights, and the actors took their places on stage. The technician then bathed them in soft light, and the audience applauded politely. Most were friends of George and Dot's, his students from the college, a few colleagues, and others who had read the announcement in the *Gazette,* or at least George assumed so, as he did not recognize them.

George sat at the piano, situated just below the stage, and prepared to begin. He had monitored people as they entered, their conversation—"Did you hear about those kids, lost out there all night," "Can you imagine," "It looks like it's Johnson's to lose"—and tried to determine the mood. The night was cool, yet the theater felt unnecessarily warm; there was nothing that could be done now. Nearly a decade after the idea first occurred to him, George Latham took a deep breath and launched into the overture.

The overture was composed with a full orchestra in mind, so like everything else on this night, the effect was minimized. George ran through the four-minute piece, nothing too bright to start—this was no comic romp, after all—but then a sampling of the show's more energetic numbers, "Remember Yale," "A Voice Full of Money," "So It's All True," followed by the dark "Careless People" and finally "One Fine Morning," just a hint of it. He finished and the crowd applauded, more than politely. George Latham bobbed his head a bit (the audience could not see him, except those in the front row) and felt that it worked. And imagine how it would be with French horns, and tubas, and cymbals!

Robert the technician placed the spotlight on the actor playing Nick, who rose to speak. George had long determined that he would not attempt to capture Fitzgerald's voice. Another actor was going to read the stage directions. Both men were longtime local actors who had appeared often at the Encore and had graciously agreed to participate. Dot was on stage as well, not as Daisy or even Jordan (both of those roles were being handled by students from the college) but for a variety of parts—flappers, guests at Gatsby's parties, needed harmonies. A high school music teacher whom George had known for a long time was handling Tom—and George worried about him. That is, he worried that the man would *overplay* Tom. In his day-to-day life, the teacher was not a man of subtlety—are music teachers ever?—and George feared he would turn Tom's privileged aggression into something closer to a rabid dog or crazed prizefighter.

"Do you know the way to West Egg?" the man playing Nick called out, to no one in particular.

And they were under way.

For the next seventy minutes they read and sang George Latham's *One Fine Morning*. They did it without intermission. There were no sodas to be sold or any reason to take a break. The songs were roughly handled—naturally, as they had been rehearsed only a few times—and at the piano George cringed from time to time (Dorothy had been right about George being ill-suited for the job of choir director: he was a taxing perfectionist), but he resisted the urge to rise and say, "We're going to do that one again. This is all just a Whitman's sampler, you know." Certain songs confirmed his instincts. "Bootlegger's Blues" was written as a good old-fashioned ragtime number but sounded strained. "Vigil" probably needed to be punctuated with more lyrics. And of course there was no "America," no signature song that rang the cash registers.

After they finished—and the ending was perhaps not as emotionally blended as George might have hoped, but these were eight actors on stage without props or a set, and one could expect only so much—George rose to speak.

He had not dressed formally for the occasion. He looked much like he did when he taught: a pair of slacks with a sweater, a slender necktie the color of the Pacific Ocean, loafers. He had planned on thanking them all for coming, that their presence was abundantly useful in working out kinks, that he knew they had better places to be (*ha ha*) on a Friday night. But the words did not come. He felt practically paralyzed. And all he said was, "Let's beat on."

What self-promoting artist has not experienced what George Latham experienced next—the obligatory, the half-eagerness, the genuine affection. Your friends invited—"nothing big, just a small theater off the—, you know the one, we're going to be doing a reading, if you can make it." The worshipful students who, seeing their favorite professor's work performed in front of them, by them, suddenly realize the mortality of the man who so often judged *them*.

Some of the audience filed out immediately; others spoke to him in turns.

You've got a winner on your hands, George.

I really loved that one number.

Thanks for inviting us.

I can't wait to see this. Have you tried sending it to so and so?

And then one colleague, a man who had been hired at the college a few years earlier, a man whose opinion George valued, said to him, "Good stuff."

Good stuff.

George could not tell if the man was lying or speaking euphemistically or being subdued. He was not a man to whom praise came highly anyway. During faculty meetings he tended to stay reserved. While other professors lauded this student or that, sang the virtues of some piece of music, the man withheld comment or sat staring out the window of the conference room window. George thanked him for coming and each said he would see the other on Monday.

Good stuff.

The phrase troubled him.

Before long everyone was gone except Dot and the technician

who was locking up for the night. George helped him put away the chairs—"I got it," the technician assured him, but George insisted—and then he put the heavy plastic cover over the piano. It would be too easy to say that it was like the placing of a funeral shroud, and the evening had not been disastrous, not at all. George Latham was not without talent. But the covering of the piano (a concert grand but not a Steinway & Sons) felt like a ceremonial closing of some kind, the extinguishing of the Olympic torch or the grave voice of a test proctor intoning, "Pens down."

Dot told him she would go on ahead. He promised he would be right behind her.

The small audience had really liked "It's All True," hadn't they? He had been surprised. He thought it was a throwaway number, when Nick realizes that there is truth to Gatsby's fantastical claims, but the crowd, the assembled dozens, that is, had laughed and found it jaunty.

He would send it off, *again,* the book, the recording, *One Fine Morning.* Music and lyrics by George Latham. Book by George Latham, based on F. Scott's Fitzgerald's *The Great Gatsby.* A bottle into the ocean with a note attached. Spaghetti against a wall.

Good stuff, the man said to him.

George felt miserable.

The Fairfax Apartments (Present)

The Actor managed to recover his phone with only a modicum of discomfort. "It's unlocked," said the woman from unit 2. Despite the Actor's attempts at sex—she had chickened out, wasn't that what happened?—her voice remained cheerful, full of tequila and lime and triple sec and whatever else went into her "special recipe." The Actor stepped back into her apartment, found his phone on the counter, and left.

He was hungry. It was midday. So instead of returning to his poolside chaise lounge, he left the Fairfax Apartments in search of food. Maybe it was just the lingering taste of margarita, but he decided he wanted a burrito, or maybe a taco, something spicy. In his swim trunks and white V-neck T-shirt he made the short walk to Melrose Avenue and headed toward Dean's Tacos. Even here, on a day when the pavement was as hot as hades, the Actor was aware of his movements. You never knew who you would encounter. Everyone was someone's favorite barista, assistant, second cousin. He moved confidently down Melrose, striding like a god. Forty, fifty years earlier he might have been Jon Voight in *Midnight Cowboy* or John Travolta in *Saturday Night Fever,* except instead of Tony Manero's red boots the Actor was wearing blue flip-flops.

Dean's Tacos was your standard hole-in-the-wall. Because it was lunchtime the place was crowded, and the Actor thought he might get his food to go, take it back to the complex and eat by the pool. He was waiting in line when he saw someone he knew, an actor from one of his classes, not his current one but an earlier class, through a small studio off Sunset. If this other man was not quite the Actor's doppelganger, he was certainly close, the same physical type, bruising not effete. Through a mnemonic trick the Actor remembered the man's name was Rick (like Ricky Martin), and they greeted each other warmly, shaking hands in the manner of brothers. "You got anything in the works?" Rick asked him.

The Actor did not tell him about the FX show, about how the Actor hoped to hear any minute about the pilot. You did not want to share that kind of information, did not want Rick running out to call his agent and saying, "Can you get me a read for that?" The Actor told him about the CBS show (even though it had been a while) and that he was up for a commercial (no harm in that) and about a few other things he hoped would pan out. "You still doing background work?" the Actor asked.

"Oh sure," Rick said. "Need to pay the bills, you know, but I'm using a call-in service, picking my spots. You?"

"The same," the Actor said.

They chatted for a few minutes longer while they waited for their orders, then wished each other well, good to see you, hope the commercial comes through, the usual exchanges.

The Actor walked back on Melrose with his burrito in the

bag before deciding he did not want to wait. He wished he hadn't done the shot of tequila. The margaritas were one thing, they practically evaporated in the heat, but the shot had him buzzing in a way that he did not like. He pulled the burrito from the bag and began eating. This part of Melrose was a strange mix of bars and shops and yoga studios, and there were derelicts at all hours—people strung out on drugs, loitering in entryways. The Actor walked past an art gallery where a group of people milled around. Some were drinking wine. In most places in the world it might have seemed a strange matter, an artist's reception in the middle of a piping hot Friday, but not here, not on Melrose Avenue, in Los Angeles.

Yes, there was no need to tell Rick about the FX show, the Actor thought, no need to jinx it or create turbulence. The acting brotherhood was a strange one—sometimes a kinship, sometimes Cain and Abel. The Actor tossed the empty burrito bag into a green metal garbage can and turned back toward the apartment complex. He could not have known that Rick was up for the same role.

Gatsby, the Musical (1964)

On the night of the staged reading of *One Fine Morning*, Dot lay in bed, restless. George was asleep. When he got home, he uncharacteristically poured himself a drink, a bourbon—they kept some around for visitors—drank it, and then crawled into bed. Dorothy was normally a good sleeper. If she was awake and alert, sometimes she would go into the front room and watch the *Tonight Show* (she liked Johnny Carson well enough but missed Jack Paar), but on this particular night she had no urge or motivation to move. And yet she couldn't sleep. She worried about George. She knew his demeanor. He had not been pleased with the reading, or at least he had misgivings. And she thought about those poor kids, lost in the woods, with the temperatures dropping. She and George were not skiers, but they had gone to the mountains from time to time, just to smell the fresh pine air and see the snow. Once a colleague of George's had offered his cabin, and they had stayed for three days, the children building snowmen and playing card games around the fire. "Happy" was the purest word to describe how she had felt during that time. George, too, had taken his customary walks and returned looking ruddy and invigorated. But those kids, the two teens, headed for a second night in those same mountains. How their mothers must feel. Dot didn't know the families—they apparently lived a few towns over—but she wanted to reach out to them. Would it be strange to take them food, she wondered? Who could prepare meals at a time like this? She even entertained the notion of rising early in the morning and driving up there, to help look for the kids. Her own children were asleep down the hallway. It would be a Saturday. George could watch them. At one point she even said, "George," but the word was a whisper—he needed his sleep, she did not want to wake him—and she tried to put it all out of her mind, but she couldn't. How their mothers must feel. And the cold, the bitter mountainous cold. When she arrived at the Encore Theater, she had sat in the car, listening to the radio. George had gone on before her—she needed to wait for the sitter—but the report came on that the search had been called for the night and she felt heartsick. But she had steadied herself, walked into the theater, and proclaimed, "Oh, it looks beautiful." And she had meant it. She loved the theater, loved their trips to New York City, loved that George would finally hear his words and songs. She even liked the Spartan feel of it all—the aluminum chairs, the carefully placed microphones. In bed she turned and tried thinking of a song, like counting sheep, but her mind kept returning to the kids, those lost kids. And their mothers. How their mothers must feel.

Felicity (2008)

Felicity was getting annoyed with the girl with the red hair, dyed red hair. She was dancing with Pauline, and this other girl kept leaning in, bellowing in Pauline's ear, moving her body in an erotic way. Typically Felicity did not feel jealous. *No jealousy.* That had been one of their rules. "Even if I am dancing with another woman, it doesn't mean I want to have sex with her," Pauline had told her once, though Felicity was not so naïve to believe her completely. But they agreed that jealousy was a deal breaker and had promised to check it at the door. And until this girl with the red hair began to bug her, Felicity had managed over the course of many months to avoid suspicion and worry.

That morning she had received her acceptance into the PhD program. She had been on pins and needles. Big envelope? Small envelope? Felicity's envelope barely fit into the narrow confines of the metal mailbox. The postman had crumpled the acceptance letter a bit in order to fit it alongside Pauline's various magazines—*Spin, Cannabis Monthly*—but Felicity did not mind: the point was to get accepted, not frame the letter.

Pauline was not home when Felicity got the news, but as soon as she returned and found out, she kissed Felicity's hand and pronounced her "Herr Doktor." Pauline meant it in good fun. And Felicity took it that way. "We are going dancing tonight," Pauline announced, "to celebrate the next in the ranks of the billionaire professors!"

All day long Felicity basked in the afterglow of the acceptance. The university was thirty, forty minutes away, depending on traffic, so she would not have to move. She still needed Imelda's help and, God forbid, maybe her mother's, and even Tony had taken to stepping up a little bit, rides home here and there or taking the boy to go do *something*. Maybe he's finally growing up, Felicity hoped. And Aunt Pauline. Felicity did not require much from her—Nick was not her child, after all—but her schedule was flexible. She remained in the habit of enrolling in classes and dropping them after a few weeks, but she could lend a hand and, well, it would all work out, wouldn't it—she had gotten accepted into a PhD program.

And so Felicity and Pauline set out for their favorite club. They dressed like they were headed to the Academy Awards, and Pauline even offered to drive (it almost always fell to Felicity to handle the driving). They decided to take a cab instead, and on the ride over Pauline squeezed Felicity's hand a few times and told her "way to go," "you deserve this."

As the cab approached the front of the club, Pauline leaned forward and said to the cabbie, "You can drop off Herr Doktor right here."

Felicity could not have felt better. But once inside the club something changed, changed the way lighting can change a mood, from bright to dismal, dismal to bright, or the way music can color an entire episode. (Felicity would always remember that the DJ was playing "Your Love Is My Drug" as they entered.) They found a table, and Pauline said, "I'll get us some drinks."

The club was crowded and Pauline took a long time. Felicity assumed there was just a line and she stood and waited. Finally she set out to find Pauline. She was not at the bar. She was not in the bathroom. She was not on the dance floor. At last Felicity located her sitting at a table talking to the girl with the dyed red hair. "What happened to the drinks?" Felicity asked. There was nothing mean-spirited in her voice.

"I got waylaid!" Pauline cried.

And she and the girl busted up. They must have gotten stoned, Felicity judged.

"All right, I'll get them," Felicity said, and she turned to the red-haired girl. "Do you want something?"

"Alabama Slammer," the girl said.

Felicity had never seen the girl before, she was sure. And she quickly decided that she did not like her. Maybe it was petty to resent the girl not offering her any money, either before she bought the drinks or after, but it was more than that—there was an aggressive quality to her. She had a face that said, "I don't give a shit what you think," a feature Felicity had admired in Pauline but fucking hated in this girl. Later Felicity would recognize that her hatred had less to do with the girl and more to do with Pauline herself. Well before that night she was losing her. Like any relationship there were fewer romps through abandoned zoos and more dull routine. They were, in a word, becoming *roommates.*

That night, when Felicity returned with the drinks, Pauline said, "Thanks Herr Doktor." But the phrase was biting.

Then came the dancing, the red-haired girl leaning into Pauline, and Pauline responding in kind. Felicity could have joined them on the dance floor, marked her territory like a dog. And besides, she and Pauline danced plenty with other women, at this club and elsewhere. It was one of the qualities about women that Felicity liked: you could dance with a woman and it was just that, dancing; men were always so transparent in what they wanted. But she did not join them on the dance floor. She wanted Pauline to realize that she needed attention. She had gotten into a PhD program. She wanted to be queen for the day. I'm being a child, Felicity told herself, while the girl and Pauline romped to "Dynamite."

During the cab ride home, Felicity thought about saying something. *You spent the whole night with that girl. You two seemed to get along.* Something along those lines. But she beat back the feelings. Jealousy, a deal breaker. They had agreed.

And when they got home and into bed, Felicity wanted to have sex, if only to feel reassurance. But Pauline rolled over and muttered, "I'm wiped."

It was a few weeks later when Pauline did not come home.

Felicity was sitting with Nick, watching *Cars* for the umpteenth time, and the hour grew later and later. When the boy fell asleep she threw a blanket over him and went into the kitchen to make some tea. While the water boiled, she decided to text Pauline. The exchange went like this:

Where are you?
With friends.
Which?
You don't know them.
What time are you getting back?
Am I past curfew?
Just wondering.
Soon.

But Pauline never came home. About two in the morning Felicity led a sleepwalking Nick to his bedroom and went to bed herself. The alarm went off, as usual, at six thirty, and it took a moment for her to realize: Pauline was not next to her. She rose and rousted the boy and poured some coffee and took a quick shower and put on her Orchard Supply Hardware shirt and made him breakfast and helped him assemble his backpack—good God, could the boy be any more disorganized—and they were just about gone when the door opened and Pauline walked in.

Felicity said, "What the hell?"

"What?"

"Where were you?"

"I told you, with friends."

"You could have texted, called, let me know you weren't coming back."

"You had to be up. I didn't want to wake you."

Pauline's manner was beyond blasé. But Felicity did not have time to engage her, if that was even possible. Nick had to be at school, she had to be at work, and Pauline, well, who knows whether she was working that day or going to some class that she was going to drop. Nick's backpack in hand, Felicity just shook her head and went out the door.

That night, however, she decided she could not let it ride. Their arrangement had always been a loose one, Pauline staying with her for financial reasons as much as anything else. Pauline never brought home another woman, or man, that would have been unthinkable, but they had never made a commitment (even as Felicity had not been with anyone else since the day at the old zoo in Griffith Park). "You just do whatever you want," Felicity said, while Pauline sat in a chair and leafed through a magazine.

"What do you mean?"

"Come home, don't come home, work, don't work, enroll in classes, don't go, smoke some more weed."

"What the fuck's your problem?"

"I don't know," said Felicity, full of piss and vinegar. "You know, I don't need to know where you were—"

"Good."

"It's just. . . the Pauline Hall Hour all day long."

"Is that a reality show you're thinking of pitching to *Bravo*?"

"Believe me, it wouldn't be that interesting."

"I stayed with friends. I was drunk. Did you want me to drive?"

"Of course not. But I wanted you to fucking call, so that I wasn't—"

"Wasn't what? Being Mother Felicity? I've made it this far without landing in a ditch, so you can stop worrying. I don't need a mother."

She's missing a gene, thought Felicity, that's all there is to it. Who doesn't come home and then acts like she simply forgot to pick up milk or grab the mail? Felicity knew that it was her own "one foot in, one foot out" disposition, her desire to be boundless and carefree battling with her basic sensibilities and social responsibilities. Either way, she knew the end was near.

It came a few days later. A torrid fight. The kind of fight where you try and hurt. Pauline was much better at it than Felicity. "You only got into that program because you're Mexican," Pauline said.

"You don't know what the fuck you're talking about," Felicity told her.

"You're like one big bundle of affirmative action."

They were facing off in the front room during Felicity's lunch hour. She had come home because she forgot her lunch and she did not want to buy from the trucks. Pauline had been out of bed for maybe only an hour, and the powder keg was ready to be lit. Felicity said, "You have no idea how anything works, other than I suppose a bong."

Then Pauline drummed out the beat to the "Mexican Hat Dance."

Felicity felt her blood boiling.

"Oh precious Felicity. Are your feelings getting hurt? Did somebody yell at you about their paintbrushes?"

The bottom was out, and for as mad as Felicity felt, she

wanted it to be over. They had been going at it for fifteen minutes, maybe longer. They could pick back up that night, after she got home from work. She said, "I don't want to fight anymore." Conciliatory.

And Pauline reached for it. She was better at this than Felicity. She knew which card to play, the one with Felicity's childhood nickname. Mockingly she said, "Whatever you need, Betty Cakes."

Felicity's right hand met Pauline's left cheek.

And that was the end of that.

The Fairfax Apartments (Present)

By the time the Actor got back to the Fairfax Apartments, the woman from unit 2 had disappeared, her belongings with her. Good, he thought. Let her take her tequila shot-taking self back to the world of medical supply sales. The Armenian man was gone as well. The Actor had a full stomach and the pool to himself, and it was still only early afternoon. Outside of a certain phone call, he could not have wanted anything more.

An inflatable mattress stood propped against a door to the small structure that housed the pool equipment. It had been there for days. Who did it belong to? Some kid visiting his grandmother perhaps, though you rarely saw kids in this complex, or just one of the residents who left it out there for community use. The Actor had the notion, so he retrieved the mattress and carried it back to his chaise. He removed his T-shirt and left his flip-flops (*stayin' alive, clip clop, stayin' alive, clip clop*) at the pool's edge and attempted to navigate himself onto the mattress. Who among us can do this gracefully? It's like boarding a bobbing canoe—you're bound to rock a little and think you are going in. But the Actor managed, and soon he was drifting, barely, across the rectangular pool of the Fairfax Apartments.

The heat was still oppressive, more so if anything, but he splashed himself now and then and that was enough to keep cooled. He wished he had some music, but everything was on his phone and his phone was at the chaise, turned up as loud as it would go in case the call came through. He imagined that he was at a resort somewhere down in the Cayman Islands—that's where they stashed money, right?—or at one of those tony mansions up in Los Feliz or Beverly Hills, where he *would be* one day. The Actor believed it. It happened to people. It really did. It was not some pipe dream. He replayed the audition in his head. He read for McKee, the tough-guy speakeasy owner who knows what's going on in the back of his store but looks the other way—for a small price, of course—and says things like, "I don't know nothing about nothing," or, "Listen, Doll, you come here for a soda or you come to cause trouble?" He had tried to read that book, the one about Gatsby, but there had been so little about speakeasies that it proved useless, and then he was drinking margaritas and dancing in that woman's apartment and now here he was, afloat on a mattress, and his eyes were closing and opening.

At one point he half-noticed that one of the brothers from upstairs had returned, still dressed in his hooded sweatshirt, and was walking up the stairs carrying a brown paper bag. The man entered his apartment, and the Actor went back to drifting.

He was a piece of perfectly tanned driftwood, this actor, barely moving in the rippleless waters. Now and then the slightest breeze would come through, hardly enough to push the mattress. Still, when the Actor reached the edge of the pool, he would put out his foot, size twelve if you must know, and launch the mattress back toward the middle of the pool.

The Actor was content to drift like that, running lines in his head, replaying the audition. Had he been a man of greater imagination, or a little more prescient, he might have conjured some roaring twenties law enforcement agency, with their hats, jackets, and stars, raiding a speakeasy, busting up the whole works, trying to apprehend the gangsters—just like the half-dozen Drug Enforcement agents who were now moving stealthily through the Fairfax Apartments, passing beneath the palm trees, holsters strapped to their thighs, Glock pistols at the ready in case they encountered resistance.

CHAPTER 9

The Comeback Kid (1993)

Mike rarely forgot that he was black. If he did, this was America—
someone would always remind him. Even the girl with the bangs
said to him, "I've never done it with one of you."

"Someone who does drywall for a living?"

She threw her head back and laughed. "You know what I
mean."

He did.

She was a sassy girl all around, so he shrugged it off and went
back to his omelet, and she started talking about how animals
don't feel guilt or some such shit. He felt confident that she did
not have sex with him because he was black. He was no totem.
They were drunk, that's all. She was a girl who liked to have fun.

No, what really bothered Mike were the assumptions, someone who had never met him, who had only talked to him on
the phone or communicated through e-mail, and then met him
and—

Oh, he's black. Mike could read their faces so clearly.

Then the comic overcompensation would begin, the pointed
way they would say, "African American," or some anecdote designed to demonstrate that they weren't racists ("the courage that
Jackie Robinson showed"), or the mention of a book ("do you
know Maya Angelou's *I Know Why the Caged Bird Sings*").

And school. Whenever the subject of being black came up
("Nigger Jim" in *Huck Finn*), the white faces would wheel his way
and the teacher would deliberately not make eye contact (*I am
not singling you out because you are black*), or she *would* and ask Mike

his opinion on the subject, as if he spoke for the entire black race. He remembered having to read *The Great Gatsby*, of being told that it was "the great American novel." There was a description of a "young buck." He wrote his paper on the guy who fixed the 1919 World Series, did a bunch of reading and research, even went down to the public library and grabbed a copy of the novel because he had lost his. It was one of the few times he got a decent grade in that class.

And the irony, if it was indeed irony, is that Mike was the product of a biracial marriage. His parents had struggled at times. They married in 1968, and even during those heady hippy times, they got stares. Mike was born two years later. In his early years, in the way of all children, he never questioned his parentage, never thought it strange. It took others to do that—"Are you adopted?" "Is that really your dad?" Thus he learned the word *miscegenation* earlier than most.

Maybe it was why he liked baseball so much. And sports generally. You proved yourself, your fastball against the other guy's ability to hit. Only once did Mike lose control. He swore he heard an opposing player refer to him as "a coon," and when the guy came up to bat in the following inning, Mike threw at his head, knocking him to the dirt.

The umpire stepped from behind the plate and took a look in Mike's direction. To that point Mike had shown perfect control. The man bent over the plate and unnecessarily brushed it off.

Mike stepped back on the rubber. He had planned on throwing at the kid's head again. The fucking cracker deserved it. Let them toss me out of the game. Just as he went into his windup, however, his competitiveness took over—and he threw a fastball past the kid, who was already stepping away from the plate, fearful for his life. Like Bob Gibson, Mike told himself, struck him out like Bob Gibson. And that other pitcher, Ray Corbin, his Topps '74 card sitting inside Mike's sock.

* * *

And now, seven years later, with the card again sitting superstitiously in place, Mike swung a bat and prepared to take his turn at the plate. *Let's see what you do with the bat.* Isn't that what the head scout had said. *Pro range.* And his speed had been good, he was sure. If he dazzled with the bat, was it inconceivable that he could get a contract out of the day? *The Comeback Kid: The Mike Allison Story.* The head scout actually had contracts in his car. He told them as much during his opening remarks, just before he told them not to get their hopes up. But Mike's hopes were raised. *Pro range.* The man had said so. The head scout for the entire California Angels baseball organization.

They called his number and he stepped toward the plate.

There is a story about Baryshnikov. One night he was dancing with the New York City Ballet and he just lost it. Midperformance. Tour en l'air. A move he had made a million times, a move he made in his sleep, it went away, like a golfer with the yips. Without warning or explanation, the great Baryshnikov stood on the stage, immobile. Seconds passed. A few seconds more. Some in the audience thought it was part of the dance, but then they realized something was wrong. He took a tentative step but he was out of synch with the music. The orchestra stopped and Baryshnikov looked out at the dark audience. He could hear them breathing, surely. Someone even cleared his throat. Then he nodded and the orchestra began again, and just as suddenly it was back, the muscle memory—and he was in the air, turning with the grace that had made him so great. No one, not even Baryshnikov, could explain what happened. It was as if someone had hit the pause button and then realized what he had done.

Mike fouled the first pitch straight back.

The way it worked was this: batters got ten pitches. Live pitching, from one of the guys attempting to get a contract, not from one of the assistants lobbing softballs that even a second-rate talent could drill into the outfield. Sometimes they pulled the pitcher after one batter, sometimes they let him go two. The pitcher that Mike was facing was fresh, on his first batter, and he was at least four years younger than Mike, with a pretty live fastball, as Mike had just learned.

But it wasn't that live. It wasn't pro live. Mike could hit this.

But then the kid came with a curveball, and it crossed him up. He missed it completely, the *thud* of the catcher's mitt taking him by surprise.

Two pitches. Two misses.

His timing was off, that's all. He stepped part of the way out the batter's box and took a practice swing. Stepped back in.

The kid is coming curveball again. He wants to show it off. The head scout was standing behind home plate. One night with the New York City Ballet, Baryshnikov, just plain forgot how to do the tour en l'air. Mike lunged at a curveball, missed it by a galaxy, a pitch he had hit a million times, a pitch he used to punish pitchers for throwing.

What the fuck.

What the fuck.

He wanted to turn and tell the head scout: *I'm rusty, that's all. There are no curves in the batting cages. It's been a while.* But Mike did not dare look. He tapped the plate and the kid came fastball and Mike hit a lazy ball to right field. In a game it would have been a single, a hit, but the scout was not looking for singles, he was looking for pop, someone who could drill the ball, someone worth the team's time and money.

Mike felt it slipping away.

The fifth pitch came—a curveball—and Mike looped it toward center field, where one of the position players easily shagged it.

He was onto the kid now, he was sure. And he was. He ripped the next pitch into left field, and the one after that into the gap— it would have been extra bases—and the kid came again with his curveball and Mike was ready and made him pay, floating it well beyond the center fielder's head. Just as suddenly it was back— the muscle memory. His ninth and tenth pitches were hit solidly as well, nothing remarkable but demonstrative. The assistant called out the next number and Mike stepped away.

He had looked like a clown lunging after that first curveball, as if he were a ten-year-old playing pickup ball with the Lakers, but if the head scout was as good as they said, he understood that Mike just needed to get loose. Five horrid swings, but then five solidly hit balls, once he had his groove. Mike walked toward the dugout area, where his gear was sitting. As he went, he glanced toward the backstop, but the head scout was nowhere to be seen.

The man had walked away after the third pitch.

The Fairfax Apartments (Present)

The Actor floated on the inflatable mattress and dreamt big. He saw himself behind a bar in a speakeasy, likable but tough, oozing noir, easy on the eyes. Then he saw himself on stage at the Nokia Theater accepting an Emmy. It could happen. A woman used to live in his complex, an actress. The woman was a real wildcat. The Actor liked to rise early sometimes, get to the gym as the sun was rising, avoid the crowds. He would be heading out of the apartment complex with his gym bag and she would just be getting back home from some club or party, still half-drunk. One morning they stopped to talk—predawn hours at the Fairfax Apartment Complex were not usually the time for conversation—and she told him about her new gig as the host of a morning show on one of the children's channels. Her job was to be the bouncy leader of The Playhouse, leading kids through song and learning their alphabet and cheering on visits from friendly furry animals—preschool stuff. The Actor figured her partying ways would fall curbside, but they did not. In the early evening he would still see her heading out for the night, and occasionally he still ran into her in the predawn hours, having to be on set in a matter of hours. She later moved out of the complex, and about a year after that she won an Emmy for Outstanding Performer in a Children's or Preschool Children's Series. It could happen.

The Actor floated on.

His eyes were closed, and the midafternoon sun continued to press down on him, and all of Los Angeles. At first he did not see the half-dozen drug enforcement agents move purposefully through the complex. A few wore sneakers, a few boots. All but one was in jeans, and they all had on the black jacket with DEA emblazoned on the back. Guns drawn, two of the agents went up the stairs, with another two right behind them. And two positioned themselves at the bottom, about ten feet away from the floating Actor. Then they kicked down the red door—and the sound of shattering wood snapped shut the Emmy ceremony and the Actor wheeled his head to see a DEA agent gesturing at him, *Keep still, don't do anything.*

The Actor *was* frozen.

These were bona fide DEA agents. Vince Gilligan was nowhere to be found.

There was a commotion coming from the apartment upstairs, shouting, and the Actor thought about slipping off the mattress and into the water—and then he just did it, reflexively. The DEA agent turned and looked at him and gestured again, *Keep still.* The agent looked annoyed but not panicked. The Actor could not have known, but this was an easy bust. The agents had not expected resistance, and the one at the bottom of the stairs was there *for* the Actor and anyone else who decided to come out of their apartments or wandered back home in an untimely way.

The Actor treaded water—he had been floating in the deep end—with only his head poking out, as if his chin were a bobber on some fishing line. And in a matter of minutes the two brothers from the upstairs apartment were being led away by the DEA agents. Both brothers were in handcuffs, and the one brother, the one who had returned only a short while earlier, was still wearing his hooded sweatshirt. The Actor had never spoken to him. The brothers seemed to never speak to anyone in the complex. The Actor avoided eye contact as they were led away.

And so as quickly as the thing started, it was over. A pair of agents stayed behind, to gather evidence, the Actor supposed, and by that time people had come out of their apartments—the

Armenian man, and Mrs. Brownmiller, the old lady the Actor sometimes helped, and some others (but not the woman from unit 2; she was either gone or sleeping it off)—and they shared their astonishment at what had happened, said they "knew it" or "knew something was off about those two." And the manager was there as well, shaking his head, maybe thinking about the damage, and the Actor had gone from being stunned to being frightened to being submerged to standing with the others looking up at the apartment, as if something more was going to happen up there.

Nothing did, of course, and eventually the DEA agents roped off the area with yellow tape. The door was a shattered red mess, and they spoke to the manager for a few minutes and then were gone themselves.

It was all a holy shit moment, one of those events that become an anecdote, even in Los Angeles, or maybe especially in Los Angeles, and it was really quite possible that somebody on Fairfax Avenue watching the brothers being led away thought they were watching a scene being filmed, maybe an AFI project, until they realized there were no cameras and that these were *actual* DEA agents leading away *actual* drug dealers, so that the unreal blended with the real and for the love of William Mulholland who wears a hooded sweatshirt in this heat, a dead giveaway.

Poolside the Actor gathered his things—the lotion, the water, his phone. People returned to their apartments, and he decided to do the same. It was late afternoon, and the agencies and the studios and production companies would be closing soon—all the young assistants off to be together in the Beverly Hills bars. It did not mean the call could not still come. One needed to be vigilant, ever at the ready. In his flip-flops the Actor climbed the stairs and opened the door to his unit. It was summertime, not even yet the solstice. The day was still young.

Cousin Billy (2005)

Like everyone else I have seen too many movies. If I had to be interrogated by the Federal Bureau of Investigation I assumed at least one of the two agents would have movie star looks—and there would be two agents, there are always two agents—and they would have a good cop, bad cop vibe. They'd approach me in a parking lot somewhere, announce themselves, and tell me they wanted to ask a few questions. Certainly I never thought I would have to go *to them*—to a nondescript office building in Diamond Bar, of all nondescript places.

The cubicle was less than cinematic as well.

When was the last time you saw your cousin?

About three or four years ago.

Can you be more specific?

(I thought.)

Almost four years.

And where was that?

At a house in Los Angeles, a party.

What sort of party?

I don't know. Just a party. Aldric was renting a house and he threw a party.

(The agent looked up from his computer.)

Did you see Aldric there?

Yes.

What was he doing?

When I saw him? He was mad at one of the caterers.

Why?

I don't know.

Did you talk to him?

No. I never even met him.

Okay, and what was your cousin doing there?

He worked for Aldric.

Doing what?

I don't really know. I think he was a personal assistant of some kind.

All right. How would you describe your relationship with your cousin, close, not close?

Well, we grew up together. My mother and his father were, are, brother and sister. I would see him on weekends at times.

Did you ever notice any tendency in him toward being violent?
He played football.
(The agent found that unremarkable.)
And at the party, did you see anything that was out of the ordinary, anything that might suggest that your cousin would do harm to Aldric?
(I thought about Aldric attacking my cousin and my cousin stomping past me and declaring, "I swear to God I could kill him sometimes." But it was just a saying. I was sure he had not meant it, at least not at the time.)
Not really.
What do you mean not really?
Aldric got mad at the caterer, he pushed my cousin, my cousin walked away.
(The agent made a note of that.)
All right, if you had to guess, where would you say your cousin is right now?
(I wanted to give him a good answer, I really did, but I said) I have no idea. Somewhere in Europe, or maybe China—he used to do some work there. The South Pole for all I know.
(The agent nodded.) *Well, if he gets a hold of you, give us a call.*
I will. But I doubt that will happen.
If he does—(handing me his card).

* * *

A week earlier I had been in my campus apartment, watching television, when the news came through that Aldric had been found dead in a Swiss hotel. As you can imagine, my ears pricked up. No cause of death was immediately available, though there was evidence of foul play. There was little information on what Aldric was doing in Bern or if there were any witnesses. These questions would be answered in time—strangulation, attending a trade show, none so far—but I watched CNN with a surreal and perverse interest. The Swiss police were investigating, and I kept waiting that first night to hear the name William Goodwin. But my cousin's name did not surface.

In a matter of days, however, he had become a "person of

interest." Television stations broadcast his picture, a photograph taken a few years earlier. How or where they got the picture I never knew. My cousin's face looked lean, handsome, gorgeous even. It was not the billboard photo. It was evidently taken at some social engagement, because he was talking with someone just outside the frame of the picture. Maybe Aldric, who knows.

"William always was too big for his britches," my mother said, when I phoned home in the wake of the news.

I pointed out to her that might be true, but it did not mean that he was a murderer. "What does Uncle think?" I asked.

There was a pointed silence. "He doesn't know what to think," my mother said. "No one has heard from William in a long time—weeks, months, I guess."

"Is he going over there?"

"Where?"

"To Switzerland."

"Why would he do that?"

"To find him."

And my mother said what we would all come to say: "I don't think William wants to be found."

The Swiss police agreed. So did the FBI. And in time my cousin officially became a "suspect." If he was found, he would be apprehended, arrested, not just brought in for questioning. But in those early hours he was still a person of interest. You could not turn on the television without seeing his face. Or a picture of Aldric. Or clips of those old Jean Girard commercials, the ones that had made Aldric famous—and rich. My colleagues talked about it at lunch. But I never said anything about being William's cousin. I just poked at my food and nodded vaguely during their conversation, their conjectures, their jokes even. One of my colleagues was a terrific mimic, and he would turn his head away from us at the table and look back, pantomiming Aldric's motions. Everyone laughed. I was not offended. When death is distant from us, we have a tremendous capacity to giggle, especially when the subject is of some celebrity. Had William not been my cousin I probably would have done the same. "I'm sure that guy did it," one of our math teachers pronounced. "Why else would he have run away?"

It was hard to argue with that logic.

Felicity (2009)

For her date Felicity wore a skirt and boots, a white shirt and a black sweater—she was going for something between classically smart and fundamentally sexy. They were meeting at a bar for a drink. This was not the "I'll pick you up at six sort of date"—if those even existed anymore. This was Felicity and one of the professors from the college getting together for a drink after several weeks of flirting. He was not *her* professor, so there was nothing really compromising about the meeting. Not that it would have made a difference. If professors published papers in the same numbers that they had affairs, every single one of them would be tenured; they can be libidinous beasts, and this one, Jack Hurley, might have found the perfect target in Felicity.

You would not have thought her naïve, not after growing up without a father, having a child at twenty, then the abortion, the whole Pauline affair, but Felicity had a vulnerability that could be sniffed out. Maybe she was just too trusting.

He got there late, if only by a bit. She was sitting at a table in the bar area and he approached. It was true: he was handsome, about ten years older than Felicity, hair the color of wheat and a good build. "I brought you that book, the one I told you about." And he handed it to her.

Pauline would have never brought her a book. Pauline was plenty smart, but she would have more likely brought her *High Times*. And Tony kept copies of *Playboy* magazine lying around, in between the various Xbox controllers and the empty beer cans. "It's worth reading," Jack said. "Maybe even give you some ideas for your dissertation."

When the waitress came over Felicity ordered a beer and he ordered a whiskey neat, and she felt a little foolish, acting as if she were inside a bowling alley. But she was pleased to be there, found his intellect titanic—a PhD from Stanford, after all—and she enjoyed their conversation, plain and simple. It had been well over a year since the Pauline mess, and outside of a couple of careless flings with women she met at clubs, Felicity had kept her nose clean. The last one, a massage therapist, had wanted to see her again, but Felicity was not interested. She was done with women, she was sure. Over several drinks she and Jack talked, on subjects that might have filled the schedule for NPR. Sex trafficking in Africa, the European Union, the election of Barack Obama, the philosophy of Roland Barthes.

"I guess I should get going," Jack announced after checking his watch (and even that Felicity found captivating—a watch, who wore a watch these days?).

"Oh, me too. It's getting late."

If he had suggested dinner, she would have gone.

"Department meeting in the morning. I'll be feeling these." And he gestured to his head. He meant, of course, the whiskey.

"I promise not to rat you out," Felicity said. "You look like you're getting a bad case of the flu."

He fake coughed, and she laughed. Felicity could handle her liquor, but she was a beer and two Tanqueray cocktails in—and feeling spirited.

They walked out of the restaurant together, into the spring evening. She was in the second semester of her PhD program, and she felt something being filled that she did not know was missing. What was it? *Intellectuality,* she would decide. Even at UC she had never felt part of any great enterprise, with so many of her classes being taught by graduate students in oversized halls. But Jack was different. The philosophy of Roland Barthes, for heaven's sake. It all felt so adult. She could not imagine him sneaking into someone's yard and going for a swim. "You sure you're okay to drive?" he asked.

No, take me home! thought Felicity. *I'll sober up there, stay the night!* But she said, "Oh, I'll make it." And they hugged, lingering a bit, and said they'd see each other at school.

So they didn't have sex that first night, after drinks, but the following week he asked her to his townhome, which he rented a few blocks from campus. He made them dinner and then they sat on the couch together and then they were in bed. After the sex Jack rose and went to his dresser, where he began stuffing a pipe with tobacco. He sat in a chair that was in the corner and lit the pipe, and Felicity gave him a strange look. "Do you mind?" he said. "Takes the edge off."

"It's fine," she said.

What edge? Hadn't they just had sex?

"So you were married once?" she asked. He had alluded to it during one of their conversations.

"A long, long time ago."

"What happened?"

"It was my fault. I probably wasn't ready to be married. You?"

"Am I ready to be married?"

"No," he said, laughing and taking a puff of his pipe. "Have you ever been married?"

Felicity sat up in his bed, pulling the sheets over her body. "I don't believe in marriage. It's an institution designed to subjugate woman. And who needs the trouble anyway."

"Spoken like a true feminist."

"I get my talking points from Simone de Beauvoir."

"I thought I detected a desire to take control."

"Next time, whips and chains."

"Next time? Interesting," he said. "So what grade did I get?"

She told him, "It was pass/fail."

He dumped the rest of the pipe into an ashtray and came back to bed. When he kissed her, Felicity decided that she could tolerate it. Sometimes, after Pauline had a cigarette and they kissed, Felicity would be aroused by the taste, but she had to be drunk. A pipe. So strange. She thought about the painting by Magritte, the famous words "*Ceci n'est pas une pipe.*" She had seen it at the Los Angeles Museum of Art. Had gone alone one day. "This is not a pipe."

* * *

One afternoon, about a month later, Felicity was in the hallway of the building where most of her classes were located and a woman approached. The woman was older, in her late forties perhaps, and she was dressed well, professionally. Felicity recognized her to be a professor, but that was about it. Instead of smiling or nodding hello or passing indifferently, the woman paused and signaled for Felicity to do the same. Felicity did not have time to think, *What does she want,* nor did Felicity expect anything foreboding.

"You should be careful," the woman said.

"What?"

"Just be careful," the woman said, again.

"About what?"

"All I'm saying is, watch your entanglements here. Not everybody has your best intentions in mind."

"I really don't understand," said Felicity, "and I don't like talking in code."

The woman stared at her—an appraisal that was part stern and part maternal. *I* am looking out for your best interests, it said.

"Just be careful about Jack," she said, and walked on.

Felicity turned and watched her go, down the hallway and into one of the classrooms. Who was she? Some jilted lover? Someone on the opposite side of a department feud? Someone jealous of graduate students like Felicity, who still had their youth and their entire careers ahead of them? She just didn't know. What was there to be careful about?

Felicity was tempted to tell Jack about the exchange. He might have been able to explain. But she decided to brush it off. She was seeing him two, three times a week, often during the day because she needed to be back home in the evenings to take care of Nick. Every so often Imelda or Felicity's mother would watch the kid at night, overnight even, and then Felicity and Jack would go out somewhere, once to a jazz club, once to a poetry reading, another time to a movie house that played silent films.

Afterward they went back to his townhome and she stayed the night. He never tried to roust her out of there. She never felt on the clock. They did agree not to parade their relationship around campus—no holding hands, no outward signs that they were a couple—if only to avoid the gossip mill. Still, people *knew.* Jack and Felicity were often seen together. Not so unusual for graduate students and professors, of course, but there was something there, most everybody could tell.

Then on a late Wednesday afternoon she and Jack were sitting inside Malone's, a bar about a mile from campus. The place was a favorite of Jack's, with its dark wood paneling and pints of Guinness and numerous dartboards. He always said it made him feel like he was in the Irish countryside with Joyce. Felicity liked Malone's well enough, though there was always the chance that someone from the college might see you there. And sure enough, on this Wednesday afternoon, a woman approached their table. She was about Felicity's age and build, with brownish hair and light brownish skin. She smiled wanly at Felicity and said to Jack, "Still tilling the fields, I see."

Felicity might have been naïve, but she did not need to be told: this woman was a former lover (*lover,* a word Felicity always choked on). The woman did not say any more and returned to her table on the opposite side of the bar. Felicity watched her go and then kept glancing over as she conversed with her companion. Felicity tried to read the woman's body language: was it plaintiveness, amusement, exasperation. At last she asked Jack, "What's her name?"

"Who?"

Felicity gestured, as in, Come on, you know who.

"Leticia."

"Leticia," said Felicity, and for some reason the name amused her. "Leticia, really? Leticia."

"She's a very nice person."

"Oh I'm sure she is."

"It was a long time ago."

"Uh huh."

"Anyway," Jack said, and went back to talking about a paper he was thinking about writing, making use of some just discovered records that had been found in a New England church. *These docs, they were in boxes in the basement . . .*

Felicity pretended to listen, but her mind was on this other woman. It was not that Jack had obviously slept with her. Felicity knew that he was no virgin in professorial robes. She was hardly a virgin herself. And it was not the tilling the fields line, whatever the hell that meant.

Just sitting there for all those years . . .

And most any other occasion Felicity would have listened raptly, taken as she was by Jack's interests, by the fact that he was interested in her, thought *her* intellect was of significant caliber. Was she falling in love? She occasionally asked herself that question. And if she was, was she falling in love with Jack or the idea of Jack? It was Jack himself, she was sure, right down to his habit of smoking that stupid pipe after sex.

Nobody thought to look. Seems so obvious now . . .

Leticia. What was it about her? She looked so familiar. Had Felicity met her before? Did they have a class together? Had she seen her dancing at a club?

So I'll probably head back there in the summer, do the heavy lifting then.

Felicity could not place it, not at that precise moment, but the realization would come later: Leticia looked like *her*, she looked like Felicity herself.

Gatsby, the Musical (Present)

Dot heard the front door open and thought that George was home at last from his walk. Her daughter Susannah entered the kitchen. "Hello, Mom."

Dorothy looked up from the table. "Oh, hi dear."

"What are you doing?"

"Just sitting here."

Susannah came over to the table and kissed her mother on the cheek. "Did you get something to eat?"

Dot remembered: "Yes, I made a sandwich."

"For breakfast?"

"Of course not. For lunch."

Susannah glanced up at the clock. "It's ten thirty in the morning," she said.

Dot considered that fact. "I must have been hungry."

Susannah chuckled and said, "Well, you haven't lost your appetite in your old age!"

Her mother smiled.

Susannah went to the sink, where she discovered a handful of mint. She hoped her mother had not used scissors to clip the mint. After the last time, Susannah had hidden the sharp knives and scissors, put them in her old bedroom, which was now a museum's worth of boxes and plastic bins. She picked the mint from the sink and placed it in a plastic bag, then opened the refrigerator door. "I'm putting your mint in the fridge," she said.

"Okay."

"Remember, if you want to make tea, just press this button here," and Susannah pointed to a plugged-in device that heated and dispensed water.

"It's too confusing," her mother said, shaking her head.

It had been a rough morning, Susannah could tell. They would have to hire a nurse soon, no doubt about it. Her father had taken out the insurance to cover full-time care, so it was just a matter of convincing the insurance company that her mother was ready. Without a nurse, Susannah worried that one of these mornings she would find, or not find, her mother wandering the neighborhood in her pajamas, maybe even the path that ran behind their neighborhood. She had good days and bad days, but the process was not going to reverse itself.

She came and put her hand on her mother's shoulder. Dot looked up at her. "Your father should be back soon," Dot said.

"Why don't you lie down for a while," Susannah suggested.

She liked to nap. Mornings were best. Such clarity.

Susannah followed her mother into her bedroom, where Dot positioned herself on the bed, on top of the sheets. The room was tidy. Susannah turned on the television, flipping through the music channels until she found "Broadway." Her mother liked to listen to the Broadway channel, all those old great numbers. When Susannah was a child, her parents went every year to New York City, to see shows. She hated it when they left but understood later how important those trips must have been. She and her husband liked to get away as well.

"I'll be in the next room if you need anything," she said.

Her mother was such a puzzle these days, sometimes lost in the maze, other times as sharp as a tack. It had been a rough morning, Susannah could tell. "I'll be in the next room," she told her again.

"Your father's been gone a long time," Dot said.

"He has," Susannah agreed.

CHAPTER 10

The Hikers (1964)

They were going to be out there for a second night. That was all there was to it.

They had eaten their last bit of real food, the cup of Jell-O, in the early afternoon. They waited a long time for the rescue plane to return, but it never did; so they ate the Jell-O and left the small clearing and wandered back through the woods. They tried to push downhill, thinking that if they walked long enough, down the mountain, they would have to emerge eventually. This was true, but it would have been *a lot* of miles, more than they could cover in the course of the afternoon. The first day they had moved mostly laterally; the second the density of the woods and the slipperiness of the ground slowed them. They made progress but very little. Bobby cut his leg as well, a pretty bad gash. Stacy, in her shorts, got covered in mud. And they both stepped in swampy ground, dousing their shoes. At one point they paused and Stacy asked him, "Do you believe in God?"

The question was probably inevitable. Spend two days lost in the woods, uncertain that you are getting out, and your mind will turn to God's plan for you.

"I guess," said Bobby. "We used to go to church, but we don't anymore."

"Why not?"

"I don't know. My mother just stopped, so I stopped. We never talk about it."

"I don't believe, in God," said Stacy.

"Why not?" Bobby asked. He had never known anyone to make such an admission.

"Because you pray, for something good to happen, but a lot of times it doesn't. And why would God care anyway, about me, just some high school girl?"

"Maybe you have to pray a certain way."

"Maybe. But let me ask you: have you prayed in the last day, have you prayed that we would get found?"

Saying that he *had* prayed felt silly, given what she had told him, but he admitted to it, especially the night before, when he was shivering and trying to get some sleep.

"Well I didn't pray," Stacy said. "And look, we're in the exact same spot."

Bobby bobbed his head a little. "I guess we are."

"I don't know what's going to happen. What if we don't—"

"At some point—"

"I know what you're going to say, that at some point someone has to find us. And that may be, but we might be dead by then. All those Jewish people killed in the war. And those boys down South, trying to register voters. Why would God let that happen?"

"I don't know," Bobby said.

"It's our fault, for getting lost. Our own fault. Or it was just dumb luck. I don't believe this is some kind of test, that if we do get out of here, that you're going to join the priesthood and I'm going to become a nun. If we get out of here, I'm going to go back to school, and so are you, and maybe in fifty years we'll laugh about it."

Bobby hoped so. But for the time being all they could do was press on.

For much of the afternoon they kept their downhill motion. That was the plan. Here and there Bobby fantasized about airplane sounds, the school bell, his mother's voice. He thought he heard his name. It happened more than once—a whisper. He had become accustomed to the woods making unusual noises, but he'd hear, "Bobby, Bobby," and he'd turn in the direction of the noise. But he knew it was nothing, just his tired mind tricking him. He was not the first person that the woods had whispered to. He could have told you that much.

And then his head got even funnier. He thought maybe it was spatial disorientation. He had read about it in an article on the astronauts. You couldn't get your bearings. Everywhere you looked was the same, every tree (every star) identical. Loopy. It took Stacy to keep them moving, because sometimes he would turn and start in another direction, and she would redirect him. The first few times that she tugged on his shirt, he seemed nervous about it. Later, as the afternoon dragged, he stopped caring and just followed her lead.

Nighttime crept in, the light pulling back from the trees. Stillness eventually settled around them, and even the ubiquitous woodpeckers ceased their pecking. And Bobby fell. Just dropped. The ground went out underneath him, and he stayed there like a stricken deer.

Stacy sat next to him.

"We need to stop for the night," she said.

He did not protest.

(A second night. That is all there was to it).

"Here"—and she reached into her pocket and pulled out the packet of chewing gum, handed him a stick. He did not immediately take it. "Come on, you need to eat," she demanded, so he accepted the gum and put it in his mouth, but his jaw barely moved.

Stacy chewed hers eagerly, could not resist the urge to swallow, just to feel *something* in her stomach. They were now down to three sticks of chewing gum.

Breakfast.

They decided to stay where they were, or rather Stacy made the decision. One spot was as good as the next. It was not like a bear's lair was going to suddenly appear or a tent was going to fall from the sky. As the afternoon wore on, they had spoken with less frequency. It did not pass the time as it had before. And now Bobby was completely silent. He sat cross-legged like an Indian, and Stacy watched him through the dark. Later, out of nowhere, he muttered words that she could not follow. She said "what," but he just shook his head and looked to the ground.

"What?" she tried again.

He kept staring at his crossed legs.

"Bobby."

But it was useless. He would not respond. And then he tipped over.

Stacy did not know, could not have known. The clumsiness, the apathy, the insensible speech. These were all signs of hypothermia.

The Fairfax Apartments (Present, 2009)

After the DEA agents hauled away the brothers—justice restored, America safe!—and sealed off the apartment with the yellow tape, the Actor went back to his own apartment to—

He was not sure what he was going to do. He had no classes, no auditions, no work that day. The whole point had been to spend it by the pool, waiting for his agent to make the call. He could go to LA Fitness and exercise, but he still felt sluggish from the sun and the margaritas, and after DEA agents sweep through your apartment complex, pretty much everything else is aftermath. He did not change out of his swim trunks. He thought he might practice some lines (*do something every day for your career*), or watch some show on Netflix and study the actor's movements, or try and read some more of that *Gatsby* book. None of it seemed very appealing.

He lay down on the couch and clasped his hands behind his head. At least his apartment was cool, and the Actor began to drift.

The girl had lived in his dormitory freshman year. She was not the sort of girl he typically went for. For one, she was tiny, gaunt like a model (someone else might have described her as waiflike), and she often seemed bothered or distracted (someone else might have described her as tormented). The Actor, then as now, was neither of those. Maybe that's why he was attracted to her. And strangely she reciprocated, or he believed she did. At times she appeared to be openly flirting with him; other times she seemed indifferent to his existence. It went like that all semester long. Around the time to register for spring classes, she was in one of her more flirtatious moods, and she said to him, "You should take Beginning Acting."

The Actor was eighteen years old. He heard: *You should take Beginning Acting and I will have sex with you.*

He registered for the class, but to his surprise, when he showed up for the first day of class, she was not there. She was a *theater* major—she had *already* taken Beginning Acting. He might have dropped. He had no real interest. But the school had a general education requirement, and he needed to take something to fulfill the category. Beginning Acting sounded better than Ceramics or Modern Dance.

It was not love at first sight. Many of the exercises made him self-conscious, downright embarrassed. The professor was loopy and uninhibited. Half the class seemed fruity. But he hung in there. There was no breakthrough moment, the Actor losing himself in tears as he inhabited the character of the wayward son, the class captivated and—pause—resounding applause. No, the turn came later when the professor suggested he audition for the school play. "It's *Death of a Salesman.*"

He didn't know it.

She explained. "Happy is a very physical role. He's a bit of a dullard, or can be played that way. Not always aware of his conditions. I think you'd be perfect."

The Actor took it as a compliment.

. . . The Robert L. Tilling Theatre at College Z is a bold enough affair. Seating capacity: three hundred and seventy-five. No black box job. The Actor, who at this particular moment was doing what many actors do on their first night, peering from backstage to calculate the audience, had never heard of Robert L. Tilling, and did not inquire. If he had, he might have learned that Tilling was a multimillionaire philanthropist who had attended College Z a generation earlier. He went into banking and became a patron of the arts. It rarely works the other way.

The theater was more than half full—not bad for a college production of *Death of a Salesman*. As the Actor observed the audience, he got a little panicky. Seeing his name on the casting list had not surprised him very much (hadn't his professor said he was perfect for the role), and even when he showed up for auditions and discovered that there were only a handful of people in the production, he had not appreciated the fullness of what was happening to him. Then he discovered that Happy had so many lines! But he stuck with it. The director—one of his professor's colleagues in the department—worked with him, showed him Stephen Lang in the television version, the one with Dustin Hoffman (the Actor knew Hoffman from the *Meet the Fockers* movies), and now he was peering out at an audience of two hundred, including perhaps the bone-thin girl from his dormitory.

When he told her that he had been cast as Happy, she seemed thunderstruck. "Really?" she said.

For the first time it occurred to him: when she suggested that he enroll in Beginning Acting, she had been messing with him.

"Well that makes sense," she said.

"What do you mean?"

"Nothing."

"So you'll come see it?"

"Maybe so."

She did not tell him: she had auditioned for the role of the wife, Linda Loman, and had not been cast.

That first night the Actor beat away the nerves (no Baryshnikov moments for him) and delivered his lines with a suitable amount of theatrical competence:

> About five hundred women would like to know what was said in this room.
>
> I can outbox, outrun, and outlift anybody in that store.

And of course:

He had a good dream. It's the only dream you can have—to come out number-one man. He fought it out here, and this is where I'm gonna win it for him.

He only flubbed twice, and even that seemed fitting for Happy, as if he were stuttering.

But it was during the curtain call that the thing really cemented itself inside him: He stepped forward from the other performers and was surprised to hear the applause. There was nothing extravagant about the noise, no thunderous rising as often happens, especially for the lead. The Actor had not stolen the show. But the mere fact of it—that they had not *stopped* clapping—filled him in a way he had not expected. He felt approved of (someone else might have called it approbation). He looked forward to doing it again.

Afterward he searched for the girl from his dormitory, but she was not there, or had already left, or was coming a different night. None of these were true. She had no desire to see *Death* and was still smarting from not being cast. She also took pains to avoid him in the dormitory.

That was all right. She was not his white whale, his Daisy, but he would always owe her a debt of gratitude—she introduced him to acting. He even sillily considered thanking her when he received his first Emmy.

The Actor must have dozed off. The light had shifted outside, deepened. He looked at his phone—no calls, no texts—and checked the time. He knew it was still hot. The heat had been unrelentingly oppressive. Like everybody else, he swore he would never again complain about the cold. He would *remember.* He stepped out of his apartment and leaned against the railing of the balcony. All was quiet in the complex. No more storming DEA agents. No woman from unit 2. The inflatable mattress still floated in the pool, and he figured there was less than an hour left of daylight. Then the sun would drop over the Western horizon and the lights would rise in the city, cars would move, someone would get lost on Mulholland Drive, and the Friday traffic on the way to Santa Monica would cause at least two suicides.

The Actor grabbed his towel off the railing and headed downstairs. The mattress was a little out of his reach, and in his exaggerated efforts to snag the thing, he looked like a silent film comedian. At last he got a hold of it and positioned himself. He thrust out his size twelve foot and pushed off.

Already he felt cooler, and he figured he would just float for a while. He again had the pool to himself, so why not? Maybe later he would practice some lines, make some dinner, call up some acting friends. Maybe he would just settle in and watch television. The night was wide open. The Actor floated on.

Felicity (2010)

Felicity stood inside the Museum of Modern Art, unable to move. How long had she been standing there? Five minutes? Ten minutes? Longer? She had come to New York for an academic conference and had drifted over to MOMA, made her way upstairs, where she came face to face with *Christina's World*. Like *Young Italian Woman at a Table*, when she had seen it at the Getty, the painting consumed Felicity, overwhelmed her. Why did this happen to her, she wondered. What was it about this woman, so far from the farmhouse, so helpless in the field, which pulled Felicity inside of her? The woman was scarred, clearly so, that was part of the magnetism. *Something* had happened to her.

Felicity was a few months removed from Jack's breaking it off. He was moving to Wisconsin, had accepted a position there, needed to find his footing, was going alone. "I fucking introduced you to my kid!" she bellowed at him. This was so. He had not become Uncle Jack, but the three of them had gone to dinner, played miniature golf together, went to see *Cars II*. And now Jack was gone, or going, and Felicity was again alone.

She finally moved along from *Christina's World*. She drifted among the other paintings on the other floors but looped back to the Wyeth. She wanted one more look before she left. Later Felicity would learn that the woman depicted in the painting suffered from polio; she was *physically* helpless in the field. This made Felicity ache for the woman even more, made her wish that Andrew Wyeth had painted her so that Felicity could see her face.

* * *

She withdrew from her PhD program at the end of that semester. This has nothing to do with Jack, she repeatedly told herself. I am not some weak-willed woman who can't function because I got used, tossed aside like a worn-out doll. I am just tired of school, don't have the gumption to research and write a dissertation, and I can always come back later. True enough. The department would let her reenter if she did so "within a reasonable period of time." She wondered, though, what would become of the rich gringa of her dreams, the woman Felicity imagined was watching her while she did the dishes. *Cómo se llama,* the woman asked in her tortured Spanish. And Felicity answered in perfect English. The woman asked because she recognized something in this poor girl's eyes, something bright and promising, not someone who would later break because of a *man,* a piddling *profesor.* The rich gringa plucked the barefoot girl to be a PhD, not an ABD, all but dissertation. But that's where Felicity was now, like a runner who pulls up lame just as the finish line comes into view.

On the day she withdrew from her program, Felicity drove home and pulled Nick from school. "Do I have a dentist's appointment?" he asked.

"Something like that," she said.

At the time Nick was eleven, doing better in school—Felicity at least had righted that ship—and seemed comfortable with the circumstances of his life, the shuttling between their apartment and his grandmothers and occasionally his father. Nick never asked about Aunt Pauline, the woman who had lived with them a few years earlier. Did he understand the nature of the relationship? Felicity did not know and was not eager to ask. He would figure it out one day. Maybe he had erased it from his memory like Felicity had tried to do, until she realized she preferred to remember that Pauline was part of her gestalt.

That day they drove to Go Kart Land. "What are we doing here?" Nick asked.

"Racing go-karts," she told him. "What else?"

Nick was eleven years old. He did not say, I am missing my history block because of this. Shouldn't *you* be at school? Why are we racing go-karts? He was out of the car in a hurry, checking out the track with its bridges and banked turns. "Oh awesome," he said, and Felicity's mind flashed back to the day he pushed his Hot Wheel cars through the botanical gardens, when she had tried futilely to introduce a five-year-old to West Coast flora.

Once Felicity signed the release forms, they got outfitted with helmets and were ready to go. "This is a four-banger, right?" Felicity said to the track marshal.

"That's right."

"A what?" asked Nick.

The marshal started to answer, but Felicity got there first. "It's a four-cylinder engine. I'm guessing we'll get up to about thirty, thirty-five miles an hour."

"Tops," the marshal said.

"How do you know so much about it?" asked Nick.

Felicity just smiled. "Be prepared to eat my dust."

And for the next two hours Felicity and her son raced their way through Go Kart Land, the boy growing more confident with each pass around the track. "Eat *that!*" he cried, when one time he passed Felicity on her left. "Oh you're going to get it!" she yelled back at him. And Felicity pressed the accelerator down as far as it would go, and hoped that these moments were what the boy would remember the most.

The Comeback Kid (1993)

Mike stood at third base and took a warm-up toss. He was one of the two dozen men selected to play the three-inning scrimmage, but it didn't matter. They were just playing out the string. They sent him to third base not because they wanted to see if he could handle the long throw, but only because they were filling positions. Maybe there was a pitcher they wanted to observe, or a catcher—check their instincts in live action. It sure felt super-fluous to Mike—like that race they run after the Kentucky Derby: nobody really cares.

He had blown it, plain and simple. Even after he came to bat during the scrimmage and screamed one down the left field line, he knew he was not getting a contract. When his time had come at the plate, he had waved at a pair of curveballs like he was Pinocchio, flopping around on a string, not in control of his own motions. Anyone could handle heat, but if you couldn't handle the curveball, you couldn't play in the major leagues.

They played out the short scrimmage and the head scout called them together. His words were mush in Mike's ears:

Thanks for coming out, it takes a lot of guts to do what you guys did.

We have your information on the reg cards.

Remember, keep playing, wherever you can.

You never know.

Oh, but you do know. Deep down you know. This was the miracle shot right here, the open tryout—all the teams did them, community service shit—and you either dazzled or you failed. It was an either/or proposition. With the others, Mike gathered his gear and began heading to his car. Some of the men looked like prisoners of war on the march; others seemed happy just to have made it to the scrimmage. Mike, he was thinking about drywall, how he would wake in the morning and do drywall ("hey Bambino," "hey Negra Modelo"). He didn't mind the work, liked it, in fact. He had not come to the tryouts to get away from his job. He came because he wanted to take his shot. There wasn't a man out there who didn't think he was Rocky.

At the car he changed out of his cleats and put on a pair of tennis shoes. He thought he might go get a drink somewhere. Maybe he would even ring up the girl with the bangs, tell her he had taken her advice. No regrets. Like an animal. Maybe he would just go home.

As he was driving out of the parking lot, the head scout crossed in front of him, headed toward his car as well. He looked at Mike and gave him the thumbs-up. But it was not a "heckuva job today, Kid, we'll be in touch" thumbs-up. It was a "well, you came out and did what you could" thumbs-up. And Mike already knew that.

Cousin Billy (2008)

On a gray morning in the middle of February, just about three years after Aldric was discovered in the Bern hotel room, I made my way home. *Home.* Is there any more troubling word in the English language? More than love or even death, we cannot pin it down—its meaning elusive, its presence ineluctable.

Like a Joad I crawled along Foothill Boulevard and headed north, over the Grapevine and up the gut of the state, past the stinking pastures and the drought-ridden fields. I took Interstate 5, some would say the least interesting of the two available highways, but that is like preferring sauerkraut to rhubarb.

I was headed home for my grandmother's funeral.

I was sitting in my small apartment and preparing for classes when my mother phoned. I knew my grandmother had been ailing, the simple effects of age, but the news still shocked and rattled me. I distractedly went through classes that day and the following morning made the trip. It took about six hours before I saw the familiar sights of my hometown, the essentially unchanged streets full of fast-food chains, the old bowling alley, the Montessori school, the KinderCare. By saying unchanged I don't mean to suggest that my hometown was in any way quaint. It was inert. That should have suited me, someone who has lived for years in the same apartment, but on this day the town seemed especially full of dead-endedness, lacking color. No wonder my cousin had sought to escape: my hometown was not so very different from his, twenty miles to the north. Just most of the time, I was unaffected by it.

At the service my uncle spoke of my grandmother's mostly quiet life. I sat in the front row with my other cousins, and we nodded appreciatively. My uncle reminded us that our grandfather, his father of course, had been "a layabout," "had died and left her high and dry," but that "she had shown good Scottish grit and carried on, enjoyed a resurrected life in fact." He added, "She looked younger at seventy than she did at fifty."

"And she loved you grandchildren, loved to hear news of what you were up to."

It need not be said that she especially loved to hear news of William. But my uncle did not mention William's name at the service, no one did, and I half-expected that there were FBI agents wandering the parking lot and jotting down license plate numbers.

The get-together at my uncle's house afterward was a different matter.

"Belize maybe."

"I bet Morocco."

"Just a momentary lapse of reason, right? That's the only explanation."

Most of these offerings were in a hushed manner, the irresistible passing of gossip, fishing for news. But no one knew *anything*, or if they did, they did not share it with me. William was gone into the ether, a D. B. Cooper or perhaps a Tom Ripley.

After everybody left and we were just down to family, several boxes of my grandmother's belongings sat between us. We were in my uncle's den, an elegantly decorated room with a large oak bookcase and an expensive globe. Had William grown up in this house, I suspect he would have slipped into this room often, spun that globe and dreamt of his future. "I don't want them," my cousin Barbara said. She meant the boxes, which were filled with old photographs, itineraries (my grandmother had not travelled much, but she had taken a couple of cruises), and dozens and dozens of Christmas cards and postcards. Barbara was not alone. Having been picked through, the items were detritus to my cousins and my uncle, the Bartleby-like bits of my grandmother's life. "We'll just toss them out then," my uncle said.

"No, I'll take them," I announced.

I had already noticed what they had not.

The following morning I returned to Southern California. Again I barreled down boring old Interstate 5, saw surprising flurries of snow as I made my way over the Grapevine, dropped into Santa Clarita, and then pushed eastward toward the San Gabriel Valley. It was a Saturday, so the campus was quiet—a few students kicking a soccer ball, but that was about it. I parked the car in front of my apartment, connected to one of the boys' dormitories, and carried in my travel bag and the boxes of my grandmother's belongings.

The postcards were handmade—pictures of nature on the one side, sometimes of the ocean, sometimes of trees, Kodak prints taped to heavy stock paper. On the opposite side, my grandmother's name and address were carefully inscribed. My cousin's handwriting was impossible to miss. I had seen it any number of times in my life, the *W* announcing itself, the almost painstaking way the other letters were presented. I suspect a handwriting expert would have a field day. The FBI as well—for there were postmarks from across Europe, a dozen of them that announced William was in a certain place at a certain time. The implications were obvious. William had been communicating with our grandmother over the years. Nothing but her name was written on the postcards, but it was his way of telling her that he was alive. Had she said anything to anyone? I doubted it. And William knew she wouldn't. Imagine that! My grandmother, our beloved Nana, a probable accomplice to a crime, a keeper of secrets.

For a long time that afternoon, I stared at those postcards myself, just as she might have done. Occasionally I could hear the cries of students playing ball on the nearby field. I remembered the day William drove us to the store, his elbow projecting confidently out the car window, some forgotten band playing on the stereo. *Such an unnecessary light.* That is what he said when I told him there was no right turn on red. But of course a man was dead. I thought of Aldric, and I thought of my own uneventful life carried out in three hundred square feet, adjacent to a dormitory where ruddy-faced boys dream of the future. I gathered up those postcards, remembering my cousin and his childhood map.

Gatsby, the Musical (1967)

If only they had moved to New York. Maybe things would have turned out differently. Shakespeare had not stayed in Stratford, had he? He had moved to London where the action was. If you really wanted to make a go of it, you went to New York.

Not that they lived in the boondocks. They were only an hour east of Los Angeles, where plenty of musical scores were being written. Still, the San Gabriel Valley was not Hollywood. You could live in Pasadena and still be in the action, but where they were, well, there was a difference. Every now and then George would meet someone from the movie industry, but nobody ever said to him, "You teach musical composition for a living. Here, write the score for *Lawrence of Arabia*." But New York. That might have been different.

Once he proposed, seriously, that they move. It was during one of their visits east, two years after the staged reading of *One Fine Morning*. They stayed at the Belvedere as usual and saw *Sweet Charity*. Bob Fosse directed the production, and George had been moved by the choreography, the inventiveness. Back at the hotel, as they settled into bed, George said, "We should move here."

"Every time we come, you say that!" Dot laughed. She was in a festive move; she had enjoyed the show as well.

"I know, but we should. The children are young enough. I can apply for a job at one of the colleges. Lord knows there are enough of them here. We'll get an apartment."

Dot knew her husband well. She detected the earnestness. "It's so expensive here," she said. "How could we manage?"

"We have savings. And we wouldn't come without a job. I'm not suggesting we move into some fleabag."

"Oh I do love New York. But I'm not so sure that I would like living here. It's different, visiting somewhere and living there. And we have a house, a beautiful house. And friends. And my mother. What about my mother?"

"Damnit, Dot!" he said, almost violently. "What are you so afraid of?"

"I'm not afraid of anything," she told him. Her tone was tart.

She did not like being cursed at. "But you just don't up and move to New York, not at our age. We're not kids, George. We have children. And I like my home."

George rose from the bed and walked to the window. He looked out at Forty-Eighth Street—the moving cabs, the people headed to late-night meals. Everything was tame where they lived, so utterly reliable. George Latham might not have admitted it in that moment, but he liked that tameness, liked being able to find parking at the drugstore, liked running into people he knew at the coffee shops. But he felt tugged. Dot did not understand, could not understand. She enjoyed singing, but she felt little need to *create*. He was certain she wanted nothing more than to sing in the church choir, root him on in his ambitions, raise their children in the suburbs, not the city. She had never been disingenuous about this, never sold him any false goods.

Without turning from the window, he said, "Sorry." He never brought up the idea again.

* * *

One night, not long after they returned from New York, Dot rose and walked barefooted through the house. It must have been midnight, maybe later. These were not the quiet predawn hours of a composing George, Dorothy bringing him coffee ("a baby, George, a baby"), but there was stillness, solitude. Dorothy stepped tenderly—her mother had told her not to shuffle her feet—and she unlocked the back door and stepped into the yard. The oak tree, as ever, loomed, and the mint field and the clothesline both in their proper places. The moon was full. She considered whether this might be the cause of her sleeplessness—the full moon. Perhaps her body was reacting. For some reason it made her think of the War. She had been a little girl during those years, and they lived in Salinas. They had so little. Everybody was sacrificing. Then the War ended and they had so much. Enough to send her to Berkeley. Why did people want so much? George owned a wanderlust that did not afflict her. They had fought in New York. Well, a fight was not it, really—an exchange of words.

Sometimes she thought that they should fight more often, like letting air out of a tire or something, yet they rarely did. Dot knew that she was pretty even-tempered about matters. But if they fought more, maybe it would be cathartic for George—he could blow off steam, rejuvenate. He was struggling, she understood, with a roil, not the light cloud that just then blew across the face of a full moon, rendering it even more beautiful and then moving on, but a more sinister force. Standing in her bare feet, she tried to put a word to what it was he was feeling, or worrying about feeling, what wind was looking to blow him out to sea. She knew the word she wanted to use, but would not. The night was too still and the moon was too full for Dot Latham to whisper: "failure."

CHAPTER 11

Gatsby, the Musical (1977)

Thus George Latham lost his idols one by one, like branches cracking from a dying tree. Novelists he admired as a young man published disappointing books late in their careers. Athletes turned out to be rapists and tax evaders, and the whole industry of sports was just that, an industry, a giant money grab. And politicians—well, the country was lied to, wasn't it, about Vietnam and Watergate, and Camelot was a myth carefully constructed in *Life* magazine. No one was to be trusted.

Dot noticed that George became less eager about Christmas as well. When the children were very young, he loved it, happily stayed awake late to assemble dollhouses and racetracks. On Christmas morning he would bounce around in his pajamas and slippers snapping photograph after photograph. Then the children grew older, and George would complain about the mess the tree made, the pine needles that got into every nook and cranny.

He used the baby grand with less frequency. She could not remember the last time they sat side by side belting out tunes from *Oklahoma!* or *South Pacific.* If teaching gave him pleasure, he never said so, complaining instead about having not gone into administration. "The salaries they pay these guys," he'd grumble. He'd never been much of a gardener, never been one to leaf through *Sunset* magazine, but sometimes she would see him through the kitchen window, standing in their backyard, looking for *something.* Dorothy still had her mint field, and the oak tree stood, but for George there were no crocus bulbs to be buried, no plantings to signify spring. Music had been his hobby and his passion.

Only the dog seemed not to disappoint him, the cocker spaniel they purchased from a breeder. They had been careful, researching what sort suited them. And the dog, Lady, did not disappoint. She was sweet-tempered and playful. And she occasionally hauled in dead birds, left them on the doorstep like tributes! In the evenings George would let her on his lap, and he would stroke her back while he watched television. But television, too, began to bore him—"the same old cop shows and those stupid sitcoms." Then Lady got sick and they had to put her down.

Dot really did not know what to do. If only he would start composing again, feel the sparkle. But composing required faith that you were composing for someone, not scribbling treble and clef notes in the dark, a grand shuffle of pages that landed in a desk somewhere, another stack of papers wasted, pulp on the floor of the paper mill.

He was a genius, Dot believed. How had the world not noticed? How was her beautiful George Latham not the man some eager-looking thirty-year-old shyly sought out in a New York diner? "A helluva guy," George had said, beaming, after meeting Richard Rodgers.

Rodgers, George learned later in his life, was an atheist. At least they had that in common.

* * *

The girl's name was Miranda, and she was in his office again. He had begun to think she was up to no good. Always she seemed to be dressed stylishly when she met with him, not like other students from the department who came to class and office hours looking like they had just crawled out of bed. She was a pretty thing, George thought—and just then she was sitting with her legs crossed, her bare knees extending from her skirt.

They were discussing, of all things, the musical *Tommy.* George and Dot had seen the film and found it tedious and incomprehensible (though George had told Miranda only that *he* had seen it, not he and his wife).

"I didn't much care for it either," Miranda said. "I know you're supposed to, but I think I was born in the wrong century, or a few decades too late anyway."

She was twenty-seven years old, fifteen years younger than him. George knew this because he had looked at her student file in the office. This was a minor breach—it was not her *main* student file, only one they kept on each of the graduate students. Nonetheless he felt every bit the criminal when he let himself into the office one evening and opened the cabinet, just to get a few tidbits. She was originally from Wisconsin, went to high school there, and she had done her undergraduate studies at Occidental.

"How about *Jaws?*" she asked.

Like everyone else George was familiar with the musical score. It was everywhere in those days. But they had not seen it. Dot had no desire. "Not yet," he said.

"I think it's out of the theaters now, so it may be too late."

"Ah, yet another thing I missed out on!"

"Have there been many?"

"A few," he said.

"Well, you just missed a lot of blood and gore is all. I don't see what the big fuss is about. Oh, how about *Dog Day Afternoon?*"

"Yes!" said George. "I went because it starred the guy from *The Godfather*—"

"Al Pacino."

"Pacino."

"And . . ."

"It was . . . okay."

She sighed, a deliberate and purposeful sigh. "What's wrong with us, George? All these movies that other people love."

Any other student calling him "George" would have been unthinkable, but there was a confidence to this girl that allowed her some berth. And how did they get on the subject of movies anyway, when ostensibly they were supposed to be discussing her master's proposal? And that knee, projecting from her skirt!

She left his office not long after that. "See you tomorrow," she said, before disappearing into the hallway.

My midlife crisis, George thought. I must be having it.

Certainly he never told Dot about the girl coming to his office with so much frequency. He only mentioned her name once, "one of my students, Miranda, is working on—" He was sure he choked on the name, but Dot did not seem to notice. No antennae sprang from her head. And what did he have to feel guilty about anyway? He had not done anything with her other than sit in his office talking about her research, President Ford, movies. And what would he do if the opportunity presented itself? She lived in an apartment, by herself—he knew that much, she had told him during one of her visits to his office. He even thought she had emphasized the fact that she lived alone, but then he decided it was his imagination. But what if she invited him over, for some tea or something, maybe even a drink? Why shouldn't he go? He had been rejected by every musical theater in the country, but he had kept the keel steady and not dragged down the family with him. He had provided. Wasn't he entitled to feel good for a little while?

The answer came about a month later. George was in his office, listening impatiently to another student talk about his work. George guessed that Miranda was in the hallway, and by then he had not only grown accustomed to her visits, he relied on them. They had become the most exciting parts of his week. The other student was talking about Haydn, and George said, "That sounds good. I'd keep going that route." He all but called a bouncer to kick the kid out.

And George was right: Miranda was waiting to see him. When she entered there was something more serious about her—maybe it was the pants suit—but also some impatience. She had spent the better part of six, seven weeks coming to his office, flirting with him, praising him. He had even told her about his *Gatsby* musical, and she had called it a "genius idea" and begged him to let her take a look. But George did not say to her, *What do you say I get us a room? Did you mention you don't have a roommate?*

It was left to Miranda to do that.

She entered the office and sat, having closed the door behind her. This was not the ebullient Miranda talking about movies. She said, suddenly and clearly, "I'm available to you—if you are interested. In case you haven't figured that out."

"Oh," he said, and leaned back in his chair.

"I haven't wanted to be pushy because I know you're married. You don't talk about her much, by the way."

"Don't I?"

"No."

"I only need so many consultations on my master's thesis, you know."

"I know," he said.

I'm available to you? Is that how women talked these days? When the Summer of Love came to town, George and Dorothy were in their thirties, with three children. They were hardly the free love, hippie types. George had had his experience with admiring students over the years, even detected a crush or two, but this was different: this was a flat-out proposition. He looked at Miranda. Such a pretty thing.

That night, when George entered the house well after their five o'clock cocktail hour, Dot was in the kitchen preparing dinner. She stepped into the front room, her green apron wrapped firmly around her hips. She was in good shape, Dot. Never anyone's model, but she swam regularly at the YMCA and had been mindful of what she ate during her pregnancies. "I was starting to get worried," she said.

"I got hung up," he told her. "One of my students was in crisis."

"Well, dinner's ready."

George would have liked a drink, could have stood a drink. He might have told her "long day" and made one, but already she was bringing out the food and setting it on the table. She called for the children. *A baby, George, a baby.*

"I saw the strangest thing today . . ." Dot told them all, but already George's mind was adrift.

He thought about the girl Miranda. There were colleagues of his who would have had the girl in bed from the get-go. They even sometimes boasted about it openly. After she had left his office, her availability as evident as an exit sign off the freeway ("I'd write down my address, but I bet you can find out"), he went for a walk. There was a path he liked, leading off campus and down toward the old fruit-packing houses. If you turned around there, the whole thing took about an hour.

He wondered: Had Dot ever strayed? It was unfathomable to him. She was always so busy with the kids. But there was so much divorce around them. Everybody they knew was divorcing. Sometimes it felt like they were the only married couple left. He had been a sourpuss at times, had worn his disappointments on his sleeves, and still Dot had remained cheerful. And the children, the youngest especially, would be devastated. To toss it all away for a cheap thrill, just because she flattered him, was younger than him. She had little at stake; he had everything to lose. And yet that overexposed skin, her bright smile, and the silky brown hair. So young and joyful about the world. And he had to admit that her office-hour visits had sent him reeling sometimes. He even thought about composing again. Wouldn't that have been the greatest gift of all?

"More peas, George?"

"No, thank you, Dot."

Peas.

Felicity (2010)

Felicity sat in the examination room waiting for the doctor to enter. She was not wearing a hospital gown. She had on a sweatshirt and a skirt and tights. The nurse had taken her blood pressure (normal), her temperature (normal), her heart rate (normal), and said, "The doctor will be right in"—and closed the door.

About a week earlier Felicity had come in for what she assumed was a bronchial infection. They took a chest X-ray and saw "something," a spot on her lungs, and ordered the CT scan. And now Felicity sat on the examination table, her legs dangling off the edge, waiting for the doctor to give her the results, order up a biopsy if necessary (she had been told that was a possibility), tell her she had six months to *live*—whatever the news was going to be.

She looked up at the picture on the wall: the Sidney Harbor. Felicity thought it criminal to hang a picture of such a faraway place. Hi, here is Sidney, Australia, somewhere you will now never go! And of course Felicity thought about her mother, all those years of her smoking in their apartment, and Pauline and her marijuana—did weed cause cancer, Felicity wasn't even sure—and Professor Jack and his stupid pipe, his sitting in the corner, taking off the edge, the smoke lifting into the air like some sort of belly dancer. And Nick, who now might be raised by Tony and Imelda, who would never see the inside of a college if Felicity were gone. But at least the kid would not need the "talk"—he could just leaf through Tony's *Playboy* magazines and figure it all out. She had a cry over that one already, but this hour she was steeling herself for the worst.

Illness is so boring, Felicity told herself. If she were ever a character in a movie, she would not want to be one who got sick. Who wants to hear about it? Every day the same questions and comments: *How are you feeling? Can I get you anything? You look great.* She had no desire to be tragic.

She had come alone to the doctor's office, had not in fact told anyone about the CT scan. Who would she tell? The kid, get him all worried? Her mother? Remember those twenty-one years when you smoked in the house? Well, guess what? Felicity had no lover (*lover*, a word she always choked on) to hold her hand. She was a woman in a sweatshirt and a skirt and tights, her legs dangling off the edge of the examination table, looking up at the Sidney Opera House.

The knock finally came and the door opened slowly.

After Felicity left the doctor's office, she drove to Inland Tattoo on Foothill Boulevard. She had passed it many times in her life. Pauline had wanted the two of them to get matching tattoos, but Felicity retained enough skepticism not to bite. Deep inside she must have known that their relationship was not going to be permanent. But now Felicity pulled into the parking lot, ready. What was she waiting for?

Inland Tattoo was located in a rough-and-tumble strip mall, adjacent to a liquor store and a taqueria with an adult toy store on the opposite side. So Felicity was surprised when she entered: The parlor was as clean as the doctor's office—brightly lit, too. There was a black leather chair, and the walls were full of designs and sample work. The owner, Jake, greeted her warmly. He looked to be about thirty, younger even, and he wore a T-shirt that displayed two arms full of ink. "I want to get a tattoo," Felicity said.

"Good, because I don't give haircuts."

"Oh shit, I totally misunderstood. I thought I could get both done!"

"Have a seat," Jake told her, smiling, and he grabbed her a beer from a mini-fridge.

Pauline or not, why had she delayed so long before getting a simple tattoo? It was practically the zeitgeist. Though maybe that was the very reason. "If everyone was jumping off the Brooklyn Bridge," her mother was fond of saying. Just what to get, however, was the question. She leafed through the folders. She considered a bird, an open book, her initials. She thought about a pipe with the words, *Ceci n'est pas une pipe.* This is not a pipe. She wondered if he could do *Young Italian Woman at a Table.* Or the Virgin Mary. Put the genie back in the bottle. In the end she settled on the words "Betty Cakes" in cursive.

Jake went to work. She studied his arms to keep her mind off the gun. It was just her ankle, but still. Ray Bradbury had died earlier that year, and Felicity remembered the Illustrated Man—all those tattoos. She thought about Neil Armstrong. What it must have been like up there, what earth must have looked like. Armstrong had died that year as well, and Felicity had read his obituary, how he had been reluctant to talk about the moon landing, did not want to be defined by that moment. The needle dug in. Her mind turned to the doctor, a Pakistani woman. She thought about Nick, still at school, junior high.

"You doing okay?"

"How much longer?"

"You need another beer?"

"I'm fine."

Don't think about the needle . . .

Then Jake was patting the area with ointment and telling her to "keep it moist for a couple of days." Felicity looked at the tattoo through a mirror and rose from the black leather chair. "Looks good," she said.

"What's it mean?" Jake asked. "Betty Cakes?"

"It was my nickname, when I was a kid."

Jake nodded, understanding, indifferent. Felicity let it go at that.

She took Foothill Boulevard back toward her apartment rather than hopping on the freeway, which would have been the faster way. She wanted to take her time. This was the old Route 66, the road that everybody used when they came to California, made famous in a song that Felicity could not stand. She had read *The Grapes of Wrath,* but it had been so long ago that she scarcely remembered a thing, only the bit about the woman breastfeeding the old man at the end. They did tours now along Route 66. Felicity had seen the advertisements. She wasn't interested. For her Route 66 was just Foothill Boulevard, the road she lived off of for so many years, the road she took to Orchard Supply Hardware and to Tony's apartment. Unless you caught a glimpse of a sign, like the one in the window of an ancient service station, you would never know you were driving along anything historical.

No music had been playing in the doctor's office. And when she got into the car to go to the tattoo parlor, she decided not to switch on the radio. But now, with the words "Betty Cakes" causing her ankle to sting some, she put in a cassette tape (yes, her car was that old) and forwarded to a song, "The Whole of the Moon." Maybe because she had been thinking of Neil Armstrong, or maybe because she deserved something uplifting, even as the lyrics were regretful and melancholy, she wanted that song. Driving westward on Route 66, Felicity reached Leary Road, where she should have turned left. Instead she banked like a jetliner, made her way north to the freeway, and headed east. By then the song was over, but Felicity had gas in the car and a brand-new tattoo.

The Comeback Kid (Present)

The girl was only ten years old and already the other parents were murmuring about how much better she was than their children. Wearing ribbons and colorful socks with stars—their "crazy socks," the girls called them—she was standing at shortstop and fielding grounders, making crisp throws across the diamond. Most of the other girls had to one-hop it or lob it in the air, but this girl threw the ball on a line. It was certain: she was going to be an all-star, play travel ball. If you were an astute observer of the game, you would see also that she had a quality, *the* quality, tenacity bordering on the unhealthy. She loved to play softball, no doubt about it (and a number of other sports), and she had fun when she was out there, but she grew angry and feisty when she made a mistake, let a rare grounder get under her legs, missed a pitch at the plate. Most of the Red Robin Rockers would laugh off a mistake, but this other girl became angrily determined. If she did strike out, the next time at the plate she would be loaded for bear, driven to rip the ball and run the bases. It was an inherited gene no doubt, this refusal-to-lose mania.

The coach, her father, was standing at home plate and hitting the grounders. He hollered, "Come on, girls, I want to see you having fun!"

He discovered that he liked coaching, was learning a whole lot about girls softball, the strange rules—how they played against time rather than innings, how the pitcher could not step back before she threw to the plate, the no stealing home before the midseason tournament rule. The game was and wasn't different from the baseball he grew up playing. He had been a very good player, all-league, played a year of college ball. If you got a couple of beers in him after practice or a game, he might tell the story about how he tried out for the California Angels. He had done well until he took batting practice, and then he'd say, "I looked like a spastic. To this day I don't know what happened."

Baryshnikov.

But he was not one of those guys who prattled on about his playing days, and he was not one of those fathers determined that his daughter would succeed where he had failed. If she wanted to play ball, that was her choice. Sure, he played catch with her from an early age, but he was not Earl Woods practicing his golf swing while the prodigy Tiger sat in the stroller and watched.

"Stay down," he yelled encouragingly to one of the girls who had just let a ball roll into the outfield.

Best of all, he had never made his daughter cry over sports—and he never would. He lost the game of baseball for a long time, lost it like people *must* do, whether because of a lack of talent, or disinterest, or a matter of age. For a good ten years he did not pick up a bat or even root on his once beloved Dodgers. He did drywall for a living and later got his contractor's license, started making good money, and got married. They had two daughters (the younger, who was seven, liked to dance and draw) and bought a small house in Huntington Beach. He was happy.

"All right, girls, let's bring it in."

And like puppies these nine- and ten-year-old girls came racing toward home plate. Already they were hollering to play "Rabbit," a game where they sprinted around the bases opposite of one another. It's how they closed most practices.

"Line up," he said.

That night, after practice, he and his daughter would stop and grab a pizza before heading home. This had become their tradition—take-out on the two nights a week they had practice or a game. His wife also worked, and nobody wanted to cook. Later he would settle in, maybe watch some ball on ESPN. Ronnie, his daughter, might watch with him; his other daughter might want to show him her drawings. He's a good father, especially now because he drinks less. That too got old, and, well, his wife insisted it was time.

But if you do get a couple of beers in him, he might tell you about trying out for the California Angels. If he does, he'll tell the story good-naturedly, not painfully or wistfully. It's a story now, a thing that happened.

What he won't include is this:

It was late afternoon when he left Trinity College. He decided to go to a sports bar, where he had a burger and fries and a beer. A woman, she might have been a traveling salesperson, sat next to him, but he said hello only. He already knew: He would not go back to school and use up his eligibility. He would not try and join an independent team. It was behind him now.

Still.

The sky was lit up pink and orange when he left, and he had to drive Route 57 to get home. As he approached Angels Stadium, he could see the Big A sign, the enormous halo, the full parking lot. The Angels were playing at home. He thought about turning off, buying a cheap ticket, and catching a few innings. He had done that in the past. He hadn't minded going to a game alone.

But tonight he drove on. He glimpsed the fans in the upper deck, the stadium lights. God they were gorgeous. Mike Allison rolled down the window of the car, and the Ray Corbin baseball card fluttered in the wind. He thought he heard the public address announcer call his name. Then he did not.

He let go.

Cousin Billy (Present)

When I think of my cousin I see him as a reenactment, like one of those documentaries on the Crime and Investigation channel. The door opens at the Hotel Allegro in Bern and a bellman steps through, my cousin right behind. The bellman pushes a cart carrying my cousin's belongings, Aldric's as well. The bell-man hangs their clothes, sets out the suitcases, asks my cousin if he needs anything else. My cousin tips him handsomely. And he is left alone.

He removes his shoes, purchased in Italy no doubt, and puts on the hotel-supplied slippers. He orders room service and pours himself a glass of Perrier. And waits.

He and Aldric have separate rooms. They always have sepa-rate rooms. (At one time they may have been sexually involved, but if so, that is long past.) They are in town for a trade show, and my cousin is feeling restless—he is tired of these trade shows. The following night Aldric will be the keynote speaker, and my cousin will hear the same speech he has heard dozens of times before: the chronicling of Aldric's rise from impoverished Pari-sian boy to wealthy and world-famous perfumist. Throughout all of it Aldric will act entitled, as if it were inevitable that he should become wealthy, that the world rewards those who deserve to be rewarded. It will also be my cousin's job to make sure Aldric stays sober, so that he doesn't slur his way through his address like he did a year earlier in Rio de Janeiro.

My cousin feels trapped. He has asked Aldric for a greater role in the company—my cousin wants to *run* the company—but Aldric has balked. "Someday," he tells him.

William is staring at the Bern skyline when the door opens and Aldric enters.

He is drunk. He has been drinking from the time they left London that morning, and he stopped at the hotel bar before coming upstairs. My cousin turns from the window and Aldric says something. The reenactment is without sound, so I can't hear what, but it hits the wrong nerve and William says something sharply in return. Aldric responds in a way that says, *That's that, I have spoken,* but William is not done. The thing is eating at him. Aldric moves toward him. I remember the night at the party at the Los Feliz mansion, when Aldric pushed my cousin and tried to knock him against the wall. It did not work then and it does not work now, and—

William snaps. He is done being Aldric's whipping boy, he is tired of slow progress, tired of Aldric's drunkenness and arrogance and abusing people (only that morning he had yelled at the flight attendant), and for the first time he pushes back. Aldric stumbles and becomes even more vicious. He barks at William, calls him horrible names, says something like, *You useless bitch,* or *Know your place,* or *I could cut you off with a snap of my fingers,* and so it happens—

William rages and places his hands on Aldric's throat. It happens quickly, too quickly, within seconds it seems, so that my cousin can hardly believe what he has done. The rage lifts and he is alone in the hotel room, Aldric dead on the floor, asphyxiated. My cousin wonders whether anyone has heard them fighting. He has only a few moments to make a decision.

* * *

One time I did see such a reenactment. I was in a hotel room myself traveling for work when *The Unsolved Murder of Jean Girard* came on the television. It was late at night, and I was feeling uneasy. I dislike travelling—it induces insomnia in me—and I do so only when I must. In this case, a teachers' conference insisted on by our dean. I was sitting on the uncomfortable bed flipping channels when the unsolved murder show came on. There was my cousin, a shadowy character being portrayed by a nearly faceless actor: William is described as an internationally successful model, hyperbole if there ever was one, and it is suggested that he is the puppet master behind Aldric's empire. Before he commits the murder, William is stalking Aldric, practically rubbing his hands together, his steps as stealthy as a well-trained assassin. Then almost immediately he becomes a petty thief, cold-bloodedly rifling through Aldric's possessions, tossing his wallet aside and methodically leaving the premises. I do not recognize my cousin. And I don't believe it would have happened that way.

You already know that I did not go to the FBI.

What good would it do? I suppose forensics experts could piece together leads from those postcards, the postage stamps, the color of the oceans and the types of trees, but even if they did, my cousin is long gone, available now only to the imagination. So you see, mine is a sin of omission, like a shirt missing from a store receipt when you get home or the failure to stop some damning gossip. You should. *You should.* But you don't—even if you don't always know why.

For many years I have lived in this same small apartment. It has suited me well. I am a man without ambition. Perhaps you would like to see me walk out the door, go to Europe, and, through some magnificent means or coincidence, find William myself. He and I switch places, William the hermetically sealed one, unable to leave his small hotel room, me finding love and adventure. Believe me, I have thought of doing so. I have seen the planes flying overhead. I have heard, every night in fact, the sound of trains passing through the southern end of town, the *chug* of their engines. And perhaps one day I might find the gumption to hit the road, though I have no chiseled jaw, no gorgeous good looks to ensure safe passage across a crowded continent. Weeks later I make my way to a coastal village where William has just stepped off a bus. He wears a chambray shirt, a pair of linen pants, a straw hat. It is summer and people sip wine at an outdoor cafe. William walks into the hotel and strolls to check-in, confident that he will not be recognized. The clerk greets him warmly. My cousin says he wants a room, and he signs whatever name he has adopted and calls out, "Hold the elevator, please!"

I am already in the elevator when I hear my cousin's voice. I hold open the door, and he enters. "Coz!" he says, not the least bit surprised to see me. And so he is reunited with his family.

My grandmother would not have liked the thought of William sitting in jail. She would not have liked it at all. Those postcards are in the back of a small closet, if you ever care to look for them. It has been a long time since anyone has heard from Billy. Really, it has.

The Hikers (1964)

Bobby was sitting on a deserted island looking out at the sea. He could no longer tell how long he'd been stranded—months? years? His hair was shaggy and his clothes rags. He felt malnourished. It might be scurvy. He had resigned himself to his fate, when off in the distance he saw something cresting toward him. A ship. It was true. *Rescue.* But they needed to know he was there. He had to reach them. He needed to reach water's edge and wade into the sea, a sea that no longer felt endless because a ship was there. He heard a noise from the woods and worried that the cannibals were back. So he rose. His energy was low. Certainly it was scurvy. But if they could not see him, he would die on this island, beneath these trees. He began racing toward the water. He could feel the sandy ground beneath his feet, feel himself splashing through the waters, the waves. They knocked him down, but he rose again and pressed toward the ship. It was slow going, like a nightmare, and the cannibals were there now, too, directly behind him, giving chase. They were almost to him. He lurched forward and fell to the ground, and the cannibals landed on him, pinned him to the ground. Bobby screamed out—

* * *

They had been sitting for hours when Bobby's breathing started to come in short bursts. At first Stacy thought he had fallen asleep, the difference in the rhythm of his breaths, but she could see that his eyes were open. He had not spoken in a while, and he was staring off into the distance, his eyes fixed into the dark, when—

He rose.

Stacy did not ask, What are you doing? She assumed he was trying to get his circulation moving.

Then suddenly he burst forward, like one of those sprinters at the Tokyo Olympics. Began running. Not very fast, but running. The act of it surprised her—why in heaven's name would he be doing this—and when he had gone perhaps ten yards, she

knew intuitively that something was wrong. Panicked, she rose
and started after him.

He slipped and got back up, continued his mad racing
through the woods.

She called his name, "Bobby! Bobby! What are you doing!"

The sound of her voice seemed to propel him. He was trying
to escape her.

He plunged forward.

She was almost to him.

He fell.

And she landed on him—not quite a tackle but an attempt
to stop whatever strange and dangerous impulse had overcome
him. He squirmed beneath her body. They were both exhausted,
without much strength, but she knew that she had to hold him
down. He screamed, a guttural, desperate sound.

"Bobby!"

As he began crawling through the woods, she rode his back.

"Stop!" she cried.

He crawled a little more.

Then he gave out and collapsed.

He began speaking mumbo jumbo: "I don't care," "kill me,"
"the ship." And Stacy could tell that he was far away.

She put her mouth close to his ear and said, "It's me, Stacy.
Bobby, it's me."

It did not seem to register, but at least he stopped moving.

She held fast to him, like a tortoise shell.

Stacy Moriarty was seventeen years old and had never experienced death, a goldfish she brought home once from a school
fair but that was it. Her grandparents were still alive. Her dog as
well. She had told Bobby her thoughts about God, about her lack
of belief. The human body, she thought, was a container. It held
the heart, the brain, the lungs, and when it ceased to function,
the universe went dark—as dark as the forest where she blan-
keted Bobby Taylor as he lay on the cold ground. He planned
on working at the grocery store after they graduated. Isn't that

what he had said? Such a nice boy. She remembered the day they met, when they were assigned to be lab partners. There was a quietness about him that attracted her. He did not need to hear his own voice. He was shy, but all boys were shy until they got to know you—and he was always solicitous of her, even that first day. She remembered his saying that he liked the song "Walk on By." Everybody else was gaga over the Beatles and Jan and Dean, but he liked this lovely, emotive tune. It was sad, really, when you listened to the words, when you really listened, bent your ear past the music and heard what the song had to say. It was like stopping and pressing your ear to someone's chest. If you froze out the world, you could hear the heartbeat. She had done so once with her brother, when they were younger, pressed her ear against his chest and heard the thump, thump, thump of his heart. The sound surprised her—such evidence of life. She never forgot that moment, not then and not there, in the San Bonaventure Mountains, where the indifferent sky would eventually lighten. Yes, Stacy Moriarty did not believe in God, did not believe in magic or hoodoo, did not believe that witches could conjure spells, but she knew that if you listened past the silence, it could give you hope. If you held fast to what you needed to do, a sound might come from above, something like a squeal, then a tap, the red-headed woodpecker beginning its morning movements, tap tap tap, like a drummer warming up for a show, lazily at first, but then more earnestly—as the darkness moves to blue, and with it the feeling that the whole forest is about to come alive.

Felicity (2010)

It's possible to leave California. Not all migrations must go west. Just hop on Interstate 210 and head out past the Miller Brewing Company ("Miller, the Champagne of Beers"), cross the Los Angeles County line, and drive through the Inland Empire with its vast swaths of rock and dead earth. If it is wintertime and there has been rain, the reigning mountaintops might be dusted with snow, almost California postcard pretty. Ignore it. You have other destinations, beyond San Bernardino and Redlands. You can cut up the 15 and head toward Barstow, and before long Las Vegas, that gangster mirage in the desert, will appear. Or you can keep going to where the 210 merges with the 10 and head out to Cabazon, where people ride dirt bikes and other off-road vehicles and gamble in Indian casinos. You'll come to the Banning Pass, with the windmills and the trains moving along a mountain ridge that is now on your right, and you could go all the way out to Indio or you could cut up through Joshua Tree and really feel like you are leaving, like you have entered alien territory, that it is all behind you.

Felicity did just this, drove and drove and drove. Failed relationships and parenting responsibilities and health scares and the nagging fear that no matter what you do, someone will do it better and the cosmos could give two craps anyway about you. They sit in telescopes in those mountains and look at quasars millions of light-years away, and you could take comfort in the astronomer's claim that we are all stardust, or you can feel like a confused woman listening to the soundtrack from a sad movie you saw recently until you pull off the road and get out of your car and examine a Joshua tree, a lone Joshua tree with its crown-of-thorns look, standing amid the dried tumbleweeds.

It's not that the Joshua tree makes you feel any better—*Oh, Yucca of the Desert, I too am*...You don't have much Walt Whitman in you on this day.

Running away. Such a childish thing to do. And of course you had not packed a bag. You took off on a whim. Maybe you were thinking you would just get away for a day or two, call the kid's grandmother and have her pick him up and for one solitary afternoon not have to worry about the math that you cannot help with and reminding the kid to read a goddamned book, *The Gamer's Guide to Life*, anything, and not have to sit up until two in the morning doing your own work for a dissertation that is never going to happen, and rising to another day of peanut butter and jelly sandwiches, oh wait, the school has sent home a note that you can no longer pack peanut butter and jelly sandwiches because some kids have allergies but your thirteen-year-old won't eat any other kind of sandwich, and this Joshua tree doesn't want anything from you—so you just stare for a while, sorting, sorting, sorting.

You can leave California. You can.

So glad we bought that property back in '82, they say; now we can cash out and move to Oregon or Colorado. But Felicity has no property to cash out, no man in the East beckoning her to come, the reel of Manifest Destiny playing in reverse, the stagecoaches moving backwards, the spikes flying out of the Transcontinental Railroad, the cities shrinking and the *Arbella* backing out of the harbor, no more City on a Hill, no more nagging notion that you must do better, no more America.

Felicity got back into the car and turned across Thousand Palms Canyon Road and headed home.

CHAPTER 12

Gatsby, The Musical (1979)

George was sitting in his campus office when a colleague ducked in and said, "Did you hear? Richard Rodgers died."

The colleague did not wait for George's response. He was just passing along a tidbit of news. He did not know how important Rodgers had been to George Latham.

George rose and closed his door. The weather was beautiful in California, almost into the seventies. He wondered what it was like in New York, New Jersey. Probably snowing, certainly cold. Typically George would not have been in his office this time of year—it was winter break—but he had forgotten to bring home some papers, and he always went a little stir crazy after a few days around the house and—Dot understood. She was probably glad to get him out of there for a while, give her piece of mind.

Richard Rodgers. Dead.

George kept a small couch in his office, and he slipped off his loafers and stretched out his body. His feet just dangled over the edge. George was not a tall man, but the couch was that short.

Richard Rodgers. Dead.

He thought back to the first time he had seen a Rodgers show. It was the first time George had seen *any* Broadway show. He was a boy, eleven, and his parents announced that the three of them (George was an only child) were going into the city to see a show called *Oklahoma!* George didn't know what to expect; he only knew Oklahoma was a state far from New Jersey. And very different, he presumed.

They took the train into the city, then a cab down to Forty-

Second Street. His parents were in a joyful mood. The War had just ended, and they could spend a little more money. His father was a salesman, and even as a young boy George always sensed his nervousness about money. Not that he was a morose man, far from it—George's father was playful, jubilant. It had been a happy childhood. But with the War behind everybody, some of the uncertainties had faded, and here they were, marching under the lights, going to see this show about cowboys.

They ate dinner at an Italian restaurant. George felt so grown up, wearing his church clothes and romping around the city. The waitress had doted on him, calling George her "little man," embarrassing him by asking, "When are we getting married?" His parents got a huge kick out of it.

Finally it was time for *Oklahoma!*, and they settled into the seats at the St. James Theatre. George could not have known at the time, but he would come here often over the years, as a college student home on break and later with Dot, during their yearly visits to New York. "What should I expect?" George asked his mother.

That had been the question everyone was asking, though the young George could not have known—his was simply a boy's curiosity. *You won't believe Oklahoma! Wait 'til you see Oklahoma! Unlike anything you've ever seen.* His mother said, "I don't know. The Hoppers saw it. They said it was different."

These days *Oklahoma!* does not feel so different. The adult professor George could have told you why: there was pre-*Oklahoma!* and post-*Oklahoma!* The show changed everything for Broadway, for young George as well. The lights dimmed and a woman was on stage churning butter and suddenly a man was singing ("Oh, What a Beautiful Mornin'," of course), and George sat up in his seat so he could see a little better. Then came "The Surrey with the Fringe on Top" and the kick-in-the-pants "The Farmer and the Cowman" and the rousing "Oklahoma" itself (*if only he could find his "America"*), and George and everybody else were on their feet, hooting and hollering while the performers took their curtain calls.

Few of us are lucky to find it, our life's work in a single instant—the boy who marvels at the tadpole and determines that he will become a scientist, the girl who stares up at the moon one August evening and insists she will become the first female astronaut. Leaving the St. James Theatre that night, the pure exuberance of it all, the show and the audience and being out past your bedtime, George Latham knew what he wanted to become. He already had a good start: he could play piano. His mother was musical, not professionally so but she could sing and play, and even during the War she had insisted that they keep up piano lessons for George. He would make music. Compose music. The future began unfolding before him.

They grabbed a cab back to Penn Station and took the train home. He fell asleep on the ride, and it was well past midnight when his father was shaking George by the shoulder and saying, "Up, we're here." He was too big to be carried, so George rose and lumbered besides his parents, the song "Oklahoma" in his head, half-humming in his sleep. And then they were home, George back in his bed, his father shutting off the light and telling him, "You can sleep in tomorrow" (it was a school day, for God's sake), and George would always remember what he overheard his father say to his mother out in the hallway as they headed to bed themselves: "A damn good day."

The day of Rodgers' death, George did not stay late in his office. He made the commute home, stopped off at the store to buy a dessert—he thought he might surprise Dot—and pulled into the driveway of their modest three-bedroom home. A number of years earlier they had converted the garage into a playroom, to help with space (this was California, cars could be outside year round), so George parked in the driveway and made his way into the house. As soon as he was through the door, Dot asked, "Did you hear?"

"Yes." George set his bag down. "Martin told me."

"I guess he'd been sick again."

"That's what they said on the radio. I got you something."

And George gave her the square pink box with the dessert, a pineapple cake that Dot liked.

She looked inside. "Oh, that's lovely. Thank you, George."

He kissed her on the cheek and said, "Let's have our drink. I know it's early, but I feel like having something."

It was midafternoon and George and Dot typically never had their vodka and tonic until five o'clock. "Let's," she said. "It's practically dark outside."

This was true. It was December 30, and even with all the good weather, nighttime still came early. George walked to the portable minibar and mixed their drinks: a jigger and half each of vodka and diet tonic and a squeeze of lime (the neighbors next door grew them and regularly left a bag on George and Dot's porch). They sat on the couch and George kicked off his shoes. "He was seventy-seven," said George. "That's a good long life."

Neither of them had to say: Remember when we walked Shattuck Avenue together and sang, "I'm in Love with a Beautiful Guy"? Remember when we saw him in that diner and you introduced yourself? Those memories were the cornerstone of George and Dot's relationship. It would have been like saying, Remember that time we breathed. "Where are the kids?" George asked.

"At school, watching the basketball game. They know to be home by dinner."

"They play on break now?"

"I suppose so."

George let out an "hmmm" and took a sip of his drink. Probably tonight he would have a second. He was always skeptical of those people who had gotten so broken up over Elvis Presley's death two years earlier, especially the ones who felt the need to make the trip to Graceland. Not that George was opposed to Elvis's music. George might have been classically trained, but he was no snob. It was the excess of adoration, the willful surrendering of your own self to celebrity, that made no sense to him. He felt saddened by Rodgers's death, and there was an empty feeling that he could not quite place, but tomorrow night he and Dot would go, as usual, to their friends Robert and Ginny's for their

THE WHOLE OF THE MOON

annual New Year's Eve party. George and Dot would function.
They would not fly east to sit shivah in Manhattan.

After he finished his drink, George rose silently and crossed
the room to the baby grand. It had been a while since he had
used his own piano. He opened the keyboard and began playing. He did not need the sheet music. He played "The Surrey
with the Fringe on Top" slower than the song was meant to be
played, and Dot rose from the couch as well and came to the
piano bench. George slid over, and she settled in next to him.
Dot's alto voice was still in good shape, kept at the ready by her
singing at the church every Sunday, and she picked up midsong:

> *Don't you wisht y'd go on ferever?*
> *Don't you wisht y'd go on ferever and ud never stop*
> *In that shiny, little surrey with the fringe on the top!*

George swayed slightly, his motion somewhere between melancholy and fond remembrance, and together like that they played
and sang, a baby grand piano, they had saved and saved, a helluva guy, a baby, George, a baby, Music by Richard Rodgers,
Lyrics by Oscar Hammerstein. George played. Dot sang.

> *I can see the stars gittin' blurry*
> *When we ride back home in the surrey,*
> *Ridin' slowly home in the surrey with the fringe on top.*

Dot sang.

The Fairfax Apartments (Present)

They were filming late on the Paramount lot. It was the thirteenth episode of season one, and the showrunner absolutely
wanted to get it right. The network had not yet renewed the
series. The ratings were lackluster but the show was acclaimed,
and the showrunner, a man in his forties in jeans and a Chicago
Cubs cap, thought they could get a second season order if someone in the big black building believed in them enough to pull

the trigger—and so everyone, except the minors who had to be sent home, were logging late hours.

Blocks away, down near Melrose and Fairfax, the Actor dangled his legs over the side of the inflatable mattress. It was dark now, and the lights in the Fairfax Apartments were not particularly bright around the pool. Some of the residents had complained to the manager, said it was dangerous, but the Actor was glad to be floating in mostly darkness. He figured it must be past nine o'clock. He had been in the pool a long time. The heat had finally broken a little bit, once the sun dropped through the haze, and the air now was sufferable, almost pleasant. The call had not come that day. It could come tomorrow. The Actor had decided to stay in for the night, fix himself a late dinner— some pasta and a bag of vegetables—and watch a network show he liked. He had done some background work on the show, and the showrunner, a man in a Chicago Cubs baseball cap, had paid him a compliment, told the Actor he had a "good look." But background work was background work. The Actor wanted to be Brendan Fraser. "Speakeasy owner, McKee, late twenties, tends bar. McKee is tough-minded, no nonsense, but has a weakness for women and a vulnerability that they like."

The Actor's phone sat on the chaise lounge, like a passenger at a bus stop. The call had not come today. It could come tomorrow.

The Actor floated on.

Felicity (2014)

Dust was flying, and Felicity's brown hair was sticking out from the back of her helmet. She revved the throttle and brought the Kawasaki into a hard skid, controlled, so that dirt shot out like an ocean wave. She was in the hills, alone, and she could see the Los Angeles skyline. It was not the most magnificent of skylines, but it was hers—the city where she had gone to college, the city where she had been young. She pulled the bike back upright and went tearing across the dry open field.

About a week earlier her mother had phoned her. "Your father wants to see you," she said.

Felicity was sitting on her couch, reading. Nick was in his bedroom doing homework. "Does he?"

"He's got something for you."

"What do you think?"

"Whatever you want to do," her mother said.

It had been years since Felicity had seen him. He came to her high school graduation but not her graduation from UC. Two other bits of contact had been inconsequential. She did not want to hurt her mother, did not want to be one of those kids who so longed for the missing parent that they sacrificed the one who stuck around. But she did not think her mother would be too wounded; it was not like Felicity was leaving home and moving in with her father. She was a grown woman. She had survived a health scare some years earlier, a spot on her lungs that turned out to be nothing. Those kinds of scares make you less rigid. If her father had something to say, she would listen. "All right, give him my number," Felicity said.

Now in his fifties, her father had never remarried. Once was enough. He liked his freedom too much, and Felicity always thought that this desire had been imprinted in her genes. But unlike her father, she had parented, had been absent from the kid's life only for the couple of years when she went to UC.

Before her father arrived, Felicity sent Nick off to some friends. She had no interest in her father swooping in and proclaiming himself a "grandpappy." When he showed, it was in a red pickup truck, a Kawasaki 150 strapped in the bed. They embraced, and her father said, "Hello, Betty Cakes."

"So where do you live now?" she said immediately.

"Lancaster," he told her.

"That's crystal meth country. Are you a dealer?"

"No."

"Well, what do you do out there?"

"Jesus, the third degree. I work for a pipe supply company. And I brought you something."

How could Felicity not think of her childhood, riding dirt bikes with her father, those happy memories—and then her father leaving and taking the Yamaha with him? He leapt into the back of the truck and undid the bungee cords that held the bike in place. "Give me a hand with this," he said, and together they brought the bike to the ground. "Do you still ride?" he asked.

"No," she said, flatly.

"You can start back up. It's a present for you. Brand new. Seventeen miles is all."

"Where did you get it?" Her eyes shifted between the dirt bike and her father. "I don't want anything stolen."

"Listen, I was a shitty father, I know that. I just want to do something nice for you, so you don't think I am a total—"

"Loser?"

"Right." And he laughed a little.

Felicity considered it for a good long time, the gift, her father's reappearance, what you do with all those lost years. "Okay," she said at last.

Her father seemed pleased. Time had softened him, as it will anyone, and he said, "Who knows, maybe one day you'd be willing to go riding together."

For a week the bike sat in Felicity's parking space. "I have a grandfather?" Nick said, when Felicity showed him the bike.

"I don't talk about him much."

Nick was unaffected by the news. He had not grown up in a nuclear family anyway. But the bike—holy cow, he was a teenager! *Can I take it out? When can I take it out? What good does it do just sitting there?*

"You don't even have your license," Felicity reminded him.

"It's a dirt bike," he said.

"Yeah, I know."

She *would* let him ride, once she showed him the ropes. But for a week she was busy with work, teaching classes, grocery shopping, being Betty Cakes. She was in her second year at the school, the Westfield School for Girls. It surprised her that she liked it so much—the camaraderie, the girls' curiosity, the single-sex classroom. The girls found her interesting; they liked that she was a single mother, possessed a teenager's taste in music, had a tattoo. And this was all before they found out she owned a dirt bike.

She finally took it out on a day when she had no afternoon classes. She drove home to the apartment, grabbed the keys, and slowly drove the back roads into the hills. The Los Angeles skyline was visible. She turned the throttle and the bike jolted underneath her, jerking her forward. It took a few tries to get the feel of the clutch (dirt and road driving are different), but when she did, Felicity raced around like a lunatic, alone, the city below her, her hair spilling out from her helmet, flopping against her shoulders.

Why do you like riding motorcycles?

A colleague would ask her that.

And Felicity said, *Because you have to concentrate. You have to think about the throttle and the clutch at the same time. If you stop thinking about what you're doing, you'll crash. You can't think about anything else.*

Once upon a time "anything else" had meant being a single mother, sorting out her sexuality, putting up with men like Professor Jack, coping with the fact that she had not become a doctor of letters. Had she let down her imaginary benefactor, the rich gringa whose house she used to clean, the one who recognized her intelligence and sent her to school? If you are riding a bike, you don't have time to think about failure, if it is failure, or about money or mortality, or whether you have royally screwed up your kid with your shenanigans. You can think only about the bike or you will crash.

Of course Felicity did not tell her colleague any of this. She said, *You can't think about anything else.* Her colleague seemed to understand. And her students, once they learned that she rode a dirt bike, thought she was badass.

High in the hills that first day out, Felicity thought she was badass too—the Kawasaki kicking dust everywhere, blowing dirt into her nostrils, Felicity confident that she was never going to crash.

The Hikers (1964)

The radio was out in the man's Ford Fairlane—again. How many more times could the same fuse blow? For the past two days he had been near the summit, winterizing their cabin, and he had gone alone. They had no television up there. They did keep a small transistor radio, but reception was spotty and he had not turned it on anyway. He preferred listening to the sounds surrounding him. All of this to say, he had no idea that two children had been lost out there.

Even as he came down the hill, headed home, and saw a pair of ranger trucks parked off the side of the road, his interest was not piqued. They were rangers—their job was to *be* in the mountains. Then he passed a collection of cars and people, but he figured it was some nature group headed out for a hike. It was a beautiful morning, cold at the summit, but wonderfully clear, and he imagined that they were from somewhere in the valley, like him. He had been coming to these mountains since he was a child (the cabin had been built by his father), and he used to love to hike himself, before he got lazy and out of shape.

The Ford Fairlane eased its way down the hill, the car in low gear against the pull of gravity. About fifteen minutes past where he had seen the people and the cars, he came around a bend and his eyes caught something off the side of the road. At first he thought it was a mother bear and her cub—that would not have been unusual—but as he drew closer, he could see that they were human forms. He pressed his brakes to get a better look. Call it mountain instinct, as he later would, but there was something in their movements that made him slow down. They were teenagers, a boy and a girl, but they looked like urchins, a couple of pickpockets from *Oliver Twist*. Neither waved at him, but he pulled over nonetheless.

He opened the car door and stepped out. They began moving slowly toward him. The boy was limping. And what was the look on their faces? Surprise? Relief?

"You two need a ride somewhere?"

An eternity seemed to unfold before the girl said, "Yes."

The boy nodded in agreement, or at least it seemed so. His head barely moved.

"Well, get in."

They did. It took all of the girl's strength just to open the back door, and the man could see that they were in a bad way, worse even than he first noticed. In addition to being caked in dirt, the boy's senses were out of whack, and there was a distance to both of their faces.

The man put the car back in gear and continued down the hill.

He figured he would drive them to Gardner, get them to a payphone and find out where they belonged. He once had kids their age. As they headed down the mountain, the man blasted the heat in the car and glanced in his rearview mirror. The boy was facing the girl, his head jutting toward her, and the man said, "You two look like you've been up to no good."

CHAPTER X

813.52 FIT (Then, Now)

Helen Garrity moved silently but purposefully through the Carrollton Branch of the County of Los Angeles Public Library system. It was an hour before the library opened and Helen was shelving books. Some of the other librarians complained about this part of the job—it felt as boring to them as making meatloaf—but Helen liked it. She liked the smell and look of books in general, and she especially liked shelving a new book, the sense of possibility, of where it was headed. On this particular day, in 1957, with soft early light making its way through the library's windows, she was holding a copy of F. Scott Fitzgerald's *The Great Gatsby*. Helen knew the book—she was the one who suggested they order a copy—and she knew that Fitzgerald had died about an hour away, in an apartment complex off Sunset Boulevard.

Alone that morning among the library's holdings, Helen shelved the copy of *Gatsby* and moved along; and for more than a half century, well after Helen Garrity died herself, the book would change hands. Only once did the unwitting readers ever meet.

Felicity sat in the gymnasium of the Westfield School. She had come down the hill to watch her students play volleyball. She liked to do this sometimes, stay after school and give her support to the girls. She was in her fifth year at Westfield, and she had just become department chair. Her own child would be heading to college soon, and though Felicity would be alone then, she had no looming feelings of abandonment, no anxiety about an empty nest. She was only in her late thirties, still young by most any measure. That, she often reminded herself, was one of the advantages of getting knocked up at twenty.

A few minutes before the game began, a man sat next to her on the bleachers. He was ordinary looking, bookish if anything, with plastic framed glasses and hair that fell across his forehead in a neglected manner. He nodded at her, and Felicity introduced herself. The man had driven the team van to Westfield— he was a teacher at the other school—and when they got to talking about their classes *The Great Gatsby* came up. Hang out at a high school long enough and *The Great Gatsby* always comes up. "I had a cousin like that," the man said.

"Like what?" asked Felicity.

"Like Gatsby. He was a real dreamer. Impatient, you know. We grew up together, and he could not wait to get out."

"Where was this?"

"Up north. In the Central Valley."

A few feet away the girls were running through their pre-game rituals, the setting and spiking of balls. Suddenly the music began blaring, intended to supercharge the girls' adrenaline systems. "What happened to him?" Felicity asked. She had to practically scream to be heard.

The man nodded again; he had a habit of nodding. He said, "Oh, he modeled for a while and then did some building designs, and then got mixed up with this guy."

"Mixed up. He sounds criminal!" Felicity was joking.

"A little bit. Maybe."

"Then he disappeared. He got accused of something and just took off."

Felicity looked away from the court, where the girls were moving to a contemporary tune unfamiliar to her. Fleetingly she studied the man with the ordinary looks, the neglected hair. "Did he do it? The thing?"

The man thought for a long time and said, "Yes. I guess. I think so."

"Ah," said Felicity.

"Anyway, he's gone, and no one knows where."

"I understand," she said. And she did. She knew about people disappearing, how they can go away, how they can come back. She also felt like the man wanted to tell her something. She had good instincts that way and a face that invited trust. But the man let it pass, and it was loud in the gymnasium anyway, and whatever it was disappeared into the musty air. Later they said "nice to meet you" and "maybe I'll see you again at one of these things" and parted ways. They never knew: at one time they had checked out the same library copy of *The Great Gatsby,* held the same book in their hands. Our lives intersect that way, little coincidences that we never know.

A man floats in a pool. He is waiting for a phone call. He is an actor. It is hot outside but the city is not burning. There are no Santa Ana winds to blow him back to the Midwest. His feet dangle off the side of the mattress, and the sky above assumes its hazy darkness.

Another man sits on a couch with his two daughters, laughing and eating pizza. He wanted to be a Major League baseball player, but that did not happen. That's okay. He is a husband and father now, has no regrets, but if you get a few beers in him, he'll tell you about the time—

Dot Latham would outlive her husband by ten years. She died to the sound of old Broadway tunes while she was taking a nap, her daughter in the next room. Her husband George had wanted to be a famous composer, like Richard Rodgers. Had even met the man once in a New York City diner.

Stacy Moriarty was seventeen years old when she ditched school to go hiking with the boy, Bobby Taylor. They got lost, but they survived. Stacy would go on to college and become a nurse. Bobby would become a butcher and join the union. For the rest of his life he would have a limp, a result of his hypothermia. The injury kept him out of Vietnam. But he never did kiss her. And they did not fall in love that day. This is not that story.

A book sits on a table inside a Los Angeles apartment complex, just down the road from where the author died. Can you see it through the window, like a baby grand piano ready to be played?

On a brilliant October morning in 1964 two kids emerged from the California woods. Lyndon Johnson was about to be elected.

The Actor is asleep. The phone—

ABOUT THE AUTHOR

Brian Rogers lives with his wife and two children in Orange County, California, and teaches in Claremont. His work has received a gold medal prize for fiction from the Pirate's Alley Faulkner Society, the George Bennett Fellowship (Writer-in-Residence) from Phillips Exeter Academy, and the Best Ten Minute Play award from the Manhattan Repertory Theatre in New York. His work has appeared in numerous journals and magazines, and he previously worked professionally as a stand-up comedian. He received his MA in creative writing from San Francisco State University and attended the University of the Pacific in Stockton, California.